CONTENTS

Rebel Raiders	2
Copyright	3
Dedication	4
The Beginning	5
Chapter 1	16
Chapter 2	34
Chapter 3	52
Chapter 4	67
Chapter 5	94
Chapter 6	112
Chapter 7	129
Chapter 8	145
Chapter 9	163
Chapter 10	177
Chapter 11	191
Chapter 12	208
Chapter 13	224
Chapter 14	237
Chapter 15	248

Chapter 16	264
Chapter 17	282
Chapter 18	299
Epilogue	304
Charleston Christmas Day 1862	310
The End	311
Glossary	312
Historical note	314
Other books	317

REBEL RAIDERS

*Book 1 in the
Lucky Jack's Civil War series*

**By
Griff Hosker**

Published by Griff Hosker 2013
Copyright © Griff Hosker First Edition

The author has asserted their moral right under the Copyright, Designs and Patents Act, 1988, to be identified as the author of this work.

All Rights reserved. No part of this publication may be reproduced, copied, stored in a retrieval system, or transmitted, in any form or by any means, without the prior written consent of the copyright holder, nor be otherwise circulated in any form of binding or cover other than that in which it is published and without a similar condition being imposed on the subsequent purchaser.
A CIP catalogue record for this title is available from the British Library.
Cover photograph by the author

Dedication

Dedicated especially to my American readers who have encouraged me to write this series. I hope you like it. Thanks to Rich for his advice and Mike for his patience and hospitality. A huge thank you to the re-enactors of the 150th Gettysburg Battle- I admire your dedication to detail.

THE BEGINNING

London 1842

The Right Honourable Reginald St. John Beauregard looked to be at least ten years older than he actually was. One of the Prince Regent's drinking cronies, he had lived the high life until the king had died in 1830. After that, his life went downhill rapidly and the enemies he had made while in the king's company now gathered like crows around a corpse. He had married well on the strength of his friendship with reprobate Prince but the years following King George's death had seen his fortunes plummet. Once Victoria ascended the throne in 1837 then his life became even worse as a more austere tone was adopted by most of the gentry. By the time his wife died in 1840 then all of his connections with money and power went leaving him and his only son, Arthur, to eke out a living. By the standards of most of the people of Britain eking is the wrong word for they had servants and ate well but it was not the lifestyle to which both father and son had become accustomed.

As he sat in the one club which still accepted him

as a member, he knew that he had to do something quickly or the creditors would close in and he would be thrown into a debtor's prison. His royal connections had all been severed. Sitting at the card table he saw a chance to rescue his fortunes. Young Lord Fitzgerald was drunk and he was a poor card player. Beauregard had learned how to cheat well during his days as a rake. The unfortunate young lord had been deserted by his friends, who could have warned him of his opponent but they had departed with the ladies of the night. Having played cards for ten hours, the Right Honourable Reginald St. John Beauregard had already taken five hundred guineas in cash from Lord Fitzgerald and now the young drunk made the cardinal error of staking one of his family's many estates in Ireland on the turn of a card. Reginald had only one small house in London and the thought of being a landowner in Ireland appealed. He reasoned that it would be cheaper to live in Ireland than in London. When he threw his winning hand face up Lord Fitzgerald merely stood, shrugged his shoulders and said, "You are a lucky fellow Beauregard. Now, where are those doxies?"

Beauregard clutched the piece of paper tightly in his fist. He and his son now owned a manor house and twenty farms in some place called Tallow in County Wexford. He had an income at last. He would be able to buy Arthur, his son, a commission in a decent regiment and assure his future. His luck had changed for the better, at last.

Tallow, Ireland 1850

The Hogan house was little more than a pile of rocks with a door. Mary kept it as clean as she could but everything within it had been made by her or her husband and tending the land took every waking minute of every day. It was hard farming in Ireland and the potatoes had failed so many times lately that they had not even been able to feed themselves. The odd cabbage they grew had to augment their frugal diet. Mary had had to rely on the good offices of the church to help provide food for her four children. Now that Caitlin, her eldest, was older she could help with the younger children and Jack helped his father in the fields but, even so, it was hard to provide anything beyond a hand to mouth existence.

She stirred the cabbage and rabbit stew as she waited for her husband John and her two eldest children to return from the fields. It was raining again and they would be soaked when they eventually arrived. That would mean they would have to dry their clothes on the peat fire while they shivered in their nakedness. At least the two young ones, Colm and Eileen were both safe and dry inside the one-roomed hut which passed for a home. The turf roof kept out the rain but the wind had a way of finding gaps in the un-mortared stones which made up the walls. She smiled wryly; at least it blew the smoke up the chimney and stopped them coughing all night. She peered into the pot. This was the third meal that had been made from the rabbit Jack had trapped and it was now just a thin soup with a few nettles and cabbage stalks to add to the flavour. She hoped the warmth would bring a little colour into the cheeks of the two youngest children. They had looked like ghosts for the last two days and their coughs had become worse.

When John arrived back with Jack and Caitlin, Mary knew that they had toiled long and hard with little reward for their labours. John gave a sad smile, "We have a couple of taties and that is all my love."

"Never mind. Jack's rabbit still has a little life left in it."

Jack swelled with pride. "Sure, and I can check me traps again ma, if you like?"

"No, sweet boy, you are wet enough as it is. Wait till the sun comes out."

John shook his head as they huddled around the miserably weak peat fire. "I am sorry to say that this miserable land rarely sees the sun. Perhaps we ought to go to America like cousin Paddy."

"No John. This is our home; we'll talk when the wee ones are asleep." She inclined her head with a sharp stare. It did not do to cross the fiery redhead.

Later when the exhausted elder children slept and the younger ones coughed in their fitful sleep the two parents cuddled and huddled together. "We will not have a crop, my love. It is ruined again."

"We'll have to see the squire then and ask for some help. He cannot keep taking and taking. We are due some help. This has been five hard and lean years."

"He is rarely here and the Englishman he has running the estate is a hard bastard."

"When does the squire return?"

"When the crops are in."

She nodded firmly. "Then that is when we shall see him."

The Manor House

The years had not been kind to St. John Beauregard. He looked haggard and drawn. He now drank more than he ate and his visits to Ireland were becoming more necessary than ever to allow him to escape his creditors.

There were fewer men willing to gamble with him and all of his influence had evaporated. He was grateful to the ruthless estate manager, Andrew Neil, whom he had appointed to run his only source of income.

He ran a bored eye over the columns of figures. "Damn it, Neil. All I need to know is, did we make money this year?"

Andrew Neil knew his master well. Lies would only come back to haunt him He delivered the truth but he already had a solution in the back of his mind. "We will be lucky to break even my lord. The crops have failed again."

The Honourable Reginald, or, as he liked to style himself these days, Lord Tallow, sank deeper into the chair and quaffed the glass of port he held. "So, I am ruined."

"Not yet, my lord. We will get little if we sell the land but we could turn it over to sheep. They are cheap enough and they do not need many men. I could evict all the tenants and hire a couple of shepherds."

"But that costs money!"

"Not so much. I can get you a flock for a hundred pounds. Next year we would clear five hundred with the lambs and the year after..."

The image of an income in excess of five hundred pounds a year was attractive. It would help support Arthur in the Guards and he could live off the remainder in this rambling manor house that he had acquired when he had cheated Lord Fitzgerald. He had enough credit left to be able to buy the sheep and it would at least stop the whining of the peasants who seemed to think he owed them some responsibility.

"Good. See to it." He suddenly wondered how his

manager would go about it. "You'll tell them they are evicted then?"

"Aye." He hesitated. "Some of them may be a little angry my lord."

There was an unspoken request in the big man's voice. "You need help then?"

"A couple of lads with muskets would keep them in order. I can get some old soldiers for a few pence."

"A few pence then." A sudden thought struck the English man. "Wait until after Sunday then; my son Arthur will be over. He can keep an eye on things."

"As you wish my lord."

Arthur St. John Beauregard was a tall and distinguished looking officer. His red uniform had been especially tailored for him and had been cut to accentuate his fine features. Although his father had only obtained a Captain's commission for him, he was satisfied enough. It was just a pity that there were no major wars at present, for death provided the best and cheapest promotions. As he rode his black stallion along the road leading from the port, he reflected that his father's estates were no place to bring those he wished to impress. The land was dirty and dismal. The people were even dirtier and drearier. The only draw to this country was the hunting which was cheaper than in England and he would be the best dressed of the huntsmen. Here he was the cock of the walk whilst in England he was a Johnnie come lately. When his father explained what Neil would be doing it brightened the arrogantly harsh features of the captain's face.

"You mean they might actually try to stand up to Neil? How amusing although I would have thought there was little need to hire men. The two of us will do this." In his head, he was already picturing one of the Irish peasants standing up to him. He saw a riding crop in his hand as he whipped it down across the unfortunate man's face. Oh, they would remember him, of that he was certain.

They rode from the manor house with pistols in holsters on their saddles. Neil carried a cudgel whilst the young officer had a sabre and riding crop. The look on his face was one of anticipated pleasure. He was disappointed when the first three families they evicted trudged off weeping and wailing but without any sign of resistance. As they headed towards the fifth family Arthur turned to his companion. "Are they all spineless jellyfish here?"

"I am afraid that the next family might be trouble your lordship. The first four were small families with only one man to deal with but the Murphy family is more like a clan. There are some big bruisers there."

"Good, then we shall teach them a lesson, eh, about how we English deal with bruisers? What is the chap's name?"

"Michael Murphy your lordship."

Word had spread in the small farming community and the Murphy clan was ready. The three men who lived on the farm had been augmented by their three uncles. Ironically, two of the uncles were some of the very men that Andrew Neil would have hired to evict the tenant farmers. They were old soldiers and knew their way around a fight.

Captain St. John Beauregard deigned to dismount and rapped haughtily on the door with his riding crop. Michael Murphy, who had a chest as wide as the door, dipped his head under the lintel and stood there, looking the Captain straight in the eyes.

"Are you Michael Murphy?" The farmer nodded insolently. "Well, we are evicting you. The potatoes don't pay and we need the land for sheep."

"And you have paperwork for this, your lordship?" Michael was clever and he knew he had to stay on the right side of the flimsy law of the land.

The others had been easily intimidated and Arthur was slightly disconcerted. "What paperwork?"

"Well, your lordship you can only evict us if we are in arrears." He stared stonily at Andrew Neil. "And are we in arrears Mr Neil?"

Arthur looked hopefully at his manager but he saw only downcast eyes and a shake of the head. "Well, it makes no never mind anyway. I want you and your family off my father's property by midnight."

"Or?" The question seemed to make the young officer confused. He looked at his manager for aid. "What will happen if we do not move off the land?"

"We will throw you off!" This was better. Arthur might actually get a fight out of them.

"Just the two of you; mighty strong words." He sighed. "Well, I think we will just let you try." He turned to go back into the house and heard the sound of metal and leather as the Captain of Guards drew his pistol and raised it. Michael turned slowly around. His face was but a yard away from the end of the gun. No one could miss at that range; certainly not the officer who practised for hours on the range. "Ah well, I see that you have a persuasive argument." He smiled which unnerved Arthur. The man should be a quivering wreck and yet he stood confidently looking at him. "You see I have another argument of my own." He waved his arm and pointed behind the officer. Keeping his pistol aimed at the huge target Arthur turned his head and saw two Brown Bess muskets pointed at him while two pitchforks threatened his manager. The Murphy boys looked after their own.

St. John Beauregard blanched and turned back to the head of the Murphy clan. "I'll have the magistrate on to you."

"Saying what? You have no papers and you have not sought the law. You have threatened us and all I am doing is defending me and my family." He stepped up close to Arthur and said quietly but with great conviction. "Now feck off you jumped up little popinjay before I knock you off your horse."

The two men had to endure the cries of derision as they wheeled their horses and slunk away like a pair of beaten dogs. St. John Beauregard's face was now effused and red, replacing the shocked white of a few moments earlier. He had been humiliated by a peasant! He glared at his companion. "Anything I should know about the next family? Are they likely to be armed and threaten my life?"

"No, sir. John Hogan has no brothers and his eldest boy is little more than a child."

"Good! I will deal with the Murphy family another day when I have some of the local militia with me." He was certain he could use his influence to coerce the local soldiers to help him. They were all supporters of the English rule in this part of the world.

John Hogan had heard of the threat which was coming his way and he stood at the door awaiting them with Mary clinging to his arm. Her eyes were ringed with shadows and she was a shadow of her former self.

Since her two youngest had died, the week before last, she had pined and mourned. She had blamed herself for their deaths and John had had to spend every waking minute convincing her otherwise. This new threat was the last straw. John's eyes blazed with anger. This was his land and no-one had the right to throw him off it.

This time the captain had his sword in his hand. He would intimidate the man from the first. "You, Hogan, we are evicting you from my land! You and your family must leave now!" His voice became piping and screeching as he screamed his anger in the face of John Hogan.

"Your land? I haven't seen you working it. And I thought it belonged to your father or has he died and we haven't heard the good news yet?"

Had it been just John present then the tragedy might have been avoided. However, Mary, his wife was there. She saw the sabre flash in the air then her guilt about the death of her youngest child rushed into her head and she threw herself towards the wickedly sharp blade. In her head, she was trying to protect her husband. She had no way of knowing that the soldier only intended to frighten John and the blade would miss his head. It did not miss Mary and almost severed her head from her body. She slumped to the ground spraying blood on the black stallion. Arthur was as shocked as anyone. This was not how it was supposed to be. He had expected to fight a man and not kill an unarmed woman. He had intended to wave the sword in front of the farmer and frighten him. He had not intended to take the woman's life.

John reacted as any red-blooded husband would do. He grabbed Arthur's left arm and pulled him from his horse. His huge fist crashed into the nose of the handsome young officer smashing and breaking the bone. His second punch struck the bloody face of Arthur St. John Beauregard in the mouth. Andrew Neil heard the jaw crack. He had to do something. If Arthur continued to be beaten then he would lose his very lucrative job. He pulled his own pistol and fired into the side of John Hogan's head. The huge ball went through the brain as though it was butter and half of the farmer's head splashed blood and grey matter all over the fine red uniform of the officer. Neither John nor Mary had any time before their deaths to think of Caitlin and Jack but the two orphans had witnessed it all as they cowered inside the hovel that had been their home.

CHAPTER 1

Oh, Mary, this London's a wonderful sight,
With people all working by day and by night.
Sure they don't sow potatoes, nor barley, nor wheat,
But there's gangs of them digging for gold in the street.
At least when I asked them that's what I was told,
So I just took a hand at this digging for gold,
But for all that I found there I might as well be
Where the Mountains of Mourne sweep down to the sea.

Percy French

Jack

Cork

I was both terrified and horrified when I saw ma and da murdered and then a white rage took over me and I would have raced out with the small, wee knife I held in my hand and killed this Arthur Beauregard. I suddenly felt Caitlin's hands grip me and she hissed, "No! We can do nothing for them. Open the back window."

The house had but one door and the rear window was really just a board to keep out the wind and to let the smoke from the fire drift out. As I was opening it and Caitlin was grabbing the few belongings, we had I heard a voice from outside. It was the voice of the man who had shot my father. "There are two more in there; their children."

I shall never forget the icy English voice which snarled, "Set fire to it and throw in the bodies of these two. Hurry up and don't get blood on my breeches!"

"What will I use to start it with?"

"Here. Use the brandy. Pour it on their bodies and then throw them inside."

"What if the children try to run?"

"You still have a pistol and I have two. It matters not if they die inside or outside."

Without the need for further urging, Caitlin and I threw ourselves through the tiny window. We ran directly for the ditch which marked the far edge of what had been our land. Our home hid us from view and we lay in the ditch catching our breath. We were able to see the huge overseer throw, first my mother and then my father, through the door. The red-coated Englishman then fired his two pistols and there was a flash of light. The house began to burn fiercely. They watch to make sure that it caught all the way around. Satisfied that their work was done they mounted their horses and watched as the house became a raging inferno. We lay as low as we could as they trotted along the track which led to the village. They passed within five feet of us as we hid in the boggy bottom of the drainage ditch.

"What about the children?"

"They were probably hiding. It doesn't matter. They could not survive that blaze. Back to the hall, I have had enough of this bloody country and I need my nose looking at."

When we knew that they had finally gone, we rose

from our place of concealment and walked back to what had been our home. The fire had been so intense that the roof had fallen in and completely destroyed everything within the walls.

Caitlin took my hand. "We can do no more for them, Jack. The house is their grave and we must save ourselves." We both bowed our heads as we each said a silent prayer.

There was a grim determination about my older sister as she led me down the track which led south and away from the hall and the hated murderers, the Englishman and his lackey. But the memory was burned, like my home, forever in my mind; it might take some time but one day I would have my revenge. I had seen their faces and I knew their names. I would never neither forget nor forgive. After a mile or so I ventured, "Where are we going?"

"Cork. We can try to get some money there."

Cork! It was a place I had dreamed of visiting but not like this. "How will we get money?" I was already thinking about how little we had. My rabbit skinning knife and my slingshot were my most prized possession.

Caitlin stopped and I noticed that she had a Hessian sack over her shoulder. She reached in. "Here." I saw that it was da's best jacket. "It might be too big but it will keep you warm. I have ma's coat and her necklace from Nanna." She shrugged. "We might be able to sell it."

I gave her a horrified look. "Don't look at me like that. We need to eat. I am the head of the family now and will be making all the decisions."

I glowered at her. "Sure, and I am the man of the house now. I'll not be taking orders from the likes of a girl."

The slap she gave me made my teeth rattle and I saw stars. "I'll tell you when you are a man!" I found myself crying. It wasn't the pain it was just that I suddenly realised that we were alone. Caitlin, too, began to weep and she put her arms around me. "You have to trust me, Jack. We have no time to argue. Now, come along, step lively and we'll be in Cork by the morning."

Caitlin had a great way with words. Her cheerful voice seemed to diminish the pain and loss I knew we both felt. It would be hard but I was in no doubt that we would manage. My mother had always been positive and cheerful. Whenever I brought home a scrawny bunny, she would treat it as though it was a side of beef. Caitlin was just like ma; she had her looks and she had her ways. Between the two of us we would survive and then one day, I promised myself, I would find this St. John Beauregard and kill him and the Andrew Neil who had shot my father. I spoke not a word to Caitlin but I made that promise to myself and those are the kinds of promises we all keep. I was to discover that many years later.

After two days of begging on the streets of Cork, we were so hungry that I did not see how we could last a third day. We had had little to eat before that. Caitlin had tried to get work but each time she failed and I could see that even my cheerful sister was becoming increasingly depressed and disconsolate. Finally, I resorted to theft. When I stole the loaf of bread from the delivery boy, I was just glad that my mother was not there. She would have been appalled at the crime but we needed the food. It staved off the hunger for a little while longer. We had managed to find a loose plank in the stables and, each night we would enter and climb to the hayloft where we would burrow beneath its warmth. As we shared the bread Caitlin looked at me with a look I had never seen before. It was almost a look of doubt. Perhaps our dream of a new life was a vain one.

"Look, Jack, we need to leave Ireland. I was talking to some of the others and they say that there are many boats leaving every week and America is a land paved with gold. Why you don't even need to dig the gold; it lies there on the top of the ground just waiting to be picked up." For the first time in my life, I doubted my older sister. The 'others' were street urchins like us and I wondered why they had not sought their fortune in America. "I think I know where I can pick up a little work." She looked down at the bread she was eating and avoided my gaze. "You go down to the harbour and find the names of the ships going to America and I will try to get this job. I'll meet you at the quayside at noon."

"What kind of job?"

"Oh, some of the girls told me of a place which needs hard working girls." Her eyes blazed defiantly as she looked at me again, "And I will be the hardest working girl they have ever seen."

I hated it when we were not together. I was not a child but I felt lonely without my big sister close by. We were almost the same height even though she was three years older than me. There had been another baby my mother had carried between Caitlin and me but she had died and with the dead brother and sister, we were all we had. I watched her as she waved goodbye and headed into the busy town. I strolled down to the quay. It was a busy place filled with sailors coming

20

and going as well as the fishermen mending their nets or landing their catches. It was a noisy place with the constant sound of screeching seagulls which wheeled overhead desperate for scraps. We had fought them off to get some of the discarded fish heads on our first two hungry days.

I found a quiet corner of the quay to count the ships and to identify any which might cross the Atlantic. It was deserted or almost so. There was just a one-armed fisherman mending his nets and I felt safe.

I peered at the boats and ships in the harbour. When the fisherman spoke, I jumped. He had a voice cracked with the pipe he had stuck between his teeth. As he talked to me, I could see that he had more gaps than teeth. "And what would a young farmer's boy be doing watching the boats?"

I was curious. "How did you know I was a farmer's boy? I could have been a sailor?"

He laughed and it crackled and croaked. "With your pale skin and the peat in your face and your hands what else would you be?"

I must have looked angry for he held out his good hand, "I meant no harm. I am Stumpy Lannigan." He held up his stump. "You can see how I got the name."

"How did you lose it?" I realise now that an adult would not have asked such a rude question but children know no better.

"I served in Her Majesty's navy and a damned slaver slashed it off with his cutlass." He grinned. "Mind I took the bugger's head off so I reckon we are even. So why are you looking at the ships?"

"Me and my sister are orphans and we want to go to America."

He shook his head. "Fearful expensive that is. Have you money?"

I was suspicious. We had met many thieves since we had arrived in Cork. "Not a penny."

He seemed satisfied with the answer. "Then you'll have to work your passage but not your sister. Sailors are superstitious. Women on ships are bad luck."

"I am not leaving without my sister."

He looked at me with a sad expression on his face. "Sometimes we all have to make decisions we don't like." I looked sullenly out across the harbour trying to see which ships were transatlantic. He sighed, "Well there are two big ones there. They have the red flag with the union flag within it. They are British ships and they carry passengers. You could sign on as a cabin boy or a sailor. That'd get you over."

I pointed at another ship, slightly smaller. It did not appear to have a flag or if it did it was so dirty and tattered as to be indiscernible. "What about that one?"

"He is a bad 'un. That is Captain Black Bill Bailey and I would steer clear of him and his like."

My eyes lit up. "Is he a pirate?"

"Not so as you would know but he trades in some mighty funny places. He goes across to America but he does it at night if you catch my drift."

"Smuggling?"

"And other things. The one next to him is safer." I followed his gaze and saw a ship with white stars and blue and red stripes. "An American, Captain Adam Lee. A fine sailor and a fair man. You could do worse than him."

I spent the next couple of hours listening to Stumpy's tales of the navy and the sea. He made it seem a comfortable place with good mates, as he called them, and exciting times. He also shared his food with me, bread, cheese, some cockles and small beer. I learned much about life at sea and the perils of signing on. By the time I heard the church bell ring twelve, the sign to meet Caitlin, I felt better than I had before I met Stumpy. He smiled at me. "I'm always here. I can't do much with one hand but I can still mend nets and I am not beholden to any man. That's important, young Jack. Always be true to yourself and ask charity of no man. If someone offers you charity that is one thing but do not beg. I hope you and your sister have more luck. But it is a cruel and heartless world we live in and a man makes his own fortune."

I ran to the church where we had arranged to meet. It was a safe and busy place. Sometimes the nuns and the priests would slip us a little food as they left the church. We had grown up Catholics but our little village church was not a fine building like the one in Cork. Caitlin looked almost tearful when I met her. It contrasted with how happy and excited I felt. Typically, Caitlin asked after me first. "Have you eaten?"

"Aye. I met a fisherman mending nets and he shared his food with me."

She seemed relieved. She took my hand and led me towards the bread shop. "Well I have a job now and I have a little money. We'll buy a loaf of bread and a jug of small beer. I had an advance on my pay. After a week or so I may be able to afford to rent us a room somewhere."

Caitlin could never hide her thoughts from me and she was keeping something from me. I could tell that she had not lied to me but she had skirted around the truth. When we had bought the bread and the ale, we headed for the green mound near the Sallybrook Road, overlooking the wide river. It was a pretty place and as it was not raining the perfect spot to sit and avoid attention. Neither of us had forgotten that the estate manager would, on occasion, visit Cork and he would recognise us. We had witnessed murder and we were under no illusions; we were disposable and, until we left Ireland, in great danger.

After we had eaten Caitlin lay back and looked up at the clouds scudding around the sky. "Do you think ma and da are looking down on us now?"

I had avoided thinking of life after death. I knew that the priest said you had to have absolution to get into heaven and neither of them had had that but I did not think that God would refuse to let them enter. "I hope so."

Suddenly Caitlin rolled over and began sobbing in my arms. How had I said the wrong thing? "They will be in heaven! Honestly; I know it! They were good people! It is those two murdering bastards who will rot in hell and I will send them there!" They were brave but empty words but I just wanted to make my sister feel better.

She rolled off me and I noticed for the first time that she had red on her lips and blue on her eyes. I had not noticed them before but before I could ask her why she blurted out. "I don't want them to see me. I am a bad girl and sinful girl and I will be the one to rot in hell!"

The look in her eyes worried me. "Caitlin. What is this job you have?"

I held my breath for I had an idea of her answer. She looked down at the grass, twisting clumps of it into tiny strands. "I work in the alehouse."

I was relieved and then heard the deception in her

24

voice. "Serving tables?"

"Serving tables," then she looked up at me, her eyes brimming with tears, "and the men."

My voice was so quiet that I barely heard it myself, "You are a whore?"

She nodded and threw herself back onto the ground. "I will rot in hell."

Suddenly Stumpy's words came back to me. Better that I work, and my sister be saved the indignity and shame of whoring herself. "I will get a place on a ship and I will earn enough to take you to America."

"But we would be separated! I should be there to look after you."

"If you are lying on your back letting strangers take you then you will not be looking after me." It was a cold brutal statement and I had made it without thinking.

For the second time, she rattled my teeth. "You may be speaking the truth but I'll not be having my own brother talk to me like that. What else could I do?"

Both of us fell silent. She was right. The world was cruel to the Irish poor and we had been little better than slaves on the land. Now we had no rights and could be hurled into the street or put in the poorhouse if we were discovered. There we would work all day for a bowl of gruel with no hope of a life outside the grim walls of the institution. I stroked her hair. "You are right and I am sorry. This is better than the workhouse and I will see if Stumpy will teach me to mend nets. That way we will have more money." I held her chin so that she was forced to look at my eyes. "But I will go to sea and I will take you to America." I held her face in my two hands. "I swear you will not suffer this long."

She threw her arms around me and held me tightly. "So long as we have each other, brother I can endure all."

Years later I reflected on my vain words; I was young and I was foolish and I had many lessons to learn before I could call myself a man.

It was late when Caitlin returned to the barn. Her face was drawn and I saw specks of blood on the edge of her dress. Another would not have seen the marks against the many other stains she had but I knew every inch of her and knew that she had an injury. I waited for her to tell me. She gave a wan smile and held out a jug of beer; this was not small beer but the one the men drank. "Here. I have had a jug myself. It will help you to sleep."

I noticed that she did not sound as she normally did. My mother would have been shocked for she had never drunk anything stronger than small beer and tea. It had been many years since we could afford even a corner of tea. Caitlin was drunk! I took a swig of the ale and found it sharp and bitter but if my sister had drunk some then so would I. She lay in the hay with her eyes half closed. "Was it ... bad?"

"I survived... I survived."

I could not sleep for hours, despite the beer. Those words haunted me. Was this our future? My sister whoring until she was of no further use and me living off her meagre money? I resolved to ask Stumpy for help the next day. I would not ask for charity but I would seek his advice.

Although I had not said a word to him Stumpy gave me a sad and sympathetic look. "Now then young Jack and how are you on this fine morning?"

The words belied his looks. "Not so good Stumpy." I had known him less than a day but I felt that I could trust him. As I grew older, I learned to trust my instincts. They rarely let me down. I told him everything.

He nodded as he carefully mended the tear in the small net he was repairing. "Now don't be hard on yourself or your sister. We do not choose our own lives; they come to us and we have to make the best of them. Just because she's... well, she is still a good girl for she is doing it for you. And you," he stopped for a moment and he said quietly, "what would you have of Old Stumpy?"

"Could I work for you? I am a hard worker and I learn fast."

"I would love you to work for me. You are like the grandson I never had but there is barely enough work for me. This time next year my eyes will have gone and it'll be the workhouse for me. No, Jack, you need a job." He stroked his stubbly chin with his stump. "I'll ask around and see if I can find a berth for you." His eyes twinkled. "I still know a fellow or two." He looked down at the rocks below. "What you can do if you want food and maybe a bit of money is to scramble down to those rocks and collect mussels. You can eat them or sell them." He looked me up and down. "In your case, I would eat them."

"Mussels?"

"Aye the black shiny shells. They cling on to the rocks. Here," he gave me the basket he used to carry his food. "Take this and use it to collect them. I can keep an eye on you from here."

I was lithe and I had good balance but, even so, the rocks proved to be slippery. I later found out that Stumpy had known that it was a hard place from which to collect them which is why the mussels there were untouched. There were hundreds of them. They were easy to pick but the smell of the seaweed and the smell from the drain water from the town almost knocked me sick. The only thing which kept me going was the thought of what Caitlin had to do. Just putting up with the discharge from the privies in the town was not important.

I collected three baskets full. Each time I collected one I took them back to Stumpy who had found me an old Hessian sack. He nodded, "They'll do." He gazed at the glistening pile of shells. "Too many to eat. I'll tell you what; we'll go down to Megan. She has the shellfish shop on the corner. She'll buy them off you and cook them. Some you can eat and some she will pay you for. How's that?"

I was so happy I wanted to hug the smelly, one armed sailor but I was becoming a man and men did not do that. "That'll be fine." I would soon be earning money and that meant that Caitlin was closer to freedom.

The fish woman, Megan, was a broad rosy faced widow. Her red hands showed that she worked hard but she was a lovely lady. I got the impression that the two of them had something going on, I couldn't work out what. She seemed to know my story and kept shaking her head and ruffling my hair while mumbling about English bastards. She paid me a handful of copper coins and gave me a basket of the steaming mussels to take home. I thought it was a shame that Caitlin would not be able to eat them hot but at least I would have provided a meal for her when she came in.

I must have been more tired than I had thought for I fell asleep soon after eating, exactly, half of the mussels. Consequently, I was easily disturbed when Caitlin returned. "Sorry I didn't mean to wake you."

Her voice sounded slurred and sleepy; perhaps she was tired. "I have some mussels for you. They are lovely."

She hugged me and I smelled drink on her. "What a grand brother you are. I'll have them for breakfast."

With that, she promptly fell asleep. I lay awake. I was young but I was not stupid. My sister was even drunker than she had been the previous day. Perhaps she had drunk too much to help her to forget what she had been doing. I would have to wait until the morning to ask her. I didn't think I would get much sense from her in her present state.

She looked bleary-eyed when we awoke but she seemed more her normal self. "Why did you drink so much Caitlin?"

"Sure, and it was just to keep out the cold. It's a lovely drink called gin. Looks like water but tastes like the nectar from heaven."

I was not convinced but I showed her my coins. "See what I earned yesterday and Stumpy said he might get me a berth on a boat."

She grabbed me about the shoulders. "My wee brother earning money; I am so proud of you but I am also trying to find you a berth but not one where you would have to work. One of the gentlemen in the alehouse says he might be able to take you as a passenger if I can pay him some money and," she giggled, "show him some favours."

This did not please me in the least. "Tell your friend it is alright. I am sure Stumpy will come through for me and I would rather work than take charity."

Her face suddenly chilled as though frozen by snow. "And this is not charity. It is business. I am buying you a passage. That is not charity."

Fearing another rattled slap, I smiled, "We will see who makes the first offer then eh?"

Stumpy's face fell when I told him my story. He pointed his stump at the harbour. "The American ship sailed on last night's tide. That would have been the best place for you." He smiled although I could see that it was forced. "Never mind; I see the two big Indiamen are still berthed and there are always more ships coming in every day."

I went down to the rocks to collect more of the mussels but my spirits sank. I would have to rely on my sister and her dubious contact. I hated the thought of the favours and pleasures he would expect. I ate all of the mussels that I had not sold to Megan that night. With some of the money, I bought myself a cheap pair of rope-soled shoes. They would be useful if I ever gained a berth and they would protect my feet from the sharp rocks in the harbour. The rest of the money I hid. Stumpy had given me an old leather purse and he showed me how to tie it beneath my clothes to keep it hidden.

"There are many fine men on ships but there are some thieving bastards too!" He also took me to his home, little more than a roof and three walls really where he gave me some other treasure. He gave me an oilskin jacket, although torn in places he assured me it would keep out the wet. As he told me, "The sea is a fearful wet place!" He gave me a hat to go with it although it was just a woollen one. Finally, he gave me a pocket knife which folded up.

Once again, I did not see Caitlin until the next morning and this time she was full of excitement. "I told you I would come through for you! I have a berth on a ship and you won't need to work! It sails in two days' time so we will have to buy you things for the trip like some clean underwear and a spare pair of breeches."

"What about money?"

"Don't you worry yourself about that. It is your sister Caitlin who is organising this, not a one-armed old soak from the harbour."

Although I loved my sister I did not like the way she spoke about Stumpy who had shown me nothing but kindness. "Don't talk about Stumpy that way. He is kind and he looks after me."

Her eyes flashed an angry green. "Meaning I don't!"

"I didn't say that. Let's not quarrel. Which ship is it then?"

She looked suddenly puzzled and then she laughed. "I must be soft; I forgot to ask. I'll ask tonight." She reached into her purse and took out a silver sixpence. "Here, put this with your money."

"Where did you get this?"

"Never mind but I bet it is more than the sailor gave you."

As I left her to prepare for her work, I realised that she was jealous. I shook my head; Stumpy was a kind old man but she was family and blood was thicker than water. Stumpy was not as happy as I had thought he would be about the news that I had a berth. "I can't see officers from the Indiaman frequenting a whorehouse. But it might have been a crewman." He rubbed his stubble with his stump. "But they couldn't get you a passage. You be careful young Jack. Your sister sounds like a kind girl but she doesn't know men and the way of the world. Keep your wits about you and survive! Now you go and get your mussels. Tonight, I'll ask around about the ships again. See what I can discover."

That night as I left Megan and Stumpy, I didn't realise it would be for the last time. They both looked at me with such kindness that I felt safe for the first time since ma and da had died. When Caitlin came in, she woke me. She had the slurred speech and smell of someone who has been drinking but her eyes were wide with excitement. "I have great news, Jack. You sail for America on the morning tide. Captain Bailey will give you passage and his is a quick ship."

My heart sank down to my new rope-soled shoes. Black Bill Bailey was a smuggler and a pirate why would he offer me passage? "Are you sure I heard he was…"

"Don't you listen to gossip. He is a good man and a kind man. He is taking you to America in return for me looking after his house here in Cork." She beamed. "I am to be a housekeeper! I'll be a whore no more!" It sounded good but I was not convinced. However, I was excited. By noon the next day, I would be heading west to America to make my fortune and then return to bring my sister to the land of milk and honey. As I gathered my few belongings together to put them in the haversack Caitlin had brought me, I was sad that I would not see Stumpy and Megan before I left… but when I returned, ah, then I would reward them both for their kindness.

CHAPTER 2

Jack

The 'Rose of Tralee' had looked to be small when I had viewed her with Stumpy but now that I stood next to her, I saw that she was quite large. There were two masts and she was about eighty feet long. I later found out that she was called a Brigantine but, as with many things, I would discover that after I had been at sea for a month and was told such things. Black Bill Bailey was waiting for us impatiently at the gangplank. Caitlin was fluttering her eyes and I noticed that her lips were red and her cheeks rouged; the blue paint on her eyes was more obvious too.

When he saw us he turned his scowl to a smile. "Ah, so this is the wee laddie." He was Scottish but it was more of a gentle burr than the unintelligible gabble of a highlander.

"Yes, my love. This is my little brother, Jack."

"Not so little. Now, young Jack, you kiss your sister goodbye and then get aboard. My first mate will see to you. The tide waits for no man."

Caitlin held me tightly and I felt the salty tears

trickle down my face from my sister's eyes. "Now Bill will watch over you; trust me and we shall meet again. Of that, I have no doubt."

"Take care of yourself and, if you ever need him, go to Stumpy." She pulled back with the start of a scowl on her face. I held up my hand. "He is a kind man and if you have nowhere else to go you will be safe. Promise me."

She hesitated. "Well, I will always be safe with Bill so I will promise you." She peered over my shoulder and I suspect that the Captain must have looked angry for she said, "Now get aboard and I love you."

It was an awkward goodbye for we did not go in for such things in our home but I said, "I love you too sis." It sounded strange but, as events turned out I was pleased that I had said it.

I clutched my bag with my few belongings and hurried up the plank to the deck. I turned and saw the Captain fondling Caitlin. I was angry but I could say nothing and then he hurried up on to the deck and began to shout orders. "Hoist the foresail. Haul in the gangplank. Cast off forrard." He glanced down at me, all semblance of kindness gone. "And you, you scraggy wee shit, get yourself below deck and keep out of the way."

A huge hand grabbed me and propelled me through the hatch to the crew's quarters. "You heard the feckin captain now move!" That was my first meeting with the First Mate, Paddy Henry. He was a sour-faced bully who terrified the whole crew. He seemed to enjoy cruelty. In all the time I knew him I never saw him smile once. I would have broken something if it wasn't for the fact that I always had good balance and scrambling about on the rocks for mussels had honed that skill.

When I stood in the gloom I peered around to get my bearings. As my eyes became accustomed to the dark I saw neatly coiled hammocks and small lockers. I could also see a dim glow from further in and a small round man stood in the doorway. He smiled at me. "Welcome to the Rose of Tralee. You have just met the, always pleasant, First Mate, Mr Henry." He held out a greasy and pudgy hand. "And I am the cook, Fatty Hutton. Welcome aboard." He pointed to the corner of the deck where a locker stood open. "This is your berth and your hammock."

I was confused. Why was I bunking with the crew? "I thought I was a passenger."

He looked at me sadly. Although his English accent sounded foreign, it was not the aristocratic English of the lord of the manor. It was a rougher accent and it made me feel welcome. "Sorry son. You are now part of the crew." There was the noise of someone coming down the steps and he hissed, "I'll talk to you later. Stow your gear and just do everything that they say." He winked at me.

A huge ham of a hand slapped the back of my head. "Put your feckin gear in there and then get yourself on deck. It's time for you to earn your passage!" The laugh he gave was evil and there was no smile attached, Paddy Henry enjoyed bullying and on this ship, he only answered to the captain. The deck suddenly looked like a scene from hell and I was doomed to die there.

The sudden light of the main deck blinded me for a moment and I looked towards the stern. I could see, beyond the wheel, the harbour and, just for a moment I saw Stumpy. He must have recognised me for he raised his stump. I felt tears in my eyes but before I had a

36

chance to either cry or wave a roar came from Captain Bailey. "Grab the rope and pull you wee little shit! Let go aft!"

I was learning that my new name was *'wee shit'*. I saw three sailors on a rope and I took hold of it and helped them to pull. The sail at the bow gradually rose and caught the wind. I was amazed at how quickly the boat left the dock. I had no time to congratulate myself. One of the seamen began tying off the rope on a metal stanchion as the captain shouted, "Hoist the mainsail!"

The sailor who had been next to me, a young lad about five years older than me said, in a strange accent, "Best do as I do, otherwise Mister Henry will flay the skin from your bones!"

I could now see that the first mate had a quirt or short whip in his hands. His face left me under no illusions; if he could he would make me bleed and enjoy every red flecked drop. It looked like Stumpy was right. What had my sister done to me? I knew it would not have been deliberate but it looked as though I was not being given a free passage to America. By the time we had hoisted all of the sails on the brigantine, I was exhausted. I had not eaten since the previous night and not even had a drink. The salt air had parched my throat and the sun now chose to emerge from the clouds and I felt myself heating up.

First Mate Paddy Henry loomed up. "You, go to the captain. Now!"

Captain Black Bill Bailey was leaning on the stern taffrail. (I soon learned all the nautical terms although it cost me many a cuff of the ear to do so.) He was smoking a long thin cigar. The biggest man I had ever seen and the first negro was steering the boat his face set in a cheerful grin. "Now then you little wee shit. Your sister wants me to take you to America."

He paused, as though affording me the opportunity to speak. "Yes, sir. She said you would give me a free passage to America."

From his laugh and that of the negro, you would have thought I had told the funniest joke ever. When he had stopped laughing he grabbed hold of my ear and twisted it. "That empty-headed whore of a sister is even dumber than I thought. You are now a member of my crew until I say otherwise."

"Won't I be getting off in America then sir?"

The backhanded slap made that of Caitlin's seem like a love tap. I tasted blood in my mouth and my head rang. I picked myself up from the deck and he pointed his cigar at me. "Listen carefully. I hoped you were a little cleverer than your sister but obviously not. You are a member of my crew until I am tired of you and throw you to the sharks. Clear?"

Holding back the tears I mumbled, "Yes Captain."

"Now get below and stow your gear away."

I descended into the gloom and took my few possessions out of my bag. They seemed lost in the tiny locker. The young seaman who had been kind to me appeared at my shoulder. "Haven't got much have you boyo? An orphan, are you?"

I turned, amazed. "Yes. How did …?"

"Me too. There were two others but," he lowered his voice, "they upset the captain and they are feeding the sharks. Watch your step." He spoke with conviction. "I am Davy Thomas from Holyhead, that is in Wales. It makes us almost neighbours. We have a packet sails to Dublin and Cork every day."

38

"I am Jack Hogan. Thank you."

He put his arm around my shoulders and I noticed that his arms were knotted with muscles. "The first few days are the worst and they let you be once you know the ropes."

"Know the ropes?"

"Aye boyo. When to pull and when to lower. You stick with me." He looked worried. "Are you afraid of heights?"

"I don't think so. Why?"

He pointed through the open hatch. "Because we have to climb the ropes and reef the sails. On a day like today that is no problem. But in an Atlantic gale…"

He let the sentence drift in the breeze. I sighed. I wished that I was on the American ship. I think I would have been safer. Fatty Hutton peered around the door leading to the galley. "Here Jack." He handed me two pieces of bread with hunks of fried bacon and a mug of ale. "Eat them quick before the first mate sees you." He winked. "You are doing alright Irishman."

"Thank you." I gratefully bit off so much of the sandwich that it filled my mouth. I quickly gobbled it down and washed it down with the warm ale. Before I finished the rest off I said, quietly to the two men, "I feel like a slave and not a free Irishman."

Fatty sadly shook his head, "The Irish were never free and when you see real slaves you'll see how well off you are." Davy nodded his sombre agreement. I had barely finished the food when we heard, "All crew on deck!" I swallowed the ale and threw the mug to Fatty who grinned at me as he adeptly caught it.

There was no sign of Captain Black Bill Bailey. I could see the rest of the crew were gathered. There were ten of us and the steersman. It was not a big crew and I wondered how we would manage to sail the ship across the ocean. One of them just glowered at me and I wondered what I had done to offend him, or perhaps he was just a man who hated Irishmen. There appeared to be plenty of men who did that.

"Get down to the cargo deck. I want all the shackles oiling and securing." He pointed to Davy. "You, take the useless piece of Irish shite with you and see if he can pick it up otherwise." He gestured behind us with his thumb and all but Davy laughed.

We descended to the deck below ours. It was black as coal and, but for the oil lamps we carried, we would have seen nothing. Davy took my arm. "Come with me." He led me to the far end. There was a sudden movement and Davy's teeth flashed in the oil light. "Rats! The feckin ship is infested with them." He pointed at the chains tethered to the wall and held up an oil can. "Smear them all over with the oil. We need to make sure we can release them quickly."

"What are they for?"

He pulled me to one side. "Slaves."

"But my da and the priest said slavery was illegal."

"So it is but that doesn't mean it doesn't go on. The slave owners in America pay well for new slaves. The ones they have are like Black Jones," I looked puzzled, "the black man on the wheel. He was a slave and he escaped. The ones who were born in America have ideas about freedom. The darkies from Africa just work till they drop."

Paddy Henry's voice boomed from the dark. "If you two feckin fairies don't stop chattering like a pair of parrots I'll have the skin off your backs." We were silent.

When we returned to the deck it felt fresh and clean after the rat-infested hell hole we had visited. We spent the afternoon cleaning and tidying the ship. Davy told me that we had a few more days before we would pick up our cargo. "They'll put you in one of the watches. There are three. We all work during the day and at night each watch works three hours." He grinned. "I don't think they'll put you in my watch. They'll split us up." His face became serious. "Just so long as you avoid Eddie McNeil."

"Which one is he?" He waited until the sailor in question had turned around and then nodded. It was the scowling sailor who had glared at me earlier. "That suits me. He looks like a nasty piece of work."

Davy looked at me. "He is that boyo and watch out. He is a bum bandit."

I was young and I was innocent but as a good Catholic boy I knew all about bum bandits and I would keep my two knives sharp should he decide to choose me as a partner.

The boat gave a slight shudder and Davy looked up at the mast. "Shit! The wind's changed. We'll soon find out how good you are up the ratlines then!"

"All hands! Take in the mainsail." The first mate pointed to me. "You, the wee shit, follow the Welsh boy and try not to fall off. If you make a mess on my clean deck I'll skin you alive!" Skinning alive was a big thing for Paddy Henry.

I looked up at the mast which seemed as high as a mountain. I was afraid of the mast but I was more afraid of the first mate and I followed Davy's lead and grabbed hold of the ratlines and climbed. It is hard to believe now but as soon as my hands gripped the tarred rope I felt at ease and I leapt to the top, beating Davy and the others. They looked at me in amazement.

I heard the voice from below. "Right monkey boy; you are so feckin clever get to the end of the crosstree."

I could see a rope which was obviously meant as a walkway and I held on to the crosstree and slithered my way to the end of the spar. The ship seemed to pitch and toss, threatening to throw me at any moment but, I never thought for one second that I would fall. My body just seemed to adjust to the movement of the ship. Davy appeared next to grinning. "You are a natural. You are even better than Eddie." I looked along the mast and saw that Eddie was on the opposite end of the spar. Davy showed me what to do and, in no time at all, we had put a reef in the sail and the movement of the ship was much easier and more under control rather than the bucking horse she had been.

"Hoist the mizzen!"

We had no sooner finished than we had to slide down the lines and hoist the large sail at the stern of the boat. I had the pleasure of a grudging nod from the first mate as I passed him. My first day at sea was ending better than it had begun. As we entered the galley I was famished. Fatty Hutton gave me a big grin and gestured to a place at the swinging mess table closest to the pot. There was a piece of wood running around the edge of the table to stop the food tipping off and I was grateful for it as the dish with the sloppy stew slid towards me. I learned this was called the fiddle- I have no idea why. I found some of the terms they used to be bizarre in the extreme.

"As we have just left port, young Jack, we have fresh

bread so make the most of it. When it runs out we will be on hard tack."

"And weevils!" chimed up a remarkably cheerful Davy.

The rest of the crew joined us. The captain and Paddy Henry had the ship for the few minutes while we ate. As we devoured the welcome hot food and I suffered the glower and glare of Eddie the top man the second mate, Woody Tree gave us our watches. He was the oldest sailor on board and, in my opinion, the best. He fixed me with his stare as he conscientiously chewed the indeterminate meat. "Since you have shown yourself to be such a good man on the rigging then you shall be on my watch young Hogan." He gave the glimmer of a smile. "We have the second watch."

Davy murmured, "Midnight."

Woody glared at Davy who nodded his apology. "There are just three of us on watch." He pointed to Fatty. "Fatty here is the fourth. You work Fatty's share and we eat well." His face lit up into a smile and I felt happy. There were still three men on board who terrified me but at least eleven seemed like friendly men.

Davy showed me how to sling my hammock and then how to get in. After the mussel collecting and the rigging climbing, I found it easy but Davy assured me that most landlubbers fell out during the first week at sea. Eddie had already gone on watch and the captain and Paddy ate in the captain's cabin so I was able to look at my surroundings. The deck above our head was low and we had to stoop to avoid banging our heads. There was just enough space for ten hammocks but we only ever needed seven so it was not too cramped. Davy told me that when in the tropics, most men slept on deck as it was cooler. Some of the men sat at the mess table and carved intricate pieces of wood or bone called scrimshank. Davy told me that they could sell them as souvenirs of foreign trips and people at home loved them. I decided that, when time allowed, I would try my hand. The penknife from Stumpy would come in handy.

After Davy turned in I was about to do the same when Fatty gestured to me and I went to the door of the galley. I knew that it was a heinous crime to enter without permission but Fatty pulled me in and closed the curtain. He took me to the far side of the pot which had bubbling stew in it; tomorrow's meal. He spoke quietly to me.

"I am Stumpy's friend. He said to look out for a red-haired Irish lad who looked like he needed a good meal."

My day was getting better and better. "You know Stumpy then?"

"Aye, we served the Queen together." He shook his head in sad remembrance. "I didn't know it then but they were the best of times." He lowered his voice even more. "The crew are mainly good but there are some bad 'uns and Captain Bill, well he didn't get the nickname Black for nothing. You keep your nose clean and we'll see about getting you off this ship in America if we can."

"But he said..."

"I know what he said but you just keep safe till we reach Charleston and we'll see."

"We?"

"There are others looking out for you and all but you needn't know that. Just keep out of Eddie's way and avoid upsetting Black Bill or Paddy. Now you turn

44

in. Tomorrow is another busy day."

If I thought my new found skill as a top man would make my life easier I was wrong. Paddy Henry would lay about him with his 'starter' as he called it at the slightest and most innocent of mistakes. Davy told me in a quiet moment that he had been a bosun's mate on a Royal Navy ship and he had learned discipline there. He certainly enjoyed meting it out on me and Davy! I also had to contend with nudges and sly punches from Eddie who no longer saw me as a potential bedmate but as a rival as the best top man aboard and he tried to hurt me whenever possible. When Woody and Blackie discovered that they had a quiet word and I saw the top man sporting a bruised cheek. I know they meant well but it just stored up more pain for me. That apart, I was quite enjoying my time on the ship. My sleep was more comfortable than the floor at home and the food was in far greater quantities than I had ever seen in Ireland. That first week we ate like kings with fresh meat every day. Davy told me that we would soon be on salted pork. He said that as though it was a hardship- it was meat and far better than thin cabbage soup. The work was hard and I was not as strong as the others but, with the food and the sunshine, I soon began to grow into my clothes which had all been my da's hand me downs. Fatty told me not to worry about spare clothes as there was a slop chest. I asked Davy about that and he looked sad.

"The lads who were fed to the sharks and the ones who either ran or died, well their clothes go into the slop chest."

It was a sobering reminder of how perilous life at sea could be. That was confirmed three days out of Cork when we ran into a gale. We were summoned from our hammocks to find the ship tossing on the stormy sea like a cork. There were troughs big enough to swallow the ship and the waves were like walls of water. We scurried up the ratlines to take in the main sheet before it tore the mast from the ship. The storm was so powerful that the cross trees almost touched the sea as the wind threw us around. I had learned to climb in bare feet as the grip was better and, that night, it saved my life. As I was racing up to the mast I did not notice Eddie coming alongside me. He hit my legs, with his arm, so hard that they lost their grip and I was forced to hang on to the tarred rope. I should have fallen had I not curled my toes around the swinging rope and secure my hold. I turned and glared at Eddie who swarmed up the ropes, grinning at me. I would need to watch the top man who seemed to have gone beyond bullying to attempted murder. It took some time to reef the sail as we were holding on as much as we were securing the sail. By the time we reached the deck, Black Bill and Paddy had lowered an anchor to hold us steadier until the wind abated.

By dawn, we were exhausted. The galley fire had gone out and we had no hot food. The last of the bread had been ruined by salt water pouring through the open hatches and we were miserable but, as Fatty pointed out, you had to be alive to be miserable. We spent the rest of the day repairing the ship. I learned how to stitch canvas and repair damaged rigging. It was at this time that I learned, from Fatty, how to splice ropes and tie an amazing variety of knots. It would be my occupation during the off duty times.

Black Bill Bailey was in a foul mood about the delay

as we had a rendezvous off the Azores. I managed to avoid invoking his ire. It was Eddie who suffered the rough edge of his tongue and his hand when the bitter top man accidentally dropped a marlin spike over the side. We had plenty of them but it was the excuse Black Bill was looking for. He took another marlin spike and beat the unfortunate top man about the head and arms. Perhaps the beating was worse than we thought for it seemed to hurt Eddie more than we knew at the time.

We hoisted the storm anchor and set sail before dusk. We set every inch of canvas and the ship fairly flew across the sea. When we were off watch we just collapsed into our hammocks and it seemed no time at all until we were summoned to the deck again. Woody took the helm and I was sent to the bow as a lookout. The old sailor was not happy about the weather for the wind seemed to be building again. As we came on deck I heard him muttering. "We should take a reef or two. This is not good."

The wind began to build and I found myself almost submerged as the bow plunged into troughs and then rose like a breaching whale. Toby, my other messmate, came for me. "Woody says come to the wheel it is too dangerous here."

It was a struggle to get back along the slippery deck and we slid rather than walked. When we reached Woody he said, "Jack, wake the Captain and tell him I need him. Toby, you grab the wheel."

I made my way aft to the big cabin at the stern. I knocked timidly and wondered if I had knocked hard enough. I heard, to my relief, his gruff croak, "Come! Damn your eyes!"

I entered the cabin which looked just like our mess

deck but it only had one hammock. Black Bill was standing, putting on his sea boots. "Second Mate says he needs you, sir. The storm is getting up again."

He nodded as he felt the motion. "Rouse the crew!"

I ran along to the crew's quarters. "All hands on deck!"

I was luckier than the others for I was awake already and I reached the end of the cross tree first. I began to reef it in having learned that time was of the essence in these matters. Davy soon joined me so that the mast tipped away from us. Perhaps it was that which caused the accident, we will never know but Eddie was making his way to the position at the far end of the mast when the boat tipped alarmingly. He reached up for the stay but his arm must have been more damaged by the beating than we thought. His hand seemed to close on the stay but he continued to fall, his dying scream ended by the noise of his body plunging into the water. We had no time to speculate on his demise for we were now a man down and we had to work even harder to reef the sail. I knew that we were in danger when Paddy Henry joined us, his huge hands working like windmills as we secured the sail.

No-one liked losing a messmate, even one as unpleasant as Eddie. As we ate ship's biscuit the next morning I asked Woody. "Will the captain not say a few words over the sea for the dead man?"

Woody shook his head, "No son. Eddie is in Davy Jones's locker now and he will join the crew of the Flying Dutchman; doomed to sail the seven seas until the crack of doom."

I learned, in my time on the Rose of Tralee, that sailors are a superstitious lot and I found myself signing the cross. The thought of a watery and lonely grave terrified me. We were now a crewman short and, despite what I thought of him, a good sailor. I had no idea how we were going to cope. In the end, Paddy Henry just rearranged the watches so that Davy was moved to his watch, and, like Woody's operated with just three men.

The day that Eddie died marked a change in our fortune and the weather. The wind blew in our favour and sped us on our way to our rendezvous. I was at the masthead securing a loose stay when I first spotted the rocky island that was the Azores. It belonged to Portugal but we would not be landing. I shouted down, "Land Ho!" and I heard the order to reef sails. Black Bill wanted to arrive after dark for his clandestine meeting. There was a large mountain, Fatty said it was an extinct volcano, at the eastern end of the island and we anchored in its lee. We had no lights showing and the nearest settlement appeared to be a dot of houses some way to the east.

As we waited, Paddy ordered two deck guns to be mounted close to the wheel. I could see that they were aimed at hatches leading to the cargo deck. Woody then issued us with cutlasses and cudgels while the officers all stuck two pistols in their belts. "Are we expecting trouble?" I whispered to Davy.

"Slaves, boyo. Black as coal miners. Sometimes they come aboard weeping and wailing but sometimes they have a mad bugger with them and they try to run. We should be fine." He sounded confident but he still gripped his cutlass.

Fatty, too had come on deck and it was no surprise. Since hitting the waters far to the south of Ireland the temperature had risen and, below decks was like an oven. As his fire was out there was no need for him to be in the galley. He pointed at the cutlass I held. "I daresay you have never used one of those pig stickers before eh?"

I held the strange, curved weapon in my hand. "No, sir."

"Thought so. Davy, when you are off watch tomorrow, see Woody and ask him if you can give Jack a lesson with the blade. It may come in handy. If you have to use it then swing hard and away from yourself." I did not know when I would need cutlass skills in America but Fatty, like his friend Stumpy, had never steered me wrong.

I wondered at the tension amongst the crew but I discovered that the Royal Navy patrolled these waters looking for blackbirders like us. The night was silent save for the sloshing of the water in the bilges and the creaking of the timbers. Toby had been sent aloft and, in the middle of the dark and moonless night he whispered down, "Sail to the north."

Paddy Henry's voice sounded strangely quiet and muted as he growled, "Stand to. It may not be our cargo."

The dhow which edged close to us was obviously not the Royal Navy and even I breathed a sigh of relief. The two ships were the same height and they tied tightly to us. The gangplank was run out and Black Bill and Paddy went aboard. I saw my first Arabs and they looked strange. They were not as dark as Blackie and they wore turbans and long flowing gowns that looked like dresses. The crew were bare-chested Africans who looked dumbly at us. I saw money change hands and then Black Bill and Paddy returned.

"Get ready." Woody disappeared with an oil lamp into the hold followed by Fatty. I just stood next to Davy as our crew lined up in two lines. A line of slaves, all chained and manacled began to ascend from the dhow's deck. They shuffled towards us, prodded by the swords of the dhow's crew. About twenty had passed us, descending when one of them tried to break for freedom. He was still on the dhow's deck and he tried to jump between the ships. I don't know what he was thinking. Had he succeeded he would have been crushed by the two hulls but it mattered not for the dhow's captain took off his head with one blow. The line of slaves stopped as the headless body crumpled to the deck. I wondered what they would do until I saw a crewman bring an axe and chop off the feet. As the body and feet joined the head and were thrown overboard, the line continued to board us. I counted forty-nine slaves and I wondered how they would fare in the confined cargo hold.

We could see the first false dawn as we separated and Paddy Henry ordered full sail and we sped westwards towards America.

CHAPTER 3

Jack

The first thing I noticed about the slaves was the smell. It was the smell of unwashed and alien bodies and it was the smell of urine and excreta which ran unabated down their legs. I was spared the horror of giving them water, for they were not fed but I could hear their moaning and their keening. Sometimes Paddy Henry would tire of it and lay about them with his whip. It worked for a while but then they would continue. We also had to throw three dead slaves overboard after they succumbed to the rigours of the voyage and I noticed that the dorsal fins of sharks began to follow the boat. This displeased Black Bill and Davy explained why, "The Royal Navy knows that sharks following a ship mean it is a slave ship."

Woody agreed that we could both practise with the cutlasses and Davy and I enjoyed the bouts. Although he was stronger than I was, I had a quicker hand and we were evenly matched. When he could, Fatty watched us and ensured that we did not hurt each other. The old sailor also gave us tips about fighting. They proved to be invaluable when I joined the Confederacy. Fatty also showed me how to load and clean a pistol. It seemed that we were not the worst of the jackals of the sea and there were pirates who would try to take our cargo from us. Shot and powder were too expensive to be wasted on me but I learned how to hold and load the weapon. The six days with the slaves aboard flew by and I learned, also, to know when the land was close. The air smelled different. It smelled dirtier somehow and Davy nodded when I told him that. "Aye, we are approaching the United States and Charleston. It is where we deliver the slaves."

I became excited and worried both at the same time. I had almost reached my goal but how would I get ashore? I was certain that they would be watching me. Fatty agreed. "Now that Eddie is dead you are too valuable to lose. Good top men like you and Davy are hard to come by." He shook his head sadly. "We may have to wait until our next voyage."

My disappointment lasted until I saw my first American city. It looked totally different from Ireland. There was a fort guarding the harbour, I discovered it was called Fort Sumter and a second one guarding the other side. Most of the buildings looked to be painted wood and it looked less shabby and cleaner than Cork. Fatty shook his head, "There are still dark places there young Jack and you need to be careful." He looked over to where Paddy Henry was staring at me. "Not that I think you will be going ashore."

We anchored in the roads and a customs officer rowed out to us. He disappeared into the main cabin and returned a few moments later grinning. Davy whispered. "That's him paid off. Now we wait until the buyer comes."

It was after dark when three longboats rowed up and tied up on the far side of the ship. This was the first time I ever saw James Booth Boswell, a man who would greatly influence me as a man. He was tall and thin. He had the look of a gentleman. I know that sounds a strange thing to say but I was comparing him to the red-coated villain who had slain my parents. That murderer had obviously been a gentleman but he neither looked nor acted like one. James Booth Boswell always looked and acted like the southern aristocrat he was. At the time I did not wonder why he was engaged in the slave trade but I discovered that some years later. He came aboard with the biggest man I had ever seen, including Paddy Henry. He was the young man's bodyguard, Danny Murphy. I happened to be standing close by the gangplank coiling a rope when he stepped aboard. He touched his hat and said, "Good evening young man."

I was so taken aback that I could barely muster a, "And to you sir."

The huge man with him just grinned and winked at me. They were below deck for some time and then emerged with Captain Bailey. "I trust you have a safe voyage east. Will you be staying in port for long?"

The southern gentleman sounded so refined that I almost shuddered when Black Bill Bailey spoke. "Just long enough to get some food and swill the decks of the smell of the darkies!"

"Until the next time." As he came by me he tapped his hat and nodded. I didn't know what to do and so I gave a small bow. Both he and his man grinned. "A young gentleman in the making I see. I look forward to seeing you again young sir!"

The slaves began to moan and wail as they were led to the far side of the ship. The sun had set and the lee of the ship was in complete darkness. I could hear the crack of the whips and the cries of the naked black men and women as they were lowered into the boats. Fatty was right, I had thought of myself as a slave but I was not. I might be a prisoner on a ship but I had more freedom than the poor unfortunates who had just entered the United States of America.

Black Bill Bailey took Fatty and Woody ashore with him in the ship's longboat. I saw a sad shake of the head from Fatty. I already knew that I would not be escaping this voyage but when we returned to Cork, and then I would release Caitlin and break from her false promise of servitude.

The deck watch was kept by Paddy Henry and he positioned himself, with a musket and pistol to stop any of us trying to swim to land. It was never an option for me as I couldn't swim and the others seemed happy enough on board. They had all moaned about not being able to enjoy the delights of Charleston. As they hadn't been paid then I wondered how they could have afforded those expensive pleasures.

When the boat returned there were four men on board and the fourth was a replacement for Eddie. Mario Locatelli had barely ten words in English but he was more agile than a monkey and was keen to return to the other side of the Atlantic. I doubted that Captain Bailey would allow that but, as he was now on board the ship, it was a moot point. Fatty had done us proud and brought fresh meat, vegetables and rum. I ate something called sweet corn and melon for the first time and I wondered at the array of foods available in America. Having survived on potato and cabbage for so many years I was enjoying food for the first time in my life.

While the rest of the crew overindulged themselves with the rum and the beer brought by the cook I just drank small beer. I had seen the effects of drink on my sister and I was now wary of the demon drink; especially when Bill Bailey was around! Fatty too was careful with his intake. There were just the seamen in the mess and when the men began to gamble he took me to one side. "Sorry about that Jack. I hoped he would give shore leave but I think he was worried that we wouldn't replace Eddie. There's always the next trip. That will be in about six weeks."

"What if I jump ship in Cork?"

"We aren't going back directly to Cork. We are bound for Bristol to take on a cargo of gee jaws. We are going down to Spain to pick up slaves this time. The captain heard that the Navy is looking for us. We will need a new route." My heart sank. I was trapped aboard this ship just like Eddie on the Flying Dutchman. Fatty saw my discomfort. "Don't worry. Next time we get across he will not be as suspicious." He ruffled my hair which had grown considerably on the voyage, "You are young and have lots of time. And I will cut these locks in the morning. We don't want nits do we?"

The voyage back was, literally, plain sailing. We had neither storm nor incident and even Black Bill Dailey managed a few jokes with the crew. I managed to spend some time with the negro, Blackie Jones. I asked him if he had any sympathy for the slaves we had transported. Without taking the cigar out of his mouth he said, "The way I look at it we don't make them slaves. That's the Arabs and I hate them bastards. If we didn't take them across the sea then someone else would and the other slavers are much worse than our ship."

"Worse than being locked up in a lightless hold?"

"On the big ships, they have just this much space." He held his arms about two feet apart. "And they squat like that all the way across. Some of them are crippled for life. At least they can stand up and stretch here. They don't have to piss and shit on the slave on the next deck below. There are scuppers here for that. No, young Jack, don't you worry about them black fellahs. They will survive. My family did and I have a fine life now." He nudged me playfully in the ribs. "At least I don't have to dice with no damn death at the top of a pitching ship." He shook his head. "I swear I thought you were going to die more than once." He laughed a deep belly laugh which was infectious.

At other times I practised with the cutlass and, one fine day Captain Black Bill Bailey taught me how to fire a pistol. I wasn't sure I could hit anything but at least I knew how to do it and I wouldn't be afraid of the noise. "You have done better than I thought you wee squab. I thought you would have drowned and I would have had to give the bad news to that pretty sister of yours." He jabbed me in the chest, "You keep your nose clean and you'll make some money with me."

I was tempted by his pleasant conversation to bring up Cork. "Will I be able to see my sister when we reach Cork?"

He became more serious, all bantering had disappeared. "It will take a lot more voyages before I trust you not to run. The rest of the crew can have shore leave but you will be with either Paddy or me. Think about it!"

I almost broke into tears when he told me that. To be so close to Caitlin and not to see her was heartbreaking. I told Fatty. "Ah, it's for the best. I'll see Stumpy and find out about her. How's that?"

I brightened. "It's better than nothing. Now you'll be due some pay. Are you going to keep it or do you want anything?"

I couldn't think of anything but I remembered the money Caitlin had given me. I took out the silver sixpence and my few coppers. Perhaps if she had them she could escape her position. "Ask Stumpy to give her these few coins. If I am due pay then I shan't need them." A strange look passed over his face and he left, clutching the money without another word.

Bristol looked far bigger and had more stone buildings than either Cork or Charleston. The guns in the harbour and the Royal Navy ships meant that we spent less than four hours at the quayside and no-one left the ship. A scrawny old man in fine clothes came aboard and spoke only with Black Bill. I learned, later, that he was the ship's owner. We sailed on the tide and headed for my home.

Cork looked so comforting when I saw the old city that I was tempted to leap into the river and swim to shore. Then I remembered that I couldn't swim and I had to wait on board with Paddy Henry and Blackie while the rest of the crew went to enjoy the pleasures of that city. I did receive my pay and it went directly into my purse. When I landed in America I would not be a poor man. Blackie sensed my sadness and told me many tales of America. It seemed he had been a slave in Virginia, close to Monticello which was, apparently a fine and famous house. He said it was a hot and humid land filled with tobacco and corn but he spoke fondly of the Blue Ridge Mountains and the mighty Shenandoah. He was so eloquent that I wanted to visit that place more than any other. The time passed far quicker than I could have imagined and, before we knew it, we were heading, once more, for the islands of Spain, just off North Africa.

When Fatty returned I grilled him about Caitlin and Stumpy. He was evasive at first but I eventually learned that Caitlin had, indeed, become the housekeeper for the captain but she had become aloof and wanted little to do with Stumpy.

"He will give her the money!"

Fatty smiled, "His friend Megan will and, I daresay, put a flea in her ear!"

As with the trip back to Britain, the voyage was easy. This time we lost no slaves and no crew so that, when we anchored in the Charleston harbour we were all happy and satisfied. When the slave master and his lieutenant came aboard we were surprised when they did not descend down to the depths but, instead stood, with Captain Bailey on the main deck. I could see that Black Bill Bailey was not happy but it seemed that James Booth Boswell wished to address us.

"Gentlemen, I wish to thank you personally for your efforts on my behalf. I am beholden to you for you have made me richer than my daddy." He laughed, "And believe me that is rich. I would like you to share in my bounty." He gestured to the huge Irishman with him. "Mr Murphy here will give you a card with my address on it. Should you ever be in Charleston and need my assistance then please call upon me."

Blackie took his cigar out of his mouth. "Even a nigra, Mr Booth?"

The aristocrat smiled and stared back, "Even a nigra, Mr Jones."

Paddy Henry snorted, "A feckin waste of time. The ignorant bastards canna read anyway."

James Booth Boswell ignored the angry look thrown by his lieutenant at the first mate and said calmly, "And can you read Mr Henry?" The shake of the head was angry but definite. "Then you are all in the same boat." He smiled, "Quite literally!" Danny Murphy laughed while Paddy Henry just scowled.

He descended below with the captain and I stared at the prettily decorated piece of card. For the first time in my life, I wanted to be able to read.

Surprisingly the one member of the crew, apart from Black Bill himself, who could read, was Blackie Jones. His owner had had him taught from a young age. For the next two years, I learned how to read, I learned how to shoot and I became a much stronger and more skilful sailor. Despite the fact that I showed no sign of running Black Bill still kept me on board every time we returned to Cork. I was allowed off twice in Charleston but only under the supervision of Paddy Henry. I bridled a little but kept my anger hidden. I would make a break but it would be on my terms. My purse was now filled and was inside a money belt I had made out of leather. The time I had on the ship whilst in harbour was not wasted. To be truthful the life on board the ship did not seem that bad. It had been over a year since the first mate had had cause to strike me and now, with my frame filled out and my muscles as rippled as Davy's I

60

was not such an easy mark.

It was in the summer of 1853 that things changed. We had picked up our normal cargo and were heading west when Davy shouted from the masthead. "Sail away to the north!"

We rarely saw ships for our route was well away from the main sea lanes from Britain to America. I could see from his expression that Black Bill was not happy. "All hands on deck. Full sail!"

I could see his dilemma. The ship, which we could all now see, had the wind on its quarter and was flying. It was also heading for us and that meant one of two things, a pirate or a Royal Navy ship. Davy confirmed our worst fears. "It's a Royal Navy brig!"

A Royal Navy brig was bigger than us and carried cannons. Our two deck guns would be useless until they chose to board. As we hoisted the sail I kept looking nervously over my shoulder. Woody chuckled. "Don't worry Jack, they won't open fire. That would risk killing the darkies. They'll try to take us and the Rose can fly with the best of them."

I knew this to be true as we had careened the ship four times and scraped the weed and barnacles from her hull. But this was a Royal Navy ship and I knew from the others that they were to be feared.

The captain changed course so that we had the advantage of the wind but that route took us away from our destination. Every inch of canvas was set. Paddy Henry came on deck with the chest of weapons. "Best tool up."

As we armed ourselves Toby ventured. "Looks like we are losing her." I peered aft and saw that we were, indeed extending our lead.

Davy's voice sounded like a crack of doom. "Sail to the south. Another brig!"

"Shit!" Paddy Henry almost spat the word out. "It's a trap!"

I was too far away to hear the skipper's words but he and Blackie hurled the wheel over and we caught a sudden gust of wind. It was now a chase to the west. Although we were faster than the two brigs, they were converging on us. If the wind changed direction at all then we would be caught. Paddy and Woody both came racing down the deck. "Mario, Jack, get up the mainmast we are going to add a spritsail, see if we can get an extra knot out of her."

The sail was heavy and required two of us to manhandle it to the top of the mainmast. While Mario tied it on I unrolled it. The bottom end flapped free until Davy grabbed it and secured it to a cleat. As soon as he did so the Rose almost leapt forwards. We waited until we were sure that the sail was secured and then slid down the ratlines. I was facing towards the northern vessel and saw a puff of smoke, a few seconds later we heard a dull crump. I saw the cannonball strike the water and bounce some hundred yards in front of us. Paddy spat over the side. "All piss and wind. If they hit us they kill the darkies and they want them to take home. Then they will be feckin heroes!" He looked up at the new sail. "If that sail gets us out of this you two can have a tot of rum tonight!"

The second ship also fired across our bows and this time they were even closer. Despite Paddy's words, I felt uncomfortable. The two deck guns had been loaded although what good they would do I had no idea. It was now afternoon and we had to evade the two ships for another eight hours if we were to escape. Once it became dark we could change direction and evade our pursuers but, until then we were helpless.

I turned to Woody, "What if there is a third ship ahead of us."

"Then we are dead!"

"Dead?"

"Aye, we'll have to fight and the Royal Navy always wins. The survivors will be hanged. No jail time for slavers. So you best hope that Black Bill Bailey has a few tricks up his sleeve."

The next few hours went by so slowly that I was convinced that time had stood still. The two brigs appeared to be a little closer and each shot they fired seemed to threaten us a little more. They appeared to be firing to gauge how close they were to us and even I could see that, unless the weather intervened, they would have our range before dark. Fatty brought out salt pork sandwiches and small beer. We dare not leave our station for the slightest deviation in the wind or the weather would mean we had to react instantly. I noticed that the ship to the north of us was closing faster than the one to the south. It showed me, a novice seaman, that the wind was stronger from that quarter. Perhaps the captain had also seen it some time ago for he and Blackie began to slowly turn the wheel to port as Paddy and Woody trimmed the foresail. Suddenly the ship to the south looked closer and I wondered if the wily Black Bill had miscalculated but just as suddenly the ship to the south also had to turn to shadow us and we began to draw away. Once again we were drawing away as we had when this sea chase began.

I had had a turn at the masthead and now it was

Davy who stood watch. Suddenly he shouted. "Captain, the ship to the south is signalling."

Paddy was hurrying back to the wheel and I heard him say to Woody, "Damn his eyes! That means there is a third one out there!"

Woody shook his head, "Now we are for it. Check your pistols and reload with fresh powder. You may get a chance to fire that gun in anger, young Jack, although I pray to God not."

"Sail to the west. I think it is a frigate."

Even I knew that a frigate was almost a ship of the line. With forty guns and the brigs like two sheepdogs to herd us, we were as good as dead. I looked aft and saw that Black Bill looked quite calm. I wondered what he was planning. I kept glancing to port and starboard to ascertain the position of our two hunters. Then I heard Toby say, "Dead ahead. A big bastard."

Even seen in the distance I could see how big it was. I also knew that close-hauled against the wind it would not be able to move closer to us. But then all she needed to do was to block our escape. If we turned to port or starboard then the brigs would have us. When I glanced back to the brig on our port side I saw that it was getting closer. Black Bill was heading towards her! The brig to the north looked further away. I realised that the captain of the brig to the south had not realised that we were closing. We would have the weather gauge and would move faster than the brig. Our clean hull and extra sails would mean we could outrun her, just so long as they didn't open fire.

The captain of the ship to the north had seen what we intended and had added extra canvas to his topgallant. He would not catch us before we passed the southern brig. What I didn't know was the captain's intentions. Woody gestured to me. "You come with me." He led me to the port deck gun. It was just a small six pounder; a shorter version of the nine-pound long tom used in Nelson's navy. Normally we would have loaded it with grapeshot but Woody carefully chose a cannonball. He checked it for deformities caressing it almost as though it was a woman and, when satisfied he loaded the gun. He placed a bag of grapeshot next to it. When he saw me looking he winked and said, "Just in case we get lucky!" I saw that Paddy and Toby were doing the same with the starboard gun.

The brig was now so close that I could read her name, the Ludlow Castle. I could also see that her six gun ports were open on her starboard side and there were three marines, resplendent in their red uniforms, standing by the wheel.

"Stand by Mr Tree!"

"As soon as I fire damp the barrel down and be ready to haul it forward when I gives the order."

"Yes, Mr Tree."

The ship suddenly jinked to starboard and we were sailing parallel to the Ludlow Castle. I know that the manoeuvre threw its captain as its sailors hurried up the rigging.

"Now Mr Tree!"

Woody jerked the lanyard and there was a loud crack which deafened me. The cannon slithered back on its trunions and I stuck the damp ram down the barrel. I was almost knocked from my feet as the captain hurled the wheel around for us to pass along the stern of the brig. The wind on our quarter and the clean hull made us agile as a hare. I heard, "Fire!" and another loud crack; this time from Paddy's gun. The thick smoke from the two guns obscured my view but I heard the thin cheer from the rest of the crew.

Woody patted me on the head. "Well done son. We won't need that second shot now."

As the smoke cleared I saw that the rudder had gone from the brig and she was drifting helplessly. Her crew were busy lowering their sails whilst others tried to load and run out the port guns. The Rose was just too fast for her and we were out of range before the ports were opened. There was a desultory crack as the six guns fired but the cannonballs flicked over the water without striking anything. The other brig had tried to match our course and now found herself having to tack around her wounded consort. It extended our lead and the frigate was now a dot on the northern horizon. We had escaped.

CHAPTER 4

Jack

Charleston Harbour 1854

We arrived later than we had hoped as the captain had had to sail well to the south, almost as far as Florida, before he was certain that he had evaded his pursuers. When we reached the harbour he gestured to me. "You have been a good lad and served me well. I think you can come ashore with me." He glowered at me. "Just don't run. I know this town like I know Cork and there is nowhere a red-haired Irishman could hide from me."

I smiled a false smile and nodded as though I intended to heed his warning. I had no intention of rejoining the Rose. Fatty and Davy both knew that I would run which was why I had not bothered with a goodbye. As I stepped down the gangplank I glanced and saw them both raise their hands and smile. They knew I would run. They would understand the lack of words and Fatty would get a message to Caitlin. Part of me worried that Black Bill might take my desertion out on her but I thought it unlikely. Besides I could do little about it. I just had to worry about how to flee this dangerous man and escape in a town and a country I knew little about.

"Where are we going, sir?"

"We missed our meeting with Mr Booth so we will have to ride out to his place and let him know we are here." He smiled at me. "At least we'll have a bed tonight and a bath too. Call it a reward for a job well done. That was smart work with the sail and the cannon. I think I got the better of the deal with your sister."

He hired two horses from the stables and we rode through the town. It was humid and oppressive after almost three years at sea. I felt as though I had the weight of the world on my shoulders. There was no breeze and the humidity was incredibly high. The town appeared to be populated with slaves as every face was black. Here and there a white overseer would crack his whip at a slave who appeared to be slower than the rest. "Are there no white people here sir?"

"Not in the midday sun. They will all be in the cool of their homes. The darkies are used to this. Come on, the sooner we get there the sooner we can cool down."

Even after we had left the town the heat continued to drench us in sweat and I felt wetter than during a force seven gale. After half an hour of riding along tree-lined roads, we reached the entrance to a plantation; it had the name Briardene. Unlike the others, we had passed this one had a barrier and two guard huts at its entrance. The white guards recognised the captain and waved us through. Black Bill saw my puzzled look and said. "The other plantations grow cotton and such. This one grows slaves." He laughed at his own joke. "The guards are there to keep the slaves in until they are sold."

The drive led up to a magnificent white house which had a huge porch. Outside stood two black slaves in a green livery complete with top hats. I had seen men dressed such as this outside the biggest hotels in Cork; it was a mark of how expensive they were. Mr Boswell was a rich man after all. When we reined in the two slaves held our horses and a black butler stepped on to the porch. "Good to see you again Captain Bailey. Mr Booth is on the rear veranda. Would you and the young gentleman like to follow me?"

I almost looked around. Was I the young gentleman? Things had changed since I had left Ireland. Inside, the house felt much cooler and I could see fans in the ceiling slowly circulating the air. I later found out that they were operated by slaves. To say I was impressed by the decoration and the furniture would be an understatement but then I did not have much with which to compare it. My home had had a table and four homemade chairs. The stable had had hay and my mess had hammocks! I suspect a hovel would have looked luxurious to me.

James Boswell Booth rose from his hammock as we stepped out on to the rear veranda. Before it lay a beautiful lawn looking like a green ocean with horses being schooled by slaves. The veranda itself had four slaves wafting air.

"Ah, Captain Bailey. I trust there were no problems?"

"We had a run in with three Royal Navy ships about a day out." He grinned. "We escaped and I thought I would treat young Hogan to a day away from the ship."

He strode over and shook my hand. "And you are most welcome sir! Jarvis fetch the gentlemen a mint julep would you?"

I must have looked puzzled for our host said, "Trust me, young man, you will enjoy it. It is an alcoholic drink with mint and it is chilled. Perfect for a day such as this." He gestured for us to sit. I know it sounds absurd but I had never sat in a comfortable seat before and it felt, well it felt strange. The drinks arrived and I drank a speculative mouthful. It was delicious and sweet. I saw Mr Booth smile and then he and the captain began to talk about the voyage. I didn't mind being ignored. The drink was pleasant and I wasn't working. For the first time since I had come ashore, I felt cool.

"You will, of course, both be my guests tonight?"

The captain nodded and then gestured at me. "Thank you kindly but we will need to keep our eye on this one. I don't want him running."

Our host gave me a curious look but said, "Of course. I will have Mr Murphy keep a special eye on him. Would you like to bathe now captain?"

"Aye, I would."

"And you Mr Hogan?" I had never had a real bath before but I felt it would be rude to decline and I nodded my assent. "Good. And afterwards?"

Billy Bailey grinned. "I have a mind for a pair of buxom darkies."

"Of course and you young sir, would you like to have some pleasure with my ladies?"

I blushed and shook my head. "No, thank you, sir, I..."

They both laughed. "A gentleman I see. Well, when you have bathed how about I take you out for a ride and

70

show you my land eh? I would like to know more about you young Jack Hogan."

There were three tubs in the bathhouse and two female slaves who undressed us. I would have baulked at this effrontery but Captain Black Bill said, "Just enjoy it, Jack. They have seen naked men before."

The two young girls giggled at my blushes and whispered to each other when they had undressed me. "Why are they looking like that captain?"

"They have never seen red hair before."

My slaves took a sponge and some perfumed soap and began to wash my body. I was alarmed at how much dirt came off. I also noticed how brown, almost black my arms were. I suspected my face was too.

"Give him a shave and a haircut while he is in there." Mr Boswell's voice floated in from outside.

I had been shaving for a year but, without a mirror, it was difficult to see the effect. The two slaves attended to me while the captain lay back luxuriating in the water which he had changed halfway through the process. The girls took each lock as they cut it and put it to one side. I found out later that they gave it to a local witch who used it for charms. When I discovered that I did not feel so bad about using slaves. I thought that I had repaid them in some way.

After they had dried me and anointed my face with a sweet smelling concoction they brought me some clean clothes. They were far better than anything I had ever worn before. The cotton shirt felt light and cool while the breeches were well fitted. There was a mirror in the bathhouse and I looked at myself. It was the first time I had ever seen what I looked like and I almost recoiled when I saw the red-haired sun tanned giant who stood there.

When James Booth Boswell spoke, I almost jumped. "There. What a fine looking young man and now, sir, if you would put on these riding boots we will take a turn around my land."

Another slave helped me to put on the boots which felt tight and uncomfortable. The grey-haired slaved grinned a mouthful of alarmingly white teeth at me," Don't worry young massa, they'll soon feel like slippers. It is just you ain't used to them eh suh?"

My host awaited me with a beautiful white horse with what looked like blue spots. The first horse I had ridden had been the one from Charleston and that was a donkey compared with this one. I just hoped I would not disgrace myself and fall off. That would be inexcusable. I tried to sit as comfortably as I could but I felt like a sack of hay on the horse's back.

"Just relax son, sit on him like he is a chair. Just hold the reins with one hand. Don't worry Jack; Midnight is one of the nicest horses I have." The reassuring words helped me and soon I was enjoying the sensation which was not unlike the motion of the masthead in a gentle breeze. "Now then, Jack Hogan, tell me your story for you interest me."

For some reason, I trusted him in the same way that I had trusted Stumpy and I told him the whole story from the death of my parents to my present position. A frown appeared on his brow. "It seems to me that you have been abused a little by my friend. I shall have to see what I can do about that."

He told me of Briardene and what the plantation entailed, where the tobacco was grown, where the cotton and so forth and then we just enjoyed the ride. We rode for a while in silence and then he asked, "What would you like to do if you had a choice?"

No-one had ever asked me that before and I answered honestly. "My aim, sir, was to come to America and make enough money to free my sister from the bondage of the whore house. That is still my intention."

He nodded. "I can see that despite your background and circumstances you have nobility and you are, indeed a gentleman. There are perilously few of us about. In your position, I suspect I may have become like Black Bill Bailey or that thug Paddy Henry." He leaned over and touched my arm. "You leave this in my hands and I will see what I can do."

By the time we had returned Captain Black Bill Bailey was sitting on the veranda smoking a large cigar and drinking brandy. He smiled at us as though we were long lost, friends. I noticed a look of disapproval pass briefly across our host's face but then he smiled. "Excellent, Captain Bill. I see that you have found my finest Cubans and my most expensive Napoleon. You have good taste."

Jarvis appeared and he too had the briefest moment of displeasure before he smiled and said, "Dinner is served."

We sat in a huge dining room, just the three of us, and I felt overwhelmed. Mr Boswell leaned over and said, "Do not be alarmed, my friend. Just enjoy yourself. Regard this as your home eh? I thought we would try some local specialities. You may not have tried them before but I am sure that you will love the taste. First, we have some Chesapeake Bay Blue Crabs. They are fine eating."

When the crabs, strangely orange- despite their name, were placed before me I knew not what to do. Luckily my host did. I watched as Captain Bill literally tore into them while Mr Booth explained to me how to eat them. "Take off the legs and put them on the side and then the claws. Take this piece of shell and break it. Now, these pieces here, discard them and everything else, except for the shell, you eat."

They were delicious and I polished off six of them. Mr Booth smiled, "Save some space for the fried chicken. It is Mrs Jarvis' special recipe."

I had never eaten chicken, let alone fried chicken but it tasted like the food of the gods. It just melted in the mouth and it was smothered in a sweet sauce I found was called maple syrup. We also had ears of corn smothered in the same maple syrup; the taste was such that I thought I had died and gone to heaven. I drank sparingly as the food was so good but Captain Bill consumed glass after glass of wine and then brandy. The last course was an absolutely divine dish; it tasted of cream but it was frozen and was drenched in chocolate. I couldn't wait to tell Fatty and Davy of the taste. Then it struck me. I had to escape and I would not be seeing either of them again. Suddenly I was glad that I had not drunk too much. The captain was drunk. It would be simplicity itself to slip out at night. Then I remembered the guards who were there to stop escapes. Perhaps they would not stop an Irishman from escaping?

"Captain Bill, Mr Hogan, shall we retire to the veranda? It is cooler there and Mr Murphy will join us."

We sat around a table laden with iced sweets and bottles of alcohol. The two girls from the bathhouse came and draped themselves around Captain Bill.

"I noticed, Mr Hogan, that you did not partake of the drinks at the table. Were they not to your liking?"

"To be truthful Mr Booth, I am not used to strong liquor and I did not want to make a fool of myself." I couldn't help glancing furtively towards the gate. "And I wanted a clear head."

"Admirable Mr Hogan and to be commended but," he leaned forward and spoke quietly, "I can tell you that you can relax. You will not need a clear head for you are as safe here as though you were back in your Wexford home with your ma and da."

I sat back in amazement. He had listened to every word I had said. "Then I am in your hands, Mr Booth."

"Call me James. In that case, I think you will enjoy this. It is from Portugal and is a drink called port. Do try it." He nodded to Jarvis who brought a glass of ruby red liquor it was sweet and yet not cloying. I sipped it. James clapped his hands. "Excellent. You drink it the correct way." He glared at the captain who drank the whole glass down in one. "Unlike some."

I noticed, for the first time that Danny Murphy was seated slightly behind the captain and he was not drinking. I was so happy that I did not try to make sense of it. However, when our host spoke, my senses prickled with the tension.

"Captain Bailey I would like to bring up the issue of Mr Hogan here. I understand, from my conversation with him that his sister had an arrangement with you that in return for certain favours you would give him passage to America. Is this true?"

Bill Bailey was too drunk to sense the threat beneath the words but I was sober and could hear the underlying anger in James' voice. "Ah, she was a soft little bitch." I gripped my hands and dug my nails in to stop myself leaping up and hitting him. I saw an angry look from Danny while James just looked coldly at the drunk. "She might have thought that but I never intended to give free passage. Do I look like an idiot?"

"So you did promise her that?"

He leaned forwards and leered at James. "We all promise women things and then when we have had our way with them..."

Danny Murphy jumped up but James held his hand up to restrain him. "Please captain; answer my question. Did you make that promise?"

"Of course I did but it doesn't count. They are bog Irish and little better than slaves." He waved an arm in my direction. "He has done all right by me."

"And he is going to do even better now. Jack here, if he wishes can stay with me and work for me. Would you like that Jack? And before you answer remember that I am a gentleman and a man of my word."

Before I could answer Black Bill leapt to his feet. "Do you think I trained a good top man so he could be your bum boy, you damned catamite?"

He got no further as Danny struck him square in the face with his fist and the drunk collapsed unconscious. I could see that he had lost teeth and Danny was rubbing his reddened knuckles. Danny grinned, "God but I have been waiting for years to do that to the bastard."

James turned to me, "I am sorry for this lout's words Jack but I assure you I only intend to offer you work."

I took a breath. "What kind of work sir? All I know is potato farming and sailing."

He and Danny exchanged a smile. "When I found

Mr Murphy, all he knew were potatoes but now he is skilled in many things. Let us just say that I like the potential which is within you. Will you accept my offer?"

He held out his hand. "Of course sir. It would be an honour." Of all the many decisions I made in my life, this was the best one and the one I never regretted, despite the accidents and tragedies I had made the right choice.

I continued to sip my port after Danny had dragged away my former employer. "Sir, can I ask you a question?"

"Of course Jack. Always ask questions, it is the only way that we learn."

"Why do you sell slaves? I mean no offence sir but it seems below someone like you, who is obviously a gentleman."

He smiled, "I do not take offence for I can see that you ask out of honesty. Let us just say that all other avenues of work were barred to me because… well, they were barred to me and I treat the slaves well. I neither whip nor beat them. I clothe them and feed them. If they are ill I have them healed."

"But on the boat, many died."

He looked sad, "They would die on any boat and before they reached the boat even if I did not offer them some hope but I can only do what I do when they reach here. So long as men want slaves then people will supply them. At least Captain Bailey's ship is better than most of the blackbirders who ply their trade." He spread his arms apologetically. "It is not a perfect world but it is my world and I make the best of it."

Although my bed was soft and downy I did not sleep as easily as I had done on the ship. I missed the comfortable rocking motion. I had been at sea for more than two years and my body had become attuned to the sea. I also found the heat to be oppressive. Finally, my mind was filled with the thoughts of my new life as well as a fear of the repercussions of my action. What would Black Bill say when he woke? Would he take it out on Caitlin? Fate had decided my course and all I could do was to sail with the wind.

A slave awoke me the next morning with a jug of water and a basin. He proceeded to bathe me and I found it strange. I suspected that, once I was employed, then such luxuries would be a thing of the past. When I was dressed I made my way down to the dining room. James was seated already reading. He half stood. "I trust you slept well?"

"Yes, sir."

He nodded absentmindedly. "Help yourself to breakfast." He gestured to a table laden with silver trays and steaming food. Breakfast for me had been whatever scraps were left from the night before washed down with small beer or whatever Fatty had left over from the previous night. The coffee smelled good and I poured a cup. The bacon and the eggs also appealed and I put a small portion on my plate. As I sat down he glanced up and laughed. "That is not the breakfast for a man. Jarvis!" His butler came in. "Please fix Mr Hogan a decent breakfast I suspect he is unused to an American breakfast."

The butler gave a huge toothsome smile, "Yes suh." He whisked my plate away and proceeded to load it with all manner of food. As he put it down he nodded. "That is all good, home cooked food. My wife is the cook. Now you enjoy."

I looked at the mountain of food and wondered if I would ever make a dent in it. Fifteen minutes later, and the plate was empty. If I continued to eat like this then I would be the size of Fatty Hutton. James looked up from his reading and smiled. "That's better."

"Excuse me asking sir but what will my duties be?"

"A good question and shows that you are a thinker. I like that. As you know I deal in slaves. These days they are even more valuable than they were, what with the British embargo on the traffic. Consequently, I need to protect my investment. You will stop slaves from running and prevent other dealers from taking my goods. How does that sound?"

It sounded nothing like my life as a sailor but then until I had boarded the Rose I had known nothing but potato farming and hunting. "That sounds agreeable sir."

"You will join Mr Murphy and my other guards in their quarters. I will take you there when we have dealt with Mr Bailey."

As though on cue, Captain Bailey lurched into the room. I could see the effect of Danny's punch. His nose had been broken and his jaw was heavily bruised. He also looked angry. He glared at me. I noticed that, despite his smile, Mr Boswell kept one hand below the table. "I trust you slept well, captain?"

"You feckin well know I didn't. When I see that bastard who cold cocked me he is dead."

"I fear that you would come off worse from such an encounter. Mr Murphy is handy with his fists."

"Who said anything about fist? And I'll be taking this scraggy wee shit with me as well." He began to lurch towards me and I stood poised, fists at the ready.

I was not the weakling I had been and I would defend myself.

Before Black Bill could reach me Mr Boswell had a gun aimed across the table. "Have you seen this weapon before captain? It is what is called a Navy Colt; made by Samuel Colt. It is a fine weapon. Much better than the flintlocks you use. You see it has six bullets in a chamber which revolves. It is a veritable killing machine."

The words halted the sailor who stared at the weapon which had looked so inoffensive but now appeared dangerous and deadly. "You intend to keep him then?"

"I am merely carrying out the promise you made to his sister." He placed the gun on the table within easy reach. "I hope this does not alter our business arrangements. I am sure Mr Barker, the owner of your ship and your employer would wish it to continue." Black Bill gave a reluctant nod. "Good, then if you would return to the ship we will be along later this afternoon to take the cargo off your hands."

From the look on his face, I thought that Black Bill was going to hit me as he stormed out but one look at the Colt on the table halted that. "We cannot always choose our business associates but we can at least choose those with whom we work. Come Jack, and I will introduce you to the rest of my men."

The guard's barrack building was about a hundred yards from the main house and sheltered by a stand of trees. Beyond that, I could see another building which I later found out was the holding area for slaves due for market. Mr Boswell's own slaves were on the other side of the estate, nowhere near the newly arrived Africans. Danny Murphy strode out to meet us.

"Captain Bailey was not a happy man as he left us, Mr Murphy."

The huge man shrugged, "I have told you before sir, he is a bad man and it is a shame we have to deal with the likes of him."

"Since the embargo, I am afraid that he is our only source of slaves. Here is Jack. Fit him out and then bring him and the rest of the men to the house. We will collect these Africans as quickly as we can." He smiled at me. "See you in a while Jack and welcome to my service./"

I walked behind Danny. Perhaps it was the fact that he, too, was an Irishman or the fact that he had struck the captain but whatever the reason I found it easy to talk with the lumbering giant. Mr Boswell seems a good man."

He looked down at me and nodded. "The best. He is a good boss and he looks after us. You are lucky to be working for him."

"I know."

He grinned. "You'll do alright. Us Wexford men have to stick together. " He looked keenly at me. "My Uncle Michael still lives there." I knew the Murphy family; they were neighbours and it felt as though we were almost related.

We entered the barracks. The windows were all open and it felt cooler than it looked. There were six men preparing their equipment. "This is Jack Hogan, a new man." They all waved and shouted a greeting. There was no Eddie look and that pleased me. "Get your gear together we are off to Charleston. Harry, pick out a horse for Jack here." He led me to a rack containing weapons. He gave me a holster and a gun which looked to be identical to the one carried by my new boss. He handed me a box of ammunition. He also gave me a quirt. Then he took me to a wardrobe and selected hat. It proved to be a perfect fit. "The boots Mr Boswell gave you and the other clothes will be fine. We have a darkie here who makes clothes. He will make you a suit when we have the time."

I held up the Colt. "I have never fired one of these."

"But you have fired a flintlock?" I nodded. "Well, this is easier. You shouldn't need it today but as soon as we have the time I will show you how to use it. Now come with me and we'll join the other men."

They were all mounted with two spare horses when we reached the rest of the guards. They were all young men none looked to be older than twenty. They all wore their guns on their right hips and, as I walked up to them I adjusted mine to match them. The quirts they carried in their right hands. The horse they gave me was a roan called Copper and she turned a mournful eye to view me as I mounted her. I loved her the moment I saw her but I had no time to become acquainted with the fine horse. Almost immediately James Booth Boswell emerged and mounted his own mount.

"Morning boys."

"Morning Captain!"

I found myself next to a wiry looking character called Harry. As we trotted down the drive I asked. "Do we call him Captain then?"

He was an Englishman and he had an accent which sounded as though he had lived in the north. "Aye. He is a captain in the militia and it is easier to say that than Mr Boswell."

The ride through Charleston showed me that the

82

Captain's trade was frowned upon by the gentrified folks of the Carolinian town. Women averted their eyes as we rode through and the men scowled. Captain Boswell tipped his hat to each lady we saw and seemed unconcerned by the reaction he invoked. For my part, I did not understand the reaction as he seemed to me to be a true gentleman. When I knew my new comrades better I would ask that difficult question.

It had only been a day since I had seen the Rose but she seemed different somehow; like a ghost of the past. One of the men had ridden ahead to secure the boats we would need to reach her and there were three longboats and a rowing boat awaiting us. Each boat had black rowers and a white helmsman. Harry and I boarded the last boat and sat in the thwarts. The small rowing boat headed for the side of the ship facing the harbour while we went, discreetly to the ocean side where we could load the slaves out of sight of curious eyes. Having seen the reaction of the people of Charleston I could not see the point and I suspect that the landing of the slaves was an open and necessary secret.

It felt strange to be looking up at my old shipmates as they threw down mooring ropes. I waved at Davy but he gave a slight shake of the head and ignored me. The rest of the crew did the same. Why was I a pariah? As chance would have it we were moored towards the stern and close to the porthole Fatty used to rid his galley of smoke. It opened and Fatty's head emerged.

"The lads can't talk to you, Jack. Black Bill came back full of hell this morning and said that we weren't to speak with you." He grinned. "I don't give a shit." He pointed at my new clothes. "You have done well for yourself."

"Aye. Tell Stumpy to tell Caitlin that I now work for the gentleman and I will send money when I can."

"I will do. Did you give him the lump on his face?"

"No that was Mr Murphy."

"Tell him well done." His head jerked around. "Have to go. Take care."

The first of the slaves appeared at the gangway halfway down the ship. It was only a four-foot drop into the boat but each slave was tethered by a rope to avoid any chance of flight. The loading of the boats took some time but I remembered that from my time as a sailor. Soon it was our turn and Harry and I stood at either end of the long boat with quirts at the ready. I did not like to inflict pain on another human being but I also knew that the Africans we carried needed dealing with in a firm way. Fate dictated that they were docile and resigned to their fate.

When we reached the quayside again, this time far from any prying eyes; there were three wagons waiting for us. I recognised some of the slaves from Captain Boswell's estate. I glanced over my shoulder and saw the rowing boat leaving the Rose. One of the slaves from the second ship made a sudden break for freedom. One of the other guards stuck out a foot and tripped him. Harry was quite close and he leapt from the boat and cold-cocked him with the butt of his Navy Colt. The brief interlude subdued the rest of the slaves. By the time the Captain and Danny reached us the wagons were loaded and the cargo hidden by the tarpaulin. Harry said, "You ride with the driver but face in. I'll sit at the back. Make sure your gun is pointed at them." He drew and cocked his gun menacingly. The Africans might not recognise the weapon but they understood the threat and their eyes whitened in terror.

When we reached the estate the gates to the slave quarters had been opened and we drove the wagons straight in. There were two house slaves ready with lye soap and they began to scrub each slave in turn while two others shaved their heads before they were allowed in. There were mainly male slaves but I noticed two young women. As we watched the process I asked Harry. "Why so few women?"

"They can cause problems and they don't work as well in the fields. The men bring a higher price."

"Then why bring two at all?"

"Breeding. The Captain will choose a suitable darkie and keep the three of them to breed some more and that way we are less reliant on the likes of Black Bill."

And so my first day passed without further incident. For the next five years, my life followed a similar pattern. I took my turn at watching the slaves. I escorted slaves to their new owners and the auctions. It was far easier than life on the Rose and far better paid. I got to know my way around the state and I became a confident rider. The Captain treated all of his men well and rewarded us suitably. We were all loyal to him. Sometimes the men went into town for drink and white women but others were happy to drink the estate rum and take their turn with the slaves. This was an arrangement supported by the Captain for the resulting children were the perfect material for house slaves and the like. I rarely left the plantation. I was satisfied with my life of luxury. I learned how to shoot both pistol and carbine. I was taught how to fence with a sabre rather than a cutlass and I became an accomplished horseman. We were, in many ways a small army working for the Captain and, over the five years we increased our numbers to ten.

It was during my second year that I plucked up the courage to ask Harry about Captain Boswell. I really got on well with Harry. He had left England after having poached some deer on Lord Derby's estate. He was an excellent hunter. Captain Boswell liked him and took him on. He was a broad tough man but as honest as anyone I had ever met. When we got to know each other we found we worked well together, almost without the need for words. We had both been on duty for eight hours and were the only ones in the bunkhouse, sipping some homemade liquor which was slipping down rather well. We had flavoured the powerful alcohol with blackberries and sugar cane and it tasted like one of Captain Boswell's ports.

"So tell me, Harry, what is the story with the Captain? He doesn't seem like a natural slave master."

He suddenly became serious. He started at me and drank the brew off in one. "Listen, Irish, for a bog Irish Mick you seem alright, but if you ever repeat what I am going to tell you I will cook your balls and serve them to the racoons!"

I had enough alcohol inside me for indignation. "If you can't trust me by now then feck off! I don't want to know! I have never betrayed a confidence from a mate and I won't start now!"

He laughed, "Calm down you mad Irish bastard." He poured himself another drink. "The Captain comes from an old Virginia family. They are like the aristocrats in England and Ireland. They think they are God!" He spat at a bug that was getting too close to the brew.

"He was the eldest son and seen as a future leader then he got a girl pregnant."

I shrugged, "It happens."

"True, but normally the girl isn't from the richest family in the state and the man marries her."

"Shit! So he didn't marry her?"

"No, and the poor sod topped herself with the shame. I don't know if he would have married her eventually but the silly bitch didn't give him the chance. His dad disinherited him and no-one would have anything to do with him. He was, what is the word? Ah yes, ostracised. He came here and began to deal in slaves. It was the only thing he could do, apart from gambling to make money."

We sat in silence for a while. "Poor bugger!"

"Poor bugger is right. I think he was just too young. He was seventeen and she was eighteen. It's why the people of Charleston behave the way they do. It's why he never gets invited anywhere. The slaving they can deal with but the disgrace…"

That story made me closer to Harry and closer to the Captain. I was just the same age as the Captain and I could picture me doing the same thing. I thought of Caitlin and the way she had been abused by Black Bill Bailey and I felt angry for my employer that he had been so badly treated by hypocrites. From that moment on I understood the Captain far better and my loyalty was never in doubt.

A year after I had joined his service we heard that the Rose had been sunk in a battle with a frigate and a schooner from the Royal Navy. Black Bill's luck had run out. I didn't hear if there were any survivors, but I hoped so. Fatty, Woody and Davy had been like family to me and I deluded myself that they had lived beyond the battle. I wondered what would become of Caitlin; perhaps she was deemed to be his heir and inherited. I somehow doubted that. My family were not one would call lucky. In all likelihood, she was back in the whore house with the other prostitutes.

Interlude

1854 The Crimea

Captain Arthur St. John Beauregard was less than happy. He had hoped that the war with Russia would be the opportunity for glory and, more importantly, financial rewards. So far it had been a disappointment. The experiment in Ireland with the sheep had been a disaster. Every flock they owned had managed to succumb to every disease and ailment it was possible to get. When his father had died and the bailiffs moved in he and Andrew Neil had taken all the money his father had managed to hide and left for England. With the former estate manager as his servant, Arthur had thrown himself into the life of the regiment. He was forced to live parsimoniously making the excuse that he still had to support his father. The gullible officers of the Guards bought the lie and he was held in high esteem by his comrades and they overlooked the way he cheated at cards.

They had been in the Crimea for three months and he hated every inch of it. It was dirty and disease ridden. He did not like any of his fellow officers and he positively despised his company. They had suffered more men dead through disease than through fighting and Arthur could not countenance such a waste. Neil, his servant and former estate manager, tried to make the best of the conditions and the life they led but it was hard. He knew that his master would have preferred infantry charges and *'derring-do'* rather than sitting behind entrenchments waiting for an attack. He hated the dirt and the mud; in fact, he could think of nothing he liked about this particular war. It was disappointing given the fact that he had dreamed of nothing but a war for so many years. Now that one arrived, it was the wrong type of war. He had, thoughtfully, ensured that all of his financial assets were secreted about his person. In London, the lawyers had deemed that the estate had been bankrupt and were not looking for the son of the dead bankrupt. He had enough to start a new life and India and America were his two choices.

When the young Lord Astbury, a fresh-faced lieutenant newly arrived from England, arrived in the regiment to replace the unfortunate nephew of the Bishop of Wells who had succumbed to dysentery, then things looked up for Arthur. He managed to inveigle himself into the good graces of the impressionable young man. The young lieutenant became almost infatuated with the dashing captain who appeared to be so worldly wise and knowledgeable about military matters. Even the slightly broken nose and off centre jaw were seen to be the results of glorious combat in the service of the Queen. Only Neil knew the truth. The devious Arthur managed to persuade the young man to place his not inconsiderable fortune in Arthur St. John Beauregard's strongbox. When the young lieutenant was sent on a suicide patrol by his superior officer, Captain Beauregard, and failed to return then questions were asked of the mentor and father figure to the heir to a fortune. This time the family was powerful enough to ask questions and the wily captain could not wriggle out of answering what were proving to be hard questions to answer.

Captain Beauregard and his servant disappeared one snowy night in early November the day before the battle of Inkerman. The confusion of the time meant that his loss was reported as missing in action. Many men died at Inkerman and the confused nature of the battle meant that records were not as complete as they might have otherwise been. Thus the resourceful Captain disappeared from sight. Had the war been going better for the allies then, perhaps more attention would have been paid to the relationship between the two officers, but it was Lord Astbury's family who grieved for the young war hero dying to defend his country. However, they never forgot the name of St. John Beauregard. It was not Jack Hogan only who had a score to settle with him.

Cork

Caitlin often wondered about Jack. Every time Black Bill returned home she asked him about her brother and was told that he was living in Charleston and doing well. That statement was normally a prelude to violent and aggressive sex but Caitlin comforted herself with the knowledge that she was doing it for her brother and, as such, was no sin.

When her master, for that was what he was her master, had returned to sea Caitlin found that she quite enjoyed being the housekeeper. To be fair to Black Bill, he was generous with her allowance and she had nice rather than fine clothes. She made the house welcoming and pleasant to be in for his infrequent visits home. She made sure that she took every precaution to prevent a child. Her friends at the whorehouse had given her the tips for that. She knew that a child would result in her eviction and she did not relish the thought of going back to earning her living on her back. She just wished that Jack would write to her although as she could neither read nor write she did not know how he would manage but she knew that Jack was the clever one in the family and, somehow, she knew that he would be able to read and to write.

It came as a huge shock when Caitlin found out about the death of Black Bill when the bailiffs came to repossess the house. Caitlin was not as clever as Jack but she was resourceful and she had put by some money. She had not spent all the money Black Bill had left for her on the house and she had been careful when buying so that she was not the pauper she would have otherwise been. She decided not to risk the whorehouse a second time; she had been lucky the first time and found a man to keep her but she was older now and, although still pretty, she had lost her youth and that was what men desired. She went, instead to Stumpy. He had been her one point of contact when Bill was away and she had changed her views about him. She had learned that he was a kind man and he deeply cared for Jack. They shared that view and talking to Stumpy made Jack seem closer somehow.

She found herself asking Stumpy's advice and the old man was honest enough to give her the truth, "There's nothing for you here is there? If I were you I would take my money and pay for passage to Charleston. The last I heard Jack was there."

She had looked puzzled at that. "But he has been there for years hasn't he?"

"I am afraid Black Bill lived up to his name and he

used Jack as a sailor. He left Black Bill a couple of years ago now and he lives on a plantation in Charleston."

That decided her and, with Stumpy's help, she began to seek a berth on a westbound ship.

CHAPTER 5

Jack

Charleston 1861

Things had not gone well for Captain Boswell in the years following the loss of the Rose of Tralee. He found it hard to get the slaves that were in such high demand. His home produced slaves became his main source of income. With the election of Abraham Lincoln, his fortunes took a turn for the better. The number of slaves arriving in the United States of America had dried up and the Captain's foresight inbreeding had paid off. He became even richer than he had been but he was still not accepted by society. His troop of men, now grown to sixteen, was the best armed and best trained in the whole state and that included the regulars. I was one of the more experienced members of the elite team. When the Henry Rifle Carbine had been introduced in 1860, despite the expense, Captain Boswell had purchased one for each of us. We became highly proficient with the weapon that they said they could load on Sunday and shoot all week. Danny Murphy confided in his men that they were the only men outside of the Union Army to possess such a fearsome weapon. We all became proficient in its use and all of us sported two Navy Colts in our saddle holsters and one on the hip. The sabre he gave us was attached to our saddles but none of us felt comfortable with the ungainly weapon. We did not know it at the time but the Captain must have been planning to form his own unit even then. He had the money and he was a true southern patriot. He was more than happy to use the money he had made in slaves to arm his men. We were in no doubt that he would form, as many rich men did, his own regiment and we would all be members of that regiment.

The whole company had ridden to Charleston to await the arrival of another slave ship. We had done the same thing on five previous occasions but the Union Navy and the Royal Navy were cooperating and we had sought the slave ships in vain. Our men had hung around the waterfront taverns talking about the escalating tensions between the slave states and those that wished to abolish the trade. As we peered out across the harbour we were all amazed when we saw shells raining on the fort. We were not to know that Carolina had seceded from the union and General Beauregard had demanded the surrender of the fort. It was bizarre to watch the start of a war which cost so many American lives from the waterfront bar in Charleston. It was as though we were watching a show on the stage. That day changed my life forever!

We headed back to the estate and we did not see Captain Boswell for many days. Danny Murphy kept our training regime up and we practised both shooting and skirmishing. As we lay in the meadow resting, after a particularly fierce fight he said, "I think, lads that we will be fighting soon. I know the Captain. If you wish to fight for the Yankees then let me know. I know that he will allow it. We all know what a gentleman he is. Otherwise, I think we will be for the south"

It is a testament to the loyalty that none of us thought for one moment of deserting our leader. To us, the loyalty to the man who had paid us for years was greater than that of an ideal.

When he did return he did not look happy. We discovered the details later on from Danny. It appeared that Captain Boswell had offered his services to the Confederate Government and, because of his history, had been refused out of hand. None of us could understand that. He was a great and proven leader but the spectre of his disgrace still hung over him. We wondered what would happen. All of us knew that he was not a man to let others dictate his options. A month after Fort Sumter he gathered every person on his estate together, blacks and whites alike and explained his plan.

He stood and smiled at us all. "My family, my friends, my people. It seems that the Government of Jefferson Davis does not wish to employ me and my men as a military force but, despite their views, I will not allow the damned Yankees to ride roughshod over us." He turned to the slaves and servants who were all seated together around Jarvis. "To my darkies I say, if you feel I have mistreated you in any way then please, leave my service and go north with my blessing."

There was a silence and then Jarvis looked around and said, "No suh. We are all happy to be here and work with you, Mr Boswell."

The Captain nodded. "Thank you for that and I will continue to look after you so long as you wish. And to you, my soldiers; if you feel you cannot follow me into battle and fight for the Confederacy then there is a purse of gold for each of you and no hard feelings."

We all looked at each other and grinned. To a man we chanted, "No sir. We are your men."

He grinned that boyish smile of his. "Then, Jarvis, I would like you to continue to run my estate as profitably as you can and Mr Murphy, get my men ready Boswells Raiders go to war!" We were as excited as children; this would be a great game.

We now had eighteen men with the Captain and Danny Murphy as our leaders. The estate tailor made us all grey uniforms and somehow the captain procured kepis for us. He had the three gold bars designating the rank of Captain sewn on to his collar while Danny had the three stripes of a sergeant. I have to confess I found the wool to be both uncomfortable and hot but I felt proud to be wearing the uniform. Finally, he had a small cavalry standard made. In the top corner was the national flag with the seven starts whilst the rest of the flag was a white background with a snarling wildcat in the middle. The Captain began to refer to us as his wildcats and, when we eventually fought the Yankees, they used the name too but they used it as an insult.

The battles that the first year of the war were far to the north in Virginia, close to Washington. Our leader chafed at the bit, desperate to be part of the action. He read the newspapers voraciously seeking out information about the cavalry and he would cut out any references to J.E.B. Stuart whom he thought the best chance the south had of defeating the northern war machine.

In October we heard that there was to be an army of Northern Virginia with three divisions. What attracted the Captain's attention was the fact that Stuart would command one of the cavalry wings. That was enough for him. Leaving Jarvis to run his estate the twenty of us took three slaves and ten horses with supplies and headed north towards the Shenandoah Valley. I was heading for the heartland of the south and I was excited. I remembered Blackie Jones' stories about the Valley and the Blue Ridge. I would be seeing them myself, first hand.

Once we left Charleston, we found ourselves welcomed everywhere as heroes marching to fight the damned Yankees. They did not listen to the name Captain Boswell, they just saw a well-armed cavalry force riding north and we were greeted with hospitality all the way from Charleston through Charlotte and on to Roanoke in Virginia. The Captain was as happy then as I had ever seen him. This was his dream, to be a hero of the south and his exile in Carolina had denied him the opportunity. The closer we came to his home in Lynchburg the more apprehensive he became. We had passed through every town on the way north and been fed and watered but we skirted Lynchburg as his face and name would be known. We slept in the tents he had brought with us.

Sergeant Murphy made light of it. "Ah sure, and it's a good thing. We would have had to learn how to put them up and sleep in them any way. This way we can do it in comfort."

During the week it took us to travel around the busy town he was sullen and withdrawn but, in hindsight, it was good training for we learned how to become invisible and become the wildcats who struck in the night.

It took us over two weeks to reach the outskirts of Winchester and we reached southern limits in December. It was cold there and we were grateful for our woollen jackets and the greatcoats we had on our horses. For the first time, we were refused shelter. We reached Kernstown towards late afternoon and the captain rode up to the farm, Pritchard's farm which stood in a prominent position above the small hamlet and church. He asked Mr Pritchard if we could shelter in his barn but the farmer told the captain that he wanted nothing to do with the war. He and his family wished to be left alone. Captain Boswell merely touched his slouch hat and led us to the valley to the west across the Opequon. There we found a clearing in the forest and we erected tents for the first time since leaving our home. We were sheltered by Sandy Ridge, there was nearby water and we were hidden from view.

There was game aplenty in the forest and we spent two days hunting while the Captain and the Sergeant left to find Stuart to discover if we could join the army. Harry was an excellent hunter and I learned much from him. I had thought I was a hunter until I met him but killing rabbits did not compare with stalking and killing a fully grown deer. We took our carbines and headed up the ridge. I noticed how he would smell the air and feel the breeze. He whispered to me. "Always have the animal smell coming to you. That way he doesn't know you are there." We reached a spot on the ridgeline which seemed to satisfy Harry. "Climb up into the trees. Animals are dumb and they look down not up." He peered at me. "Only shoot when you are certain that you can make a kill. It is better if we can shoot when there are a couple of them. You take the nearest and I will take the furthest. Right?"

"Right Harry." I was keen to climb and begin hunting. The rabbits I had trapped in Ireland seemed pathetic now that I was about to shoot my first deer. We had discarded our hats but it was cold enough to keep on our cavalry jackets. I did not feel the cold as much as the captain and those born in America. Ireland and England were always cold and normally wet. I stared at the ground intently and occasionally flashed a glance at Harry. I saw him point and I glimpsed the three deer as they approached our stand. There were two females and a young one. They were searching for berries on the blackberry bushes. Most had been eaten or were old but there were still one or two left and the treasure was sought by the hungry creatures.

I took a bead on the one at the front. Once they were level with my tree I knew that they might be able to smell us, although our position up the tree would confuse them. I aimed at a spot just behind the head. I had been told it was the best target. I took a breath and gently squeezed. There was a slight recoil and a puff of powder. A half second later I heard a second shot and then a third. I chambered another round but I could see the three animals all lay dead. Two of them had lumbered a few yards away but the one I had shot lay where it had been hit.

Harry slapped me on the back. "Well done Irishman. That was a cracking shot. Now let's get them back." He looked ruefully at them. "These are big buggers."

We cut three saplings and tied the animals to them.

When we lifted them it felt like the first time I had taken a reef in canvas; I thought my arms and back would break. The saplings bent alarmingly but they held and took the weight. There was a cheer from the men when we reached the camp. There were others there, as well as Harry, who were skilled at skinning and gutting. Harry threw me one of the skins. "Here Mick; when this is seasoned you can make a good coat from it."

One of the slaves, Aaron, walked up to me, grinning. "Here suh. I will tan it for you. Perhaps I can have the cut offs?"

"Sure thing." I was surprised to watch him lay the skin out and then piss all over it.

He saw me and smiled, "A few days of this and then stretch it out. You'll have a fine piece of hide."

One of the deer was cooked for our meal while the other two were salted and dried. We might soon have to live off the land. That was my first venison and I thought it delicious. Harry had the slaves cook one of the hearts for me and one for him and, along with the liver, was one of the best meals I had ever devoured.

Captain Boswell and Sergeant Murphy rode in two days later. They were not happy. Captain Boswell went to his tent and Sergeant Murphy gathered us around him. "It seems that General Lee has made it clear that we cannot join the regular army. It seems the captain's family are powerful and have made a stand. They have funded two regiments and General Lee is not willing to risk losing the support of such a rich family." He saw our disappointed faces and he smiled. "Sure and it is not all bad news. Colonel Stuart wants us to scout, unofficially, of course, north of the Potomac." He gestured us to move closer to him. "And of course cause a little mayhem amongst the Yankees!"

That brought a cheer. We were all young men and we were desperate to fight for our leader. His war was our war. Personally, I had nothing against the Yankees but I equated them with the English landowners who had thrown my family off our land. It made it easier for me to do what I knew I must do - kill Yankees.

We headed up the Williamsport Pike. We had no idea if the bridge would be guarded or what forces we might meet and, once we passed through Martinsburg we were given instructions from Sergeant Murphy. "You will each have another man to work with." He allocated our pairs and when I was paired with Harry I could tell that thought and discussion had preceded the decision. "I am going to send two pairs to, separately, scout the bridge. All you have to do is see if it is guarded and then get back." He glared at us all. "Do not get seen!"

I was delighted when Harry and I were one of the pairs selected to scout. We headed to the west of the pike. It was early afternoon but we were wary. We might be the northernmost rebs and if there were any Yankees north of us we would be outnumbered. We halted about six hundred yards from the bridge. We had left the pike sometime earlier and we sheltered in a stand of elms overlooking the river. To our dismay, we saw the Union flag and the unmistakable blue of Yankee infantry. The bridge was guarded.

"Ah well back to the captain then Jack."

"Hang on Harry. Why don't we head west for a while, we still have time and we can scout the river." He looked dubious. "What is there to lose? We know where the Yankees are. There might be another bridge."

He nodded and we headed west. As soon as we were out of sight of the town we headed down to the river which was to the north of the track we were on. We had travelled just a mile or so when I saw the island. It was closer to the southern bank but it showed that the bed was shallow.

"Good call Irish. We could cross here."

I suddenly had an inspiration. "Let's try it now."

"What?"

"We are here. We can try to cross the river. If we can't do it then there is no way that the whole column can. It will save time."

He shook his head. "I always thought that you Irish were mad as fish. Come on then. We will try the island first and if we manage that…"

The channel was deeper than I had thought but Copper only had to swim for a few strides and then we were on the island and she was shaking herself dry. I grinned, "That was easy now for this bit." I dug my heels into the flanks of my horse and she leapt into the water. Surprisingly it was quite shallow and she managed to get her footing quite quickly. I reached the other bank although I was wet up to my pistols but we had made it.

Harry soon joined me. "The Captain will be pleased." He looked up at the sun which showed that it was heading towards evening. "If we set off now then we can be back soon after dark. No-one will see us."

When we reached our camp close to Martinsburg we were warmly greeted by an angry Sergeant Murphy. "Where the feck have you two been? George and Dago told us that there were soldiers on the bridge."

Harry grinned, "Then they didn't tell you that we

can cross upstream and not be detected." Captain Boswell was as delighted as the Sergeant. "Well done you two. I can see that you two will be my best scouts."

We left before dawn the next day riding as quickly as we dared using the pike whenever possible but there were toll booths close to the river and we headed west as soon as we were able. When we reached the island Danny said, "Are you sure we can get across?"

In answer, I kicked hard and launched Copper to the island and thence to the other side. I knew that Harry would fill in the details. When Captain Boswell rode over he reined in next to me and shook my hand. "Well done Jack. That was well done."

We camped in a clearing in a wood some way from the river. We would be here for some time if things went well and we laid out a camp which would be hidden from view. The tents were placed under the trees and a picket line for the horses hidden away from the white tents. Harry and I were excused a watch and we collapsed into our tent, exhausted. When we awoke the camp was busy with activity. Breakfast was on the go and men were saddling their horses.

Sergeant Murphy greeted us. "You two are with Captain Boswell. You are heading towards Hagerstown. I am taking the rest of the lads towards Cumberland."

As we passed the fires I grabbed a cup of coffee and a sandwich proffered by Aaron. "Pissed on your hide again last night suh. Coming along fine!"

My mouth full I waved my hand in acknowledgement. As soon as my horse was saddled I emptied the charges in my three pistols and reloaded. The wetting in the river would make them misfire. I suspected that we would need them this day. Captain Boswell smiled and then led us north east towards Hagerstown. We had no idea how many troops if any were there but it would be valuable information for Colonel Stuart.

We were barely a mile from the camp when we were halted. Captain Boswell gathered the nine of us around him. "We don't use our voices. We use hand signals." He held up his hand, "Halt." He waved his hand one way. "Right." He waved the other way. "Left." He pointed at his eyes, "Go have a look see." He waved his hand above his head, "Get the hell out of here!" We grinned. We want to be ghosts who just appear and disappear, silently. Make sure your pistols are all loaded and when I shout charge or fire, give it all you have boys."

Hagerstown was far enough north of the river for the inhabitants to feel secure from southern raiders. We could see a gun in the middle of the road leading to the heart of the town and blue uniforms surrounding it. Beyond the town a small camp with soldiers drilling was visible. It looked to be a couple of companies of soldiers. Captain Boswell took out a notepad and wrote down some information. He called, "Dago!" Dago galloped up. "Take this to Colonel Stuart in Winchester and then return to camp." I could see the disappointment on Dago's face. There would be action soon and he would be missing it, riding back along the pike with a message. It might be an important message but I knew that Dago would rather be with us than riding to the safety of our lines.

When he rode off we waited as Captain Boswell scanned the Yankee lines with his binoculars. He waved for us to join him. "Gentlemen. Tonight I have a mind to upset the Yankees a little." We all leaned in closer, intrigued. "As soon as it is dark we will ride down to their little pop gun and capture it."

Jimmy exclaimed, "And take it back to the General sir?"

"No Jimmy. We will deposit it in the river. That way the Yankees will think it is a raid from the south and not a raid from north of the river."

It was that sort of thought which marked out the captain as a clever military man. We committed dangerous acts but we did it safely.

Later, after dusk, we rode down to the road. We did not slink up to them we rode along the road from Williamsport. As there were Union troops holding the bridge the gun crew and sentries assumed that we were Union cavalry. The dim light helped the illusion. Our grey uniforms did not stand out in the dim light of dusk. As soon as we were close enough the Captain shouted, "You men are prisoners of the Confederacy. Throw down your weapons."

Of course, they did no such thing. There were just ten of them and they grabbed their weapons. We each pulled our Navy Colts and blasted away. As soon as my gun was empty I drew my second and fired again. When the smoke had cleared there was just the moaning of the dying. "Jimmy, Jed, throw a rope around the gun and ride like the wind for the river. The rest of you take any weapons you can from the dead. Harry and Jack, you two take the limber and get it in the river."

Harry and I took a rope and threw it around the limber carriage and tied it to our horses. We fairly flew down the turnpike. We could see where Jimmy and Jed had headed off the road with the gun and we followed them. We reached the river just as the last bubbles from the cannon appeared on the water. With four of us to help we were able to drag the limber and caisson further along the river and, it too, sank without a trace. We were all grinning like kids on Christmas day. "Now what?"

"I guess we head back to camp and meet the Captain."

When we reached camp Sergeant Murphy was already there. "Where's the Captain?" There was a hint of concern in the sergeant's voice but, once we told him of our success he shook his head and laughed. "I guess that will have settled his nerves. Well done boys. The cannon and caisson, they are well hidden?"

"If the river level drops they might find them but with the winter snows due I reckon they'll end up in Washington. Just in time for General Lee to pick them out himself."

At that stage of the war, we were all in high spirits. The Confederate Army had almost beaten the Yankees in the first battle and we all knew that we had the better men and horses. It would just be a matter of time.

When the captain and the rest of the patrol came back we all cheered and he raised his arm in acknowledgement of our success. "Well boys, we have struck or first blow against the Yankees and it won't be the last. Sergeant Murphy, make sure we have pickets out tonight. I would hate to be surprised."

None of us tired of telling the story over our supper. The captain shared out the loot we had accumulated. There was little in the way of money but there were guns, watches and knives. All of us had some memento of the victory. Months later, when we found a Union newspaper, we read of our exploits. They said that the raid had been carried out by ghosts who just appeared. The garrison at Williamsport had seen nothing and there were no tracks. The only sign they discovered was the pile of neatly stacked dead bodies. It was the beginning of the legend.

The next day we were sent out in our scouting pairs, Dago had still to return from Stuart and the Captain wanted his next report to be as full as possible. Harry and I found few signs of the Union Army. We heard the sound of a train in the distance on the Baltimore and Ohio Railroad but other than that we could have been on the plantation in Charleston.

By the time we had returned, Dago was back from his ride. He had already reported to the Captain who sat in his tent with Sergeant Murphy planning our next strike. We, of course, pumped Dago for his information. "Colonel Stuart was right happy when I gave him the report. There was another fellah there, a Virginian, Colonel Jackson, he took a keen interest too."

"Well, what are our orders you numbskull?"

Dago shrugged. "I don't know. They were sealed and I give 'em to the Captain."

The Captain was smiling when he and the sergeant joined us. They were both smoking fine cigars. "Well boys we may not be in the army but the army thinks well enough of us. Our orders are to head on down to Harper's Ferry and see if can find out what they have in that area." He winked, "And cause a little mischief I daresay." We all cheered. "Pack up the tents we will head out tonight. I think we need to use the night to our advantage and move when we can't be seen."

It did not take us long to pack and we headed east to the junction of the Potomac and the Shenandoah.

Harper's Ferry, we all knew, was where the canal met the railroad and Washington was just a short hop away. It was exciting to think that we might be the front line of the Confederate Army. As Harry said, "It's just a shame the Confederate Army doesn't know we are in the army."

The trickiest part was crossing the Williamsport Pike. Since our attack, we were certain that they would be patrolling that road. The slaves and the pack horses were kept at the rear with orders to run at the first sign of trouble. The captain did not want them hurt. As he had told us many times, they were not belligerents, they were our responsibility. We were riding in a column of twos as we approached the pike. There were four soldiers guarding the crossroads. We were not attempting to hide and the soldiers were not alarmed. After all, we were coming from Yankee Hagerstown. The brazier they were using gave off little light and our uniforms could only be seen as grey when we were almost on them.

Their sergeant stepped forwards. "What is your unit?"

The captain had kept on riding and he suddenly thrust his Colt into the sergeant's face. The rest of us had our revolvers out in a trice and the other soldiers dropped their weapons. "We are Boswell's Wildcats! You are now prisoners of the Confederacy."

As they were disarmed I wondered what we would do with them. Sergeant Murphy tied their hands behind their backs and they were bundled on to the backs of four of the pack horses. Harry searched their belongings and found some maps as well as supplies which would come in handy. Once again the ghosts had struck and when the relief for the four men arrived the next day they would just find a deserted camp. We headed towards the river and avoided roads. By dawn, we were in the forest to the east of Harpers Ferry Road. Deep within its shelter, we were invisible and we spent the day resting.

We spent some time talking to the four prisoners who were men from Ohio. It seems they had only just arrived in the area and had no idea that cannon had been captured. "We thought you Rebs were the other side of the river!"

We almost laughed at the shock in their voices. Twenty men appeared to have a disproportionate effect on their imagination. There was no way they were going to try to escape for four men watched them every moment. They were amazed at our weaponry. They still had muskets. Later that night, as Harry and I talked over the events of the day I speculated about that. "You know we can fire something like one hundred and eight shots in less than a minute. That would take out a whole company and then we have two more pistols all loaded."

Harry nodded, "I know and I wonder when the captain will realise that we could cut through some of these Yankee regiments like a knife through butter. A musket can hit jack shit. Especially if Jack Shit is on the back of a horse and galloping towards you cussin' and a yellin' like there is no tomorrow!" We both went to sleep laughing at the thought of cutting through so many soldiers. What we didn't realise was that most of the Confederates had worse weapons than the Yankees. A few cavalry had carbines but nothing like we had and Colts were as rare as hen's teeth. We were fortunate, but then, we didn't realise how much.

CHAPTER 6

Jack

The next day we headed towards Harper's Ferry. The four guards who were left with the prisoners were less than happy. I was just glad it wasn't me; guarding prisoners compared with beating the Yankees, did not even come close. As we closed on the valuable crossing point we heard the whistle of a train. We were on the heights and looked down on the crossing. The captain held up his hand. He spoke with Sergeant Murphy who trotted off down the track through the forest towards the river. The captain turned to us all. "Make sure you are loaded and have a round chambered."

As we did so my worry was ammunition. Our guns did not use the same ammunition as the Confederate Army and there were only Union Cavalry regiments who had the same. I worried that tangling with a regiment of cavalry could be hazardous to our health.

When Danny returned he spoke briefly with the captain. "Right men. The Baltimore and Ohio is just below us. What say we disrupt it just a little eh?" I know that our cheers must have heartened him for he grinned and reared his horse. It was a small thing but it made us feel better. We galloped down through the forest towards the railroad.

We tethered our mounts close to the edge of the forest. We had too few men to leave a picket but we thought that it was unlikely anyone would stumble upon them. There were steep tracks all around and anyone wandering around in the dark risked a dangerous fall. Danny had brought us to a workman's hut he had found. It was next to the track. We easily broke in and took out the track tools that were kept there. "Right boys," Danny was in his element, a real Fenian. "Let's destroy this pretty little track!"

He had chosen a spot just after a curve and the sixteen of us took up four rails and walked with them to hurl them into the Potomac River. We then retired to the edge of the trees. It was getting dark when we heard the wail of the train and then the mournful whistle as it hurtled towards its doom. It was coming from the west. The driver had no chance of stopping the train, despite his valiant efforts; we heard the vain screeching of the brakes. The mighty leviathan hit the empty space and the engine slewed to the right and rolled on to its side; it slowly slid down the bank and into the river. The wagons behind were all derailed; the first three ending, with the engine, in the river. The crew of the engine died in the water and I suspect the rest of the crew, who would have been in the guard's van at the rear, fled when they heard our yells. If I had been there I would have done the same. Whatever the reason, there was no one left to stop us. We swarmed over the surviving cars and shot the locks off. Within them were uniforms and food. One of them had boxes of ammunition. We took out all of the ammunition we could use and then the captain ordered us. "Burn it and then back to the horses, boys!"

We carried the boxes between us and loaded them onto our horses. The pyre from the fire soared high into the sky. Those in the town of Harper's Ferry would wonder what had caused the disaster. Some may have thought, from the noise that it was a Fourth of July party or perhaps a northern battle. It would be some time before they realised that it had been Boswell's Wildcats.

Back at the camp, we were ecstatic at our victory. The engine, the train and the track had been destroyed. Surely the hierarchy would let us join now? We rested for a day and then left again. Two men were assigned to watch the camp now with valuable materiel of war. Once more I was lucky- I was not left behind. This time we headed for Harper's Ferry. The infamous ferry had been augmented by a bridge and that was the object of our visit. If we were to return south we would need some way to cross the Potomac and Captain Boswell said that he was tired of getting wet in Yankee water.

The blue uniforms which swarmed around the bridgehead told us that it was defended as did the cavalry horses that we saw in great numbers. This was not just infantry this was cavalry and they could travel as fast as we could. We scouted for an hour to ascertain the strengths and the weaknesses and then we returned to our camp in the forest.

The next day we were sent out in pairs to scout the area north of the ferry. I was more nervous than before as I had seen more Union soldiers in one place than we had encountered so far in our travels. We were just two men; what would happen if we came upon a cavalry patrol? The prospect of a Yankee prison did not appeal.

We saw no troops but found a field with half a dozen horses grazing. We had learned to be opportunist thieves. Horses were more valuable than gold. They could carry the captured goods for us. We quickly rounded them up and roped them together; my knot and rope skills made the task quick. The owner of the horses saw us and raced out with an antique musket in his hand. He fired at us but at a distance of over two hundred yards, he would have had more chance of hitting us by throwing the weapon at us.

The captain was delighted with our haul. Others had also found supplies, however, the worst news was that Sergeant Murphy had spotted a company of cavalry who appeared to be scouring the country for us. The captain was a brave man but he could see that we were between a rock and a hard place. The cavalry to the north were driving south and the only way across was through the garrison at the ferry. We all awaited his decision but even I could see his dilemma. With the prisoners and the slaves, we did not have the freedom he needed.

Sergeant Murphy, who was a quiet thinker, suddenly grinned. "I have it, sir. The bridge is wide enough for six men and horses abreast. We take six of us. Let us charge the bridge a-firing our pistols, the slaves and the prisoners in the middle and the rest of the lads behind. If we do it at night we will scare the bejesus out of them."

"We would have to gag the prisoners."

"Simple enough sir and we use one of us to guard

each man. Sure it'll be like a dream." Danny Murphy always sounded confident and confidence is infectious.

"I like it, Daniel! Hopefully, it will be a nightmare for them. Slaughter the captured animals and strap the carcasses to the backs of the spare horses. Spread the ammunition between the new horses we just acquired. We ride at dusk. "

The prisoners were not happy about the prospect of being gagged but I suspect it was the proximity of their comrades which galled them the most. At best they would be interrogated and exchanged and at worst end up in a rebel prison camp. They were so close to safety and yet, if we were successful, they might never see home again. I was delighted when the captain chose Harry and me to be two of those who would charge the enemy.

Sergeant Murphy came to give us advice. "Tie your reins around your pommel. That will give you two hands to fire two pistols. Use your saddle guns first and just keep pointing and firing. You don't need to aim. Besides in the dark and with the smoke you'll be lucky to see anything. All you lads need to know is that anyone in front of you is a Yank!" He turned to the four of us who would be leading the charge. "When we reach the other side of the bridge turn and use your carbines to cover the others as they come across. When I yell '*run*' then you better listen; I won't be giving any second shouts!"

The captain addressed us before we left. "There will be no noise until we charge the bridge and then I want you to sound like the Army of North Virginia. If the Sergeant or I fall then it is your duty to get to Winchester and give our information to Colonel Stuart.

God speed!"

We could see the lights of Harper's Ferry in the distance. We descended from the heights through the forest, avoiding the road. When we were two hundred yards from the bridge we emerged from the trees. The captain and the sergeant placed themselves in the middle. Harry and I were on the right and the other two were on the left. The rest of the men, prisoners and our slaves, were bunched up as close behind us as they could manage. We tied our reins on to our pommels and drew and cocked our pistols. The captain waved us forward and we kicked our horses.

Copper was a very responsive horse and she trotted next to Harry's mount easily keeping pace with the others. The guards at the bridge were lounging at their posts and looking over the side. I daresay they were watching the river and trying to spot fish. I could see their neatly stacked muskets; they were not expecting trouble. Once again, the gloom aided us for they heard the hoofbeats and assumed it was their own cavalry. We urged our mounts faster and I heard a Yankee shout, "Slow up you damned stupid…" He got no further for there was a double flash and a bang as the captain opened fire. We all fired at the same time. The rate of fire became more erratic as we all cocked and fired at different times but the defenders stood no chance. I saw at least two dive off the bridge into the Potomac. The ones at the far side had had the chance to grab their muskets and they raced to the middle of the bridge. That was a mistake for it shortened the range for our pistols. They knelt and levelled their weapons; the officer behind them raised his sword. I quickly emptied my two revolvers and slid them into my holsters. Danny had been correct for we could see nothing beyond the smoke. I drew my hip gun and aimed at a sergeant who suddenly loomed up at me in the middle of a knot of men. I must have been ahead of the rest for there was no smoke and I saw the back of his head erupt as the bullet killed him. I saw no more for the others fired and it was a wall of smoke through which we rode and then my pistol was empty and we were on the other side. I holstered my weapon and took out my carbine. I could see the flash of muzzles on the southern side of the bridge and knew that it was the garrison. I just aimed and fired at the flashes.

As the slaves and prisoners galloped by I thought we had made it and then I heard the cavalry bugle. Sergeant Murphy roared. "Skirmish line!" and twelve of us formed a stationary line. Four of us held our carbines whilst those at the sides had their pistols ready. The Union cavalry outnumbered us by at least five to one but they had their sabres out; even the poorest pistol has a longer range than a cavalry sabre and we had the best revolvers that money could buy.

"Steady. Hold your fire!" When they were thirty yards from us the captain shouted, "Fire!"

I fired as fast as I could until the carbine was empty. I was now without a loaded weapon so I put the carbine away and drew my sabre but, as the smoke cleared, I could see that the charge had faltered and failed. A wall of dead horses and men lay before us while the rest milled around leaderless. "Run!"

We needed no urging and we galloped up the road after the others. I still had my sabre out and I suddenly saw a soldier with his musket aiming at Dago's back. I raised the sabre and slashed it down. It had never been used before and was razor sharp. It sliced through his kepi, his head and his face. He fell, a bloody mess and then we were in the dark and there was just the desultory pop of a hopeful musket behind us.

The slaves, prisoners and their guards were waiting for us at the top of the heights. We slowed to a halt and looked around to see who had survived. Harry grinned at me. "The luck of the Irish again!"

Sergeant Murphy came and slapped me on the back, "Luck of the Irish, my arse. Dago, you owe young Jack here your life. He sliced through a man aiming at you as though his head was a watermelon!"

Captain Boswell looked flushed with excitement. "Well done lads. Any injuries?"

We looked around and then Jedediah said, "Tom's not here."

Dago shook his head, "I think I saw him take a musket ball in the gut."

Another voice piped up. "Yeah I saw him just after the bridge and he looked mighty dead to me."

All the elation evaporated as we realised we had suffered our first casualty. We rode in silence south, the prisoners now without gags but silenced by their prospects. As dawn broke we could see Winchester in the distance. We had seen no Yankees on our way south which was a good thing as we were in no position to fight. There was an infantry roadblock on the northern end of the Valley Pike. They could see our grey uniforms but they wisely kept their weapons aimed at us.

"Where you fellahs from?"

The Captain jerked his hand behind him. "Came through Harper's Ferry. We were scouting for Colonel Stuart."

"You must have been away some time boys; he's now Brigadier General Stuart. Are those prisoners for him or General Jackson?"

"We were sent by Stuart so I guess it will be for him."

"What is the name of your unit sir?"

"Boswell's Wildcats. Remember the name son."

We rode through Winchester to the headquarters building marked by the huge flag outside. The captain sent most of the men back to our camp close to Kernstown and retained just the prisoners, the sergeant and Harry and me. I felt honoured. While the captain entered the building we three remained on guard with the prisoners, who now stood forlornly awaiting their fate.

The eldest of them said, "We thought you boys would have let us go. We were never no trouble you know."

"I know," Sergeant Murphy nodded, "but the thing of it is that we are at war now and you can't behave as we would have before it started. I am sorry for your problems but I wish you well."

A sergeant from the First Virginia came out with two armed guards. "We'll take your prisoners off you now. Your captain will be out shortly."

We waited, what seemed like an age and then Captain Boswell rejoined us in the company of a stern looking fellow who I discovered was the famous Thomas Stonewall Jackson although at the time he had yet to make his reputation. Captain Boswell's face was flushed and angry and I knew why as we heard the tail end of the conversation.

"Sir I do not approve of General Stuart using irregulars and I can confirm, sir, that you will not become part of the regular army for you are not a gentleman." He saw us. "If you and the other boys wish to join the regular army we will be more than willing to have you. We need fine fighting men like you and you will receive a soldier's pay."

I was about to answer when Danny held up his hand. "That's a fine offer sir but you see we are Captain Boswell's men and, until he tells us otherwise we'll be serving under him." He looked at the two of us and we nodded. "Of course we all serve the Confederacy sir."

The captain led us, in silence to the east of the town. We said nothing for we could sense the anger and frustration. He was a real gentleman and his one indiscretion of youth was being used by his family to prevent him from doing what he wanted to; to serve the South. We knew we were heading for the cavalry when we smelled the horse shit. To a cavalryman, it is the smell of home. The captain rode straight up to the tent of J.E.B. Stuart. When the famous horseman came out of his tent I was surprised for he looked quite small and slight. His reputation as a fearsome cavalryman made me think he would be a giant. He had a fine beard and long hair.

He strode up to Captain Boswell and clasped him by the hand, "Well done James, well done. You have bloodied the Yankee's noses for sure."

I looked at the others in surprise. How could he have heard about Harper's Ferry? The Captain gave a wry smile. "If I might sir, give you a full report?"

"Of course. Gentlemen, please take a seat."

We sat down on the wooden chairs outside of his tent. We felt awkward but we had been invited to sit and we did although tiredness and hunger were taking over. The captain explained about the train and the horses finally describing our charge through the lines.

The little General almost bounced up and down on his chair. "Bully sir! Bully for you!" He looked at my holster. "Sir, could I examine your gun?"

"Of course," and I handed it over.

"And your men have three of these?"

"And a Springfield or a Henry carbine too."

He looked down the barrel and turned the gun in his hands. "I wish we had these for all our cavalry." He looked at Sergeant Murphy who was filling his pipe. "And you sent a company of cavalry packing sergeant?"

"Sure sir and they must have all been married men for they could not face the lads." He looked proudly at Harry and me. "With all due respect sir, these boys are the finest light cavalry in the South and it is a shame that they can't fight with the army."

"Not now Daniel."

"No James, your sergeant is right. It is a shame but the army's loss is my gain. Will you continue to scout for me? And perhaps undertake some other missions for me?"

"Of course sir. We are camped down on Middle Road, close to Kernstown."

"Good. I'll arrange for some supplies for you. Anything else you need?"

The Captain grinned. "When we destroyed the train we found some Yankee ammunition for our carbines and pistols and we have quite a few spare horses. At the moment sir, we are in profit and, until my men get paid, that will be how we will operate."

"You know Jackson calls you bandits?"

"He can call me any damned thing he likes for we

know we are patriots."

"Good. Then let us get you a wagon and some supplies."

When we returned to our men we had food, blankets, canteens and slouch hats. The latter were appropriated by the sergeant and, as we rode back he explained why. "You see lads if we are to be ghosts then we need to change our appearances; the slouch hats one day the kepi the next. We'll keep the Yankees guessing and they will think we are twice the number we actually are."

The camp was already set up when we arrived and Dago had made a rope corral for our herd. We did not need to hunt as we had supplies and, while the slaves cooked, we cleaned and loaded our weapons. One of the items we had been given by Stuart was a cartridge belt for each man. We already had one but it meant we could carry twice as many rounds now. We spent a week in camp before we were sent on our next mission. In fact, there were two missions. Dago, Smithy and six others were sent to escort Jedediah Hotchkiss to make maps for the general. This annoyed Danny Murphy. "Sure and General Jackson is a hypocritical bastard. He won't give the captain a commission and yet he will use us to carry out the jobs he needs doing."

"Never mind Sergeant, at least we are acknowledged and we are serving the Confederacy. These maps will help us to win the war. Our mission is simpler. We have to scout Romney across to Harper's Ferry. I suspect we will have more action there."

There were eleven of us who headed to the northeast that day. It was a new country for all of us and we would be in the western half of Virginia. The land rose steeply to the Allegheny range of mountains which had made such an imposing barrier to the early settlers. We hoped that we could gather much intelligence from the people of that area for most of them would be supporters of the rebellion. In that, we were proved wrong.

We headed west along the main road which went almost directly towards Romney. Pairs of us would scout on either flank to look for signs of the enemy and to find information from the locals. That close to Winchester the people knew nothing of the enemy other than they were at Harper's Ferry. Once we neared Romney we began to hear rumours of blue coats in the vicinity. Annoyingly we saw no signs of them but the farmers we met talked of blue columns in the distance. As it was March the farmers were busy in their fields and so the Captain was tempted to believe them. He sent Jedediah back to Winchester with the news that there might be a Union force close by and we headed south figuring that the Union forces might well have been heading into the Shenandoah Valley. We headed south and camped in a sheltered spot in the mountains. There were trees for shelter but we were all nervous as we were not sure where the enemy would be. We were supposed to find them and not the other way around.

Guard duty is more nerve-wracking than a watch on a ship. You know what might happen at sea- a change in the wind, a squall, a storm. Each eventuality could be planned for. Picket duty, sat on your horse watching the dark was a different beast. Was that shadow the moon? Was it an animal or was it a soldier sneaking up to slit your throat? With so few men we had a picket which was one hour on and two hours off.

It helped to keep us concentrated on the task in hand. Even so, when we rose the next day I could see the red-rimmed, tired eyes which were an indication of the stressful night we had spent.

We were just a little short of Moorefield when Jedediah found us. He was out of breath and his horse was frothing. He had ridden hard. "Sir! The Yankees are in Winchester and the General has taken the army south towards Mount Jackson."

There was a stunned silence. What did we do next? Captain Boswell was a good officer but he was an even better leader. He smiled. "Well, I hope the darkies keep the camp hidden but, for us, it changes nothing. We are heading in the same direction as the General and we are only twenty or so mile from Mount Jackson. What say we see where the Yankees are and then ride to the General?"

It seemed so simple when he told us that and we trotted down the road. There was a river running towards the town and we watered our horses. Suddenly there was the sound of a musket and a chunk of wood flew from the tree by the Sergeant's head.

"What the..."

Before we could react, a column of cavalry appeared out of nowhere. There had to be half a company at least. We didn't wait for orders. We took out our carbines and began firing. The range was over a hundred yards but they were a big target and our first volley took out men and horses. Their commander was no fool and he halted them and began to change into line formation. Captain Boswell took his opportunity. "Right boys; get across the river and into the forest. We now know where the Yanks are. Let's get the hell out of here and tell General Jackson."

Jamming my carbine back in its holster I wheeled Copper around and plunged into the icy waters. I hoped that the Yankee cavalry did not have carbines such as ours for the passage through the river would slow us up and we would be easier targets. I urged Copper on and felt a sense of relief as his hooves found purchase on the river bed. I turned to watch the rest of the patrol. Sergeant Murphy was struggling as he was a big man. I could see the eager cavalry closing on him. I took out one of my Colts and aimed at the horse of the nearest man. It was a long shot but a horse is a big target. I was lucky and the horse shied as my bullet hit it in the shoulder. It gave Danny the time he needed and he slapped his horse hard with his reins. The rest of the patrol loosed a volley and one of them struck a trooper who fell. They raised their own carbines and the captain roared, "Let's go!"

We headed into the trees which, mercifully, soon swallowed us up. It was now a game of cat and mouse. They could split up and send men in many directions. They would be bound to outnumber us. I also suspected that they might be keen to get their hands on our weapons; our former prisoners had often admired their efficiency and accuracy. We soon slowed down. It would not do to break the leg of a mount on the mountain trail and we did not wish to exhaust our horses either.

"Jack, you ride twenty yards behind us and keep a sharp ear out for them."

I was the tail of the patrol and I would be the first to know if we were being closely pursued. I turned Copper to face the opposite way. I did not want to get a stiff neck. I took out a loaded pistol and I waited until I thought the rest of the men had moved away. Then I turned to follow. Every hundred yards I stopped and watched and listened. I could hear the pursuit but it did not appear to be closing. Each step east and south took us closer towards our own army and safety. Suddenly Copper's head came up and I saw, less than twenty yards away a trooper. He was as surprised as I was for I had been still and he had no idea I was waiting. I just reacted and brought up the Colt. At that range, I could not miss and the bullet took him out of his seat and threw him to the ground. I grabbed the reins of his horse and galloped hard. Every horse was worth over $100 to us!

I saw Harry's horse. "They are right behind me. Ride!" Harry needed no urging and he kicked hard and shouted a warning to the others ahead of him. Soon we were all galloping as hard as we could manage through the forest. There was no trail and we had to just hope that we could find our way out. We heard the pop of pistols behind us. It meant that they could see us. Poor Jedediah's horse had already been tired when he had reached us and the last gallop through the forest proved too much. His hoof caught a tree root and he was hurled from the saddle. Jedediah was a good horseman and he safely rolled clear of his dying mount. "Grab your guns. I have a spare horse."

He quickly recovered his weapons and, as I fired at the approaching blue coats he sprang into the saddle. I could see from his face that he wanted to put his horse out of its misery but we had no time. He too fired a couple of shots in the direction of the pursuers and then we galloped on. I was surprised to see the rest of the patrol spread out before us. Danny shouted, "Get on the end of the line and take out your pistols!"

The Yankees were as shocked as I had been earlier, especially when twenty-two pistols fired a volley which ripped through trees, men and horses. We fired until our guns were empty. We could see nothing because of the smoke and Captain Boswell signalled that we head north and west. There was no shouted command and we all followed. By the time the smoke had cleared, we were gone and I doubted that the enemy would have seen us move. We would have appeared to have been spirited away like ghosts. We halted half a mile away and waited. We all reloaded while we did so.

Jedediah said, "Thanks for that Jack. That was smartly done. I picked up a shitty carbine but I lost my two good holsters." He had had to resort to tucking his pistols in his belt and slinging his own carbine over his shoulders. He did look comical.

There was no pursuit and after an hour we headed south again but stopping frequently to listen for the enemy. We had no idea where the Union forces had moved to and for all we knew we were behind their battles lines and trapped.

CHAPTER 7

Jack

We found that we had travelled too far north and were close to Strasburg. "Too late to find the General tonight; we'll find somewhere to sleep and then head on south in the morning."

We saw a farm with the glow of oil lamps, and, as this was the Shenandoah Valley where we might find aid, we headed there for some shelter. It was still March and the nights were as cold as Ireland. The farmer was a little more sympathetic than Mr Pritchard had been and we were offered the barn. It was a real luxury; the hay was warm and we slept well. The farmer's wife cooked us ham and eggs in the morning. This, washed down by hot black coffee, was as good as it would get. Just before we left the farmer told us that there were Union forces in Winchester. To Captain Boswell, this seemed like too good an opportunity to miss. He sent two men to Mount Jackson to tell the general of the threat from the west whilst we headed north.

We went quite gingerly; we wanted to see but not be seen. When we reached the outskirts of the town we left one man with the horses whilst the rest of us went in pairs to spy out the land. Harry and I made our way to the railroad line. There were a number of engines and cars in and there was activity around each one. It looked to both of us as though they had brought fresh troops but we couldn't see them. Our problem was that we had to hide and move surreptitiously. Luckily our grey uniforms did not stand out as much as the Yankee blue and we wore our slouch hats much as the farmers and citizens did. We had left our carbines with the horses and just carried the one Colt with the flap on the holster open. I hoped it would be enough.

We walked along the railroad for the carriages and cars looked deserted. "Look!" Harry's sharp eyes had spotted horse shit, more than could have come from one animal. We left the railroad tracks and followed the sign left by the horses. We emerged from the houses and saw tent after tent. It was a huge Union army. There were small open fires and stacked muskets. We lay behind a wall and took off our hats. We began to count flags and standards for that was always a good way to ascertain how many regiments there were. We estimated that we could see fifteen or so.

"That's a lot of soldiers."

"It sure is Jack but I can't see any cavalry. That is a bonus."

We made our way back to our horses, avoiding all the busy places we had encountered on our way there. We had a scare when we went down an alley behind a drinking establishment and three Union soldiers were relieving themselves. Harry had more brass than a twelve pounder and he just said, "Have one for me boys!" and they laughed. I suppose if they had looked up they would have taken us for their own men but a man who has his manhood out is focussed on one thing at a time.

The sergeant and the captain were both there when we reached the horses. We told them what we had found. "Good work. It seems that two divisions have left the Valley for Richmond and this fellow Shields is holding Winchester with just one."

"Aye sir but it sounds like ten thousand men. How many does General Jackson have?"

"I am not sure but it cannot be more than four thousand. We have to get the news to him."

We mounted and rode like the wind. We met the first horse pickets outside Woodstock. There was no sign of Stuart and the Captain reluctantly had to report to Stonewall Jackson. He took Sergeant Murphy with him.

We got to talking with some of the men of the Fourth Virginia, Jackson's old regiment. "We keep seeing you fellahs around but we can't work out your regiment."

They were looking at our buttons and insignia. Harry stared back at them; he was never one to back away from a fight. "We aren't regulars. We fight for Captain Boswell."

"I hear you are nothing more than bandits."

The soldier who made the mistake of insulting Harry was a big man but Harry's fist planted a punch in the middle of his face and he fell backwards, unconscious. We were outnumbered and it looked as though it could turn ugly. I just whipped my Colt from my holster and held it in the face of the Sergeant. "Now let's just calm down here. Words were said that shouldn't have been said and your man paid for it with a little blood. Do we want a bloodbath or shall we leave it at that?"

The Sergeant breathed heavily. "I guess you got the drop on me Irish so we'll back off but the next time I see you make sure your hog leg is ready because I don't forget." They picked up their unconscious comrade and dragged him away muttering threats and insults as they went. Sergeant Murphy emerged at the end and he looked at me and the gun in my hand. "Now what did I miss?"

Jedediah grinned. "We'll tell you later but these two sure are wildcats sarge. They were ready to take on the whole of the Fourth Virginia when they called us bandits."

Once again the captain left the general's tent with a red and angry face. "Come on boys we are wasting our time here. Let's head back to the camp."

We rode hard and made it back to our camp close to Sandy Ridge. The slaves had kept it tidy and fed the horses but there was no food ready. While they cooked it Sergeant Murphy opened a jug of poteen. "I think we need this tonight and we will tell you what transpired."

We were the most loyal soldiers one could ever imagine and I think that one reason for this was the openness and honesty of our two leaders. The captain took the first swig and wiped his mouth with the back of his hand. He passed it to Danny. "Well, boys it seems the General doesn't believe us. Colonel Ashby's cavalry said there were just four regiments of infantry and a couple of guns in Winchester. General Jackson believes him and he intends to attack as soon as he reaches Winchester."

"But we counted almost ten thousand!" I was angry too.

"I know, Jack, but we are not regulars and have no standing. They doubt everything we say until it is backed up by regulars."

"How many men does Jackson have?"

"No more than four thousand."

"It will be a bloodbath."

"I know."

There was an air of despondency in the camp that night and we all drank a little too much. We all felt for Captain Boswell. He had tried to do the right thing and had been rebuffed. It was hard to see what else we could do. We knew that their information was wrong and General Jackson has been misled but we were powerless. The captain decided to leave the Shenandoah Valley and find General Stuart who was rumoured to be in the Peninsula; there, at least, he had an ally.

What none of us knew was that the Yankees were moving south to meet Jackson's threat and were heading for the Valley Pike. As we lay in our tents that night we were about to become part of a battle, the only battle that General Stonewall Jackson would lose.

I had not drunk as much as the rest and had elected to take the early morning watch. Just before sun up, I roused Aaron and the other slaves to prepare coffee. I was not sure the men would be ready for food. As they got the food going Aaron went to his tent and returned with my hide jacket.

"Here suh. I finished it while you boys were away."

I was touched; he had done a remarkable job. "This is perfect Aaron. I reached into my pouch for some coins.

He waved them away. "Don't worry Mr Hogan. I had plenty left over and I can make some fine little knick-knacks. It is my pleasure."

I don't doubt that many slaves were abused by their owners and treated badly but I have to say that Captain Boswell's slaves were as loyal as any freedman. The slaves we had had with us could have easily run when we were north of the Potomac. They were in the land that was free of slaves but they elected to stay with us. I often wonder what would have happened had shells not been fired on Fort Sumter. Much later I was told that the south could have seceded and been a sovereign country but the firing on the Federal fort was an act of war. Had that happened then I do not know what my life would have been like but events outside of my control were dictating my destiny.

I was nearing the horse lines when I heard the noise of marching men in the distance. I saddled Copper and then went to wake the Sergeant. "Sergeant Murphy. I can hear soldiers. I am going to investigate."

As hungover as he obviously was, the big Irishman nodded and waved me away. I felt happier knowing that he would organise things. The sounds that had alerted me appeared to be coming from beyond Middle Road. At the tree line, I halted. I could see blue coats marching towards the top of Pritchard's Hill. As yet there appeared to be no troops on the road or towards the ridge. I wheeled Copper around and headed back to the camp.

Sergeant Murphy had, indeed, roused the camp and all was frenetic activity. Everyone halted as I galloped in to the middle of the mayhem. I pointed to the east. "Union troops are digging in on the top of the hill but the road is empty as yet."

The captain looked relieved. "Good. Well done Jack." He turned to Aaron and the slaves. "Take your boys down the road to Harrisonburg. William and Matthew, please escort them there and find a camp. We will join you whenever we can." He looked around and found Jedediah. "Jed, ride to the General and tell him that there are Yankees on Pritchard's Hill but Sandy Ridge is empty and he could flank them this way. Join William at Harrisonburg when you have done that."

In a remarkably short space of time the tents and equipment had been packed on the horses and into the wagon Stuart had given to us and they headed south to safety. There were now but eight of us left for Dago and the others were still with the mapmaker, Hotchkiss. We all looked at the captain for orders. He gave a rueful smile. "I guess we can't do much with just eight men but I think we will let them know who we are." So far we had kept our standard furled but the captain now took it and handed it to Harry. "Here Harry, let us carry this today." He grinned at us. "There are simple orders for today, follow the flag. And Harry, I want you closer to me than my underwear!"

We all laughed and Sergeant Murphy growled. "And, before you get too excited, check that you are fully loaded, today could be a hot day."

We headed east across Middle Road towards the trees which lined the base of Pritchard's Hill. We could see the caissons and limbers of artillery as they were dragged into position. Obviously, there were Confederate forces to the south of them and we could see the lines of soldiers as they hurried to form defences behind the walls of the farm. It meant that their attention was not upon us and we made it to the tree line without discovery.

We heard the pop-pop of fire from skirmishers to the east. The battle had begun. I just hoped that the captain's message had reached Jackson in time. Already we could see columns of Yankees moving from Winchester towards the hill. We made it to the edge of the trees and we tethered our horses to their branches. We were less than a hundred yards from the right flank of the Union Army and we were unseen. We could see, beyond the cannons and the infantry, cavalry skirmishing on the Valley Pike. From the direction of the church, we could see columns of grey advancing. Jackson was attacking.

"That damned pig-headed fool. Good men will die today because of his dislike of me!" He took out his own carbine. "Right boys. There are only eight of us but I want them to think that there is a company. Empty your carbines and then be ready to run at my command."

It was much easier resting our carbines on our knees or steadied against a tree than from the back of a moving horse and we were able to aim much more accurately. I targeted my carbine on a sergeant of artillery. He was standing behind his cannon smoking a cigar. I waited for the command and as soon as it came I fired. I watched him spin around the cigar flying into the air. I chambered another round and aimed at the gunner clearly identified by his lanyard. He was moving but I still managed to strike him on the shoulder. The smoke from our guns and the muskets of the enemy now made a fog of war but the Yankees were tightly packed and any rounds fired through would strike something. We heard the whinnies and neighs of horses mixed in with the screams and shouts so we knew we were hitting their mounts and draught animals as well as men. I heard the empty click. I was out of ammunition. "Jack! Move!" I turned and saw that we were falling back to the horses. We quickly mounted and I saw that all eight of us had survived.

"Unfurl the flag!" Harry shook the standard to make it flutter and Captain Boswell led us down the meadow towards Middle Road. As we galloped I could see why there was a huge column of Union infantry moving along Middle Road towards the hill.

Harry gave a rebel yell, "Yeehaw!"

Sergeant Murphy, his face filled with the joy of battle roared, "Ride you Wildcats, ride!"

There was a ragged volley from behind us but, at a distance of over a hundred and fifty yards, they might as well have been spitting at us. The Captain led us obliquely across the front of the advancing Union army. I was at the back and I could see why he had chosen this course of action. Jackson's army was marching up the hill towards the cannons and Union lines. Had we tried to join them we would have been cut to ribbons by the fire of both sides. Sandy Ridge looked to be the safest place. There we would be on the flank of the Union Army and could move in any direction.

Once we made the edge of the trees we reloaded and rested our horses. To our horror, we saw the attack repulsed and the grey coated warriors retreated down the hill. Harry attracted the attention of the Captain. "Sir, it looks like there are some of our lads heading this way."

"Good he can outflank them. Let us go down and

meet them."

We had not gone far when we came upon a stone wall, the boundary of some property. I was at the rear and as we slowed to cross the obstacle I glanced over my shoulder towards Pritchard's Hill. They had turned their lines to face the threat and I could see an enormous column of men half a mile away. "Sir you had better hurry for the Yanks are coming."

Just then the first of the Virginians reached the wall. The captain shouted to the lieutenant leading the troops. "I would get your men behind this wall lieutenant! There is a brigade of Yankees ahead of you and they outnumber you."

He touched his kepi and drawled. "Thank you suh! I am much obliged." He turned to his men, " Twenty Seventh Virginia hold the wall!"

As we crossed behind them a sergeant asked, "Are you with Colonel Funsten?"

Sergeant Murphy laughed, "No, we are Boswell's Wildcats!"

As we descended through the advancing army we could see that there were pitifully few of them. The captain recognised the General's aide, Sandie Pendleton. "Sir, there is a huge column of Yankees advancing. These boys will struggle to hold them."

"Thank you, Boswell." He closed a little and said in a quieter voice. "Sorry that the General didn't heed your advice or use you. You should know that there are many of us who think you should be fighting with the army. I will pass on your news and I am surely grateful to you." He saluted and rode back to the General.

"I think we will give these Virginia boys a little help here."

We tethered our horses and found a thinly defended piece of wall. The lieutenant we had spoken to was there. "Mighty generous of you horse boys to help us. Is that a repeating carbine?"

"It is."

"I sure wish we had them."

I could see that the soldiers were armed with muskets. They all had a bayonet on the end and the whole weapon looked to be both ungainly and inaccurate. We could fire from a prone position but they had to stand. It was fortunate that they had a wall to afford them some protection.

"Will you look at that Captain Boswell? There must be two hundred men at the front of that column and about fifty ranks deep. That is a powerful lot of Yanks."

The sergeant who had spoken before said. "Don't worry Irish we are from the Stonewall Brigade. We will hold them." He was an older man and I could see, from the resemblance, that the soldier next to him was his son. I hoped they would survive.

The captain had us all together and he spoke quietly. "I want volleys today. It will be more effective. Once these boys begin firing you will see nothing so your first shot will have to be accurate and then keep firing without moving your gun."

"Sir!"

"And remember that today we fight under our own flag. Let us not let it down!"

When the column was a hundred and twenty yards away we heard the order to fire. Where we aimed our carbines a hole appeared and we fired again. By the third shot, we could see nothing. It was as though a fog had descended but we kept on firing. We kept loading and reloading until the barrels were too hot to touch. I wondered how long we could keep it up, it was already late afternoon.

Suddenly disaster struck. The attack on Pritchard's Hill had failed and the Union General launched his men on our right flank. Men began to fall. The lieutenant shouted. "We are flanked! Fall back!"

All discipline left the Virginians who streamed away from the wall desperate to avoid the hundreds of blue-coated enemies who hurtled after them. "Right boys. Back to the horses and we'll buy these Virginians some time."

As soon as we were mounted we faced the wall and drew our pistols. "Make each shot count!" Sergeant Murphy would be watching us and woe betide any man who wasted a ball.

The men from Ohio who screamed across the wall thought that they had won for it was rare for a retreating infantryman to stop. The major from Ohio who stood atop the wall screaming, "Death to the rebels!" had a surprised look on his face as the sergeant's Colt took off his face. Our revolvers barked death to any Union infantryman who dared to clamber across the wall. Once they saw it was only eight men someone ordered them to fire from behind the wall.

"Right lads. Time to go!"

As we rode hard I saw the sergeant who had spoken to us lying on the ground his body struck by an artillery round. His son was kneeling over his body. I leaned down to grasp his arm. "Come on son. You can do nothing more for your pa." He looked up tearfully and took my arm and I swung him on to the back of Copper.

We all galloped after the sergeant and soon found ourselves amongst the retreating Virginians. We had fought our first battle, and we had lost! I lowered the boy, "Your pa did well. Honour him by fighting twice as hard."

"I will sir, and thank you. I will remember the Wildcats and what they did for me and my pa."

We joined the tail end of the retreating Confederate army as we headed south down the Valley Pike. The infantry were exhausted, having marched all the way from Mount Jackson to Kernstown. At least we had ridden. We had, for the first time since Tom's death, had injuries. None of them were life threatening but it was a lesson from which we could learn much. We had been lucky but one day our luck could run out. We pushed on along the North Fork of the Shenandoah to Harrisburg where the captain had had the foresight to send Aaron and the spare mounts. We managed to make our way through the army which was marching at the pace of the artillery. As we were irregulars we moved at our own pace. When we rode through the staff General Jackson looked up as he saw the Wildcat Standard and Captain Boswell. He acknowledged the salute with a nod. Was he thawing? After all, we had warned him of his impending disaster. Once we were through the army we kicked on and found the land full of the promise of spring. We had been on the road for almost five months through winter and it showed. Our uniforms were a little more ragged and our mounts looked in need of a good feed.

When we reached Aaron's camp, which was located just south of the town, the captain called us all together for a meeting. "When our boys come back from the map making I think we will head on home for a while." He pointed at the slaves. "It doesn't seem fair to put these boys in danger and we need to replenish our supplies."

"You mean we have lost sir?"

"No Jack. I mean that until Stuart returns to the Valley there is little point in us wasting our time here. We have learned some valuable lessons here but we need more men and more uniforms. We'll head on back."

Interlude

Even as Jackson was retreating south, still smarting from his defeat, President Lincoln pulled troops back from the Richmond campaign to counter the threat to Washington. Despite being outnumbered, the Army of Northern Virginia had almost won. As a consequence General Robert E Lee was given command of the Army of Northern Virginia and he was joined by Brigadier General J.E.B. Stuart. This would be the start of Jackson's dominance of the Shenandoah Valley.

Atlanta 1862

Arthur St. John Beauregard, now self-styled Major, arrived in Atlanta with all the pomp and ceremony of a visiting dignitary. He and Andrew Neil now had two servants although they were more bodyguards than servants. He had also acquired a little money on his travels from the Black Sea, via Tunis and Cadiz thence to Florida and finally Atlanta, the jewel of Georgia. He had been one step ahead of the law since his desertion during the Crimea. The Mediterranean was too close to Europe where there were still too many people who remembered the events leading up to the scandal. He had needed a new start and, after picking up the two other guards, he had headed west to America.

He had chosen the Confederacy for its cavalier attitude and because he thought he could hide. The British Government was still talking to the Union. He also had the arrogant view that he could be a great leader of cavalry. The infantry had not been for him and he deluded himself that the cavalry would be where he could show his élan and dash. He imagined himself on a fox hunt but hunting men! He and his three companions had rented a house which had belonged to a northern sympathiser. There were few of those in Atlanta but it meant he acquired it at a ridiculously low rent. His plan was quite simple; he would establish himself as a gentleman fallen on hard times and recount tales of heroism during the Crimean War. Eventually, he would be begged to command in some capacity and then he would be made. America would know the name of Arthur St. John Beauregard.

Boston

Caitlin had not managed to get a berth to Charleston because of the blockade and the war. Boston was an easier option but she found herself impoverished when she arrived. However, Boston was filled with the Irish who had emigrated from the poverty of Ireland. With the war on and industry booming, there were many jobs and Caitlin found herself as a barmaid again. This time, however, it was just serving behind a bar and there were no fringe benefits for the customer. The owner and his wife, Sean and Kathleen O'Donnell, appreciated the honesty and diligence of their new worker and, for the first time since her parents had been killed she found a home and was almost happy. But the cloud was ever the thought of her young brother Jack and his life in this war-stricken land.

CHAPTER 8

Jack

Charleston 1862

Late April

After two weeks back on the estate we all felt like new men. Jarvis and his wife excelled themselves and we ate like royalty. We had spare summer uniforms made and our horses re-shod. The Captain shared the profits from our raid and I found that I had a tidy nest egg. The next time we returned here I might have enough to send for Caitlin- that was still my dream.

The Captain had found three men to make our numbers up to twenty. Carlton, David and Barton were all ex-sailors. Since the blockade of the Southern ports by the Union Navy, berths had dried up and the sailors were desperate for money. The prospect of shared profits from the Wildcats appealed. We could have had another twenty but Danny was careful in his selection. He wanted men he could rely on and he wanted single men. We all joked about the married men from the Union who ran but it sounded plausible to us. If a man had a wife or girl to run to then he might desert if things went against him. We had loyalty to each other and the captain. The three new recruits were told quite clearly that we were irregulars. They had grinned and laughed at that. The stories circulating in the local taverns had blown our exploits out of all proportion.

One day the captain received a message from General Stuart. It seemed the General was back in the Shenandoah and wanted us to join him... unofficially of course. More importantly, the Confederate Government had passed a law authorising Partisan Rangers. It meant that, if we were supported by Stuart and Jeff Davis, then we could fight for the South and receive pay while still operating on our own. We said our goodbyes to the plantation. It was not suffering as much as the ones who relied on cotton. At least we had a source of income but we knew that we would need to become much more profitable or Jarvis and the others would begin to suffer.

We took pack mules this time for the tents and the spare ammunition. We left Aaron and the others behind. As Captain Boswell had told us it was not fair to risk their lives. We headed directly for the Valley and we relied on the hospitality of the countryside for shelter. At that stage of the war, when it was still remote from Southern Virginia, we had a great welcome and were fed as well as we would have been at home. Later in the war, it was not so easy.

Stuart was close to the Union positions at Front Royal with the rest of the army and we received a much better welcome from the other officers. News of our exploits at Kernstown and Harper's Ferry had been circulated. We still had our enemies; these were mainly amongst the Southern Aristocracy, but the rank and file approved of us and our deeds. Stuart had more braid about his uniform and the ends of his moustaches waxed. The captain told us later that he was styling himself on Napoleon's flamboyant marshal, Murat. I preferred the functional style of our own uniforms which had saved us on more than one occasion.

When the captain returned from his meeting he was a much happier man. "Apparently we are well thought of and we are not the only irregulars who are operating beyond our lines. Apparently, there is a John Mosby who is pursuing a similar line of work." We all laughed and cheered. We were not alone. "We don't get pay yet but the army will buy anything we capture at the going rate."

"When do we start?" Dago still resented the fact that he had had to escort Jed Hotchkiss whilst we were fighting in our first battle. He was of Italian descent and reckoned he was descended from Julius Caesar. He was always ready for a fight.

"Soon enough, Dago. The General says he will get his cavalry to do the scouting close to the army but he wants us operating in the north around Berryville and Leesburg. He wants to frighten Old Abe." I was learning about the geography of Virginia and knew that the two towns were both close to Washington D.C. "Of course it means we will be operating behind enemy lines. Does that worry anyone? "

"Sir, No Sir!" It was exactly what we had wanted.

The first thing the captain did was to give a couple of stripes to me and to Harry. "You two have proved yourselves to be capable leaders and I reckon that we might have to split up. This way we can have four groups of Wildcats. What say you, boys?"

"Thank you, sir," I muttered. This was an honour and I would take it very seriously.

We headed northeast following the line of the Blue Ridge Mountains. Berryville and Leesburg were old and prosperous towns and the loyalty to the south of their inhabitants was not a certainty. North of Berryville was the Baltimore and Ohio Railroad; this was a vital artery for the north and we could strike at the heart of Lincoln's power. There was plenty of cover for us as we travelled towards the Blue Ridge but we took no chances and travelled early in the morning and late in the afternoon. We also found that this conserved the horses for, unless we captured some more, we would soon be foot soldiers.

We reached the outskirts of the town after dusk. Harry stayed with the captain and half of the men while Sergeant Murphy and I took the rest to reconnoitre. We saw Union flags flying but no soldiers. We did not attempt to go down the main street which appeared to be busy. There were many people taking the air or just socialising. We headed around the side streets and headed for the bigger houses. We saw that some of them looked to be the houses of officers. We deduced this when we saw the fine horses outside of the imposing building.

"That looks like the billet of some high ranking officer I'll be bound. I'll go and tell the captain. "

Danny left me and Dago with the rest of the men to watch the large timber house on South Church Street while he went for the captain. The house was the first in a line of imposing homes and was separated from the smaller houses by a large empty lot. It looked to be far bigger than any other house we had seen. It was built on a raised plot making it look even bigger. It was painted a delicate blue. The glow from the lamps inside showed that it was well decorated. I knew that Danny had been right. This was the sort of house they would use for someone of status. There was a shaded road which joined the main road and it provided adequate cover for us. There were large bushes and hedges giving privacy from the neighbours too.

We had all left our carbines with our horses. If there was to be any action then our revolvers would do the trick far better than the longer carbine. As we watched I saw a cavalry officer, clearly identified by his yellow stripes breeches come on to the veranda for a smoke. It was a hot night and he was in his shirt sleeves which meant I could not tell his rank. He was not a young man. We were hidden in the tree and hedge lined road. I sent Dago and one of the new boys around to the other side of the house to hide in the cover of the neighbour's hedges. The house looked to be in darkness but Dago would be able to alert us of any danger. The road from the north passed by his position. I hunkered down and awaited the arrival of Danny.

The captain had brought another four men. I pointed to the smoking officer and whispered. "Looks like a senior officer." He gestured for me to carry on and elaborate. "That is a fine house. I can't see it being used by a lieutenant and he looks as old as General Jackson."

"Sound thinking. So he would make a good prisoner." He peered beyond the house, "Now we need someone on the other side."

"Dago is keeping watch there."

He patted me on the back. "You wait here with the men, Jack, and come a-running when I signal. Come on Daniel; it's time for an after-dinner stroll for two Union officers."

The two of them left the hedge and casually ambled down the narrow lane which led to South Church Street. It was dark and the only light came from the house which meant the officer just saw two men walking towards his home. He waved his cigar and said, airily, "Evening gentlemen. Too damned hot to be indoors, I don't know how the others can stand it."

"It certainly is sir."

"Would you gentlemen care to join me for a smoke?" He peered into the darkness trying to identify them, " I am not sure I recognise you."

Danny and the captain were now close enough to be seen clearly and the Yank gasped but before he could shout a warning to the others inside Danny had his Colt in his face. "Now just calm down sir and let's go inside."

The captain waved and we ran over. He pointed to the last two men. "You two stay here and watch the road. The rest of you come with me."

The surprised Colonel Reed of the Third Ohio didn't know if he should be outraged or worried. The sergeant took him through the hall and towards the large dining room at the front of the house. As we entered Danny hissed, "Check the servant's quarters and bring the servants or slaves here. Have the boys check the outbuildings."

I turned to Matty. "You go and tell Dago to search the outbuildings. The rest of you search the downstairs but don't be trigger happy. These are servants, not soldiers."

I led the men through the small doorway to the servant's area. The kitchen had four people in it: a cook, a serving girl and two waiters. I smiled and lowered my gun. "Would you folks be so kind as to join the family

150

in the dining room?" They were all negroes although I could not tell if they were free or slave.

Their eyes widened and they all went into the hall and then the dining room. I nodded at the food and one of the boys began to pile it into a box which looked to have been used to deliver vegetables. Danny grinned when I brought in the servants.

The captain was addressing the table. "You officers are now prisoners of the Confederacy. If you give me your parole I will not bind you."

The two young lieutenants looked as though they might object but the Colonel shook his head. "You have our word sir and I trust the ladies will not be harmed?"

"We are gentlemen, sir, despite the war."

One of the lieutenants spat out. "Bandits more like."

Danny walked over and cuffed him about the ears, "Learn some manners boy or I will teach you some."

Dago came in beaming from ear to ear. "There are six fine horses in the stables sir."

"Good saddle three of them. We have some guests. Jack, you and Jed, watch these until we are safely away." He smiled. I don't think they will give you any trouble. Sergeant, see if there are any papers or other useful articles in the other rooms." He gestured towards the front door with his Colt. "Gentlemen..." The three donned their hats. The two younger ones looked fit to bust but the Colonel was resigned to his fate. Doubtless, he would be exchanged. We had lost a couple of senior officers at Kernstown and we might now get them back.

There was just a door and a window in the dining room and Jed sat in the window while I stood in the door. I gestured at the seats and asked the servants, "Do you want to sit? We may be some time."

The young girl looked as though she might sit but the cook, an old mammy, smiled and said, "No thank you, sir. We are used to standing. I just hope my food isn't going to be ruined."

"Don't worry about that ma'am, we are taking care of it. We hate to see fine food go to waste."

Danny stuck his head around the door. "We'll be off Jackie boy. Give us ten minutes." He pointed at the clock and was gone.

The room became silent save for the ticking of the old Grandfather clock in the corner. I had never seen such fine furniture apart from at Briardene. The people who lived in the house must have had plenty of money.

The woman, she was obviously the Colonel's wife, coughed and said, as she slowly sipped her port, "And just who are you Rebels?"

"We are Boswell's Wildcats from Charleston."

She looked surprised. "That is a long way from here and you don't sound like someone from Carolina."

"No, ma'am. I am an Irish boy from County Wexford. I just happened along to your little war." I looked at the clock and I judged that ten minutes had elapsed. "And now we will leave you good people; my apologies for any inconvenience." I nodded to Jed who slipped out of the window and I turned to leave by the door. We leapt on our horses and galloped down the street towards Main Street. I did not doubt that the woman would raise the alarm as soon as she could. She had not been intimidated by our weapons. There were still many people hanging around but we were just two cavalrymen riding rapidly towards the front.

When we reached the captain the men were all in high spirits. "I will take the prisoners back to the General. I'll take Harry, Dago and the three new boys with me." He gestured to the maps, papers and other items we had liberated. "We did well. The General will like the papers and the jewellery will fetch a pretty penny. Sergeant you and Jack take charge. Scout around but stay out of sight. This looks to be a good place to camp."

They rode off with the captured horses and officers leaving the rest of us to congratulate each other on the raid; our first as Partisans. After we had eaten the purloined feast which had been superb, Danny and I lay talking. "The captain thinks highly of you young Jack."

"I know but why?"

"He had a young brother and I think you remind him of John. He was killed by a runaway horse and it broke the captain's heart. That was around the time he ... well you know the story with the young girl. I don't think he was thinking straight at the time."

We lay in silence each lost in our own thoughts. Danny puffed contentedly on his short pipe. He once told me that Virginia was the perfect place for him as there was so much tobacco. He used to soak the thick bars of tobacco in his poteen mixture so that when he smoked it gave off an aromatic smell of whisky.

He jabbed the stem of his pipe in my direction. "The thing is we have to be even more careful here than we were north of Harper's Ferry. With Captain Mosby and ourselves, there will be a hornet's nest looking for us soon. They know about us now; before we were just a myth. That's why he made you and Harry corporals. He knows we might be split up and you two won't lose your heads."

"What about Dago and Jed? They are just as good soldiers as me and Harry."

"True but you and Harry think as well as you fight. That is important. There will come a time when our luck will run out and then it will be up to you and Harry to look after the lads if... well if me and the captain..."

I almost laughed out loud. Shaking my head I said, "You and the captain are indestructible. You'll outlive the rest of us."

Danny shook his head and made the sign of the cross. It was then I realised that Danny was like many other Irishmen, he was superstitious. It would not impair his abilities as a soldier but it lurked in the dark recesses of his mind like a skeleton in the closet. It took me some time to get to sleep that night as ideas raced through my head like ghosts on Halloween.

The next day I led six men on a patrol towards Leesburg. We had decided I would just look and report back. We crossed through the gap in the Blue Ridge Mountains. There was plenty of good cover there but once we dropped down the other side it was a difficult country to traverse as the ground rose and fell giving many places where we could be ambushed. I had to smile to myself. This would be perfect for us to ambush the enemy but we, as yet, did not know the land. We knew when we approached Leesburg for we saw the smoke from fires and industry. We approached cautiously and our caution was rewarded. We saw the unmistakable signs of an infantry barracks. There looked to be at least two companies there. We spent some time watching the traffic moving along the busy road. There were many wagons and carts but they appeared to be guarded by cavalry. The effects of the Partisan Raiders raids had made them a little more careful, even this close to Washington. Although there were less than ten with each convoy it would be too many for us, we would need the rest of the troop.

"Right lads, let's get back to the Captain." The Captain had drilled into us that we should explore as much of the land as we could and so we headed back a different way. I was leading and when Copper snorted and then whinnied I knew that there was something ahead. "What is it, old girl? Smell something?" She snorted again and I raised my hand. "Keep your eyes peeled there is something or someone close by."

The men were well trained and they spread out, ten yards apart. Jimmy whistled and waved his left arm. We all converged on him and saw a corral with twenty horses. They looked to be cavalry remounts but that meant soldiers somewhere. "There will be soldiers. Spread out and keep your Colts cocked."

We approached in a semi-circle and there appeared to be no-one there. Suddenly two troopers emerged from the stables and they made the mistake of going for their guns. In hindsight, we could have easily captured them but we were all nervy and all seven of us let fly with our pistols. The two men stood no chance; each one falling to at least two bullets.

"Jimmy, ride down the road and see if there is anyone else. Georgie, check inside the building. The rest of you get some ropes and tie the horses in fours."

I dismounted and gave myself the grisly task of checking the bodies. There appeared to be no papers. I found a few dollars, a penknife and a watch. There were also letters in the pocket of the older one. I placed them back in the pocket. I did not want to know whose heart we had broken.

Jimmy returned, "No-one in sight Jack."

The men brought out a couple of guns and hats. We took them because we never knew when they might come in handy. With me in the lead and Jimmy at the back the others each led four fine cavalry remounts back to our hideout at Berryville.

The camp was in good spirits. The quartermaster had bought the six horses we had captured and the general was pleased with his prisoners. Harry told me later, "General Jackson almost had to crack a smile but the tough old bird fought the impulse."

My news of the wagons and the barracks pleased the captain. "We will leave late this afternoon and visit the barracks. Its time old Abe heard that the Wildcats are close to his henhouse." He looked at us all. "Now that we have two corporals we will operate in four sections. Me and the sergeant will have one each and Harry and Jack the other two. In the heat of battle look to your leader and they will look to me." My section looked over at me and grinned. I now had the responsibility of another four men to carry on my shoulders.

This time we did not need to worry about our camp. We tethered the mules some way from the tents where they had graze and water and we left just before dusk, skirting Berryville. I suspect the local troops knew that some officers had been kidnapped but I doubted that they suspected that we were camped less than a mile from their sleepy little burgh. In the twilight, we were almost invisible in our grey uniforms. The gap across the Blue Ridge was filled with the sounds of late spring and we could hear animals snuffling away in the recesses of the vast forest. I knew that Harry would be itching to hunt but this night we hunted men- a far more dangerous prey.

The lights of Leesburg could be seen in the distance and, closer to us the illumination from the barracks with the patrolling sentries. I wondered if my theft of the horses had alerted them if so, there was no sign of it. We halted behind the wall of the turnpike. The captain left Harry with three horse holders and, taking our carbines, we spread out and headed for the barracks. We moved in total silence and hid next to the second wall lining the turnpike. The captain removed his hat and peered over. He turned to us and held up four fingers. He pointed to Danny and held his hand palm up. Danny tapped five men on the shoulders and headed right. He pointed at me, palm up and then gestured left. I tapped five men and led them to the left. When we were in position he waved both of his hands and Danny and I led our men across the wall to scuttle across the open ground to the wall which led to the gate. As soon as we were there and I could see the way was clear I waved and the captain led his men towards the gatehouse.

I hugged the wall of the barracks building. I had picked Dago and I knew that he would be watching our rear for any surprises. I could hear the chatter and hum of conversation from within the barracks as we neared the four guards. They saw the captain just as I arrived. I placed my carbine next to the back of the head of the sergeant. "I would just lower your weapons and then you won't get your head blown off."

I saw the faces of his men looking at him for direction but Danny put his gun to another man and said, "I would listen to him. Like me, he is mad Irish."

We had brought rope this time and we took the weapons and boots from the guards and tied their hands and feet behind them. Dago put a gag covering each man's mouth.

The captain pointed to Danny and then made a circle. Danny took his men to search the other buildings. While we hid the guards in the guard hut Harry brought over our horses. We always felt happier with a means of escape close to hand.

"Sir, the Sergeant says there is powder in the next building."

"Tell him to grab a couple of barrels. Jack, you and Dago take some of these burning coals in a shovel. Then carry them over there to the sergeant and start a fire. As soon as you have done that get back here."

I found a shovel used by the guards to feed the fire and I shovelled a mound of glowing coals. Dago and I followed Danny's man. We were slower as we were carrying coals and by the time we reached him Danny had four of his men carrying two barrels each. He saw the fire and went into the powder store to smash open another barrel. He laid a trail out to us. "Right, Jack me, boy. Drop your coals and run for all you are feckin worth!"

I did so. The hot coals ignited the powder and it spluttered and sparked. I did not wait but ran. We had just reached the horses when there was an almighty whump and then a wall of flame leapt into the air and out into the night. Harry, Jed and the captain were holding our horses and I leapt on to Copper's back. Eight of the men were carrying barrels and they were in the middle.

"Right Wildcats. Ride!"

The soldiers from the barracks had spilt out to see what the noise was. Luckily they were unarmed. There was another explosion and flames leapt towards the barracks. They ran for water to put out the flames which already licked the roof of their home. They would need a new arsenal and a barracks.

Before we could congratulate ourselves we heard the strident notes of a bugle giving the cavalry call for boots and saddles. Almost immediately half a company of Union cavalry erupted from a lane to our left.

"A trap! Wildcats use your pistols and let's ride through them." I took out one of my Colts and blasted away at the blue uniforms. Luckily they had drawn swords; the Union cavalry all fancied themselves as swordsmen – give me a pistol any day- and that always gave us the edge.

I emptied one gun and drew another. Our withering fire was clearing the track and forcing the cavalry away from the centre. Danny and the captain halted. "Jack, Harry, lead the men away."

"Sir! Wildcats you heard the Captain now ride!"

I noticed that they both had a pistol in each hand and they began to fire at the soldiers to the side allowing the men with the barrels to escape. One spark could send the man and those around him to Kingdom Come! I rode hard for a mile and then halted the men. "Reload your weapons. Dago, ride ahead and check the road. Jed, go back and watch for the captain and Danny." The horses were panting with the exertion and I could see the whites of the eyes of the new men. They had had a baptism of fire, quite literally! I grinned at them. They were gripping their barrel for all they were worth. "Welcome to the Wildcats lads! It is like this all the time."

We heard hooves and I cocked my pistol. To my relief, I saw the captain and the sergeant followed by Jed. Then I saw that the two men were both hurt. I went towards Danny, he waved me away, "Just a cut, Jack, we'll be alright."

"Harry you take the rest of the men and the captain back to Berryville. Jimmy, Jed, Matty, you stay here with me."

The captain was about to object until Danny said, "Good lad Jack. Don't take any risks."

"I am a Wexford boy and I have the luck of the Irish." My voice sounded more confident than I felt.

Harry led them away, giving me a wave. I turned to the other two. "The cavalry know which way we went and they will come like Billy Bejabers." I pointed to Jed and Jimmy. "You two get behind that wall and I will go on the other side of the road with Matty. We'll have them in crossfire. Empty your carbines as they come and then ride a mile along the road I'll meet you there." I paused. "Don't shoot directly across the road eh?"

They sniffed their opinion and then we stopped as we heard hooves clattering behind us. Dago's voice stopped us from firing. "Harry said you would need a hand."

"Over here with me and Matty."

We stayed on our horses but we were partly hidden by the wall. We would have to ride through the fields or try a leap in the dark when we ran but we would cross that bridge when we came to it. I kept the carbine across Copper's saddle and we listened. Soon we heard the drum of hooves. We could not see them but we could hear them nearing. I suddenly saw an officer and a bugler at the head of a column of twos. "Fire!"

We began firing as fast as we could chamber rounds. The smoke filled the road and then we saw the flashes and heard the reports of their weapons. "Ah, the daft buggers have learned eh? A little late I would say."

I judged that we had slowed them up enough "Let's go!" I yelled. I hoped the other two had survived but I had no way of finding out. I lowered my body to lie flat along Copper's neck and urged the game horse along the side of the wall. He was a sure-footed beast and unerringly picked out the safe track. I saw a gap in the wall and wheeled her through it. We rode until I estimated we were at the rendezvous point.

My hand drew my Colt when I heard the hooves but it was Jed and Jimmy. Jimmy was leaning to one side. "Jimmy caught a slug in the arm."

"Jed, put a tourniquet on it and then ride another mile down the road. Matty, go with them. Dago, stay with me." We could hear the horses but they seemed to be slower. Perhaps they were warier. I suddenly had an idea. "Dago, are you game for a bit of craziness."

He grinned back. "Sure thing Jack."

"They will be watching for an ambush from the side. What say we charge down with Colts blazing and then wheel back up the road?"

"Sounds like a plan to me."

We tied our reins around our pommels and kicked on. Our horses were too tired to gallop but a trot would be quieter and just as effective. We were ready for the cavalry and they were not. We rounded a bend and found ourselves but twenty yards from them. We emptied our pistols in no time and then wheeled around. It was dark and it was smoky but I heard the screams of pain and the whinnies of terrified horses. I also heard a voice trying to organise them. "Draw your weapons and fire at the flashes! There must be at least six of them!"

By then it was too late for the ghosts had vanished. We trotted down the road after our companions. We could ambush them no longer but I hoped that we had deterred them enough to make them cautious. The Blue Ridge was but a mile or two up the road and once there we could always lose ourselves in the forest. Jimmy had taken the musket ball on the forearm and it had broken his left arm. The skin had not been broken which was a blessing. Broken skin could mean amputation. We pushed on over the Blue Ridge and, as dawn was beginning to break, saw Berryville loom large in the distance. It would not do to get caught so close to home and we were especially careful as we skirted the still sleeping town. When I heard Harry's voice intone, "About bloody time!" I knew we were safe.

CHAPTER 9

Jack

One of the new boys, David, proved to be a revelation. It seems that when he had served in a ship he had assisted the surgeon a couple of time. He set Jimmy's arm quickly enough and then looked at the Captain and Danny. Danny had been lucky the musket ball had just done into the fleshy part of his thigh. We were easily able to extract the ball and then clean it with poteen. The cut to his face from the sabre was not deep and poteen cleaned it up too' "Not too much now. We don't want to waste this valuable liquor."

The captain was more of a problem. His face needed stitches and we discovered a musket ball in his back. It took three of us to hold him while David dug around for the ball which had split upon impact. Our erstwhile surgeon was not happy. "I am not sure that we have got it all out. If there are any fragments left in it will cause gangrene. We can amputate a leg but not a shoulder!"

The Captain heard him. "Just wash it with whisky eh?" Then he passed out.

We rested for the rest of the day. "It looks like they put the cavalry there to watch for us."

"Sorry, Danny. I didn't think when I took those horses."

"No Jack, you did the right thing. We just need to be more cautious. I want you to take the powder and the horses to the south of Front Royal and tell the General what we saw. We will just rest until you get back. You will need half the men."

I left the next day. Harry was in charge until the Captain and the Sergeant had fully recovered. We approached via Martinsburg and skirted Winchester to the west. I knew that we had to vary our routes or be caught by our own predictability.

I sent Dago with the rest of the boys to the Quartermaster while I sought General Stuart. He was not in camp but I spoke to his aide, Jeremiah Hill. He smiled as I made my report. "I can see why the General likes your men and Mosby's. You tie up a lot of Yankees. We heard from some prisoners that they think we have two companies in their rear." He shook his head. "Yankees sure are dumb. Tell your Captain to keep it up. There will be an attack on Winchester soon and we need their lines of communication disrupted. They will be sending all sorts of wagons and men through Berryville soon. You will have to watch out and be effective."

"Don't worry sir. We will be."

Dago rode next to me as we headed back to our camp. He patted his saddlebags. "That powder paid well and the horses! We did all right out of that."

I shook my head, "I am not so sure. What about the wounds?"

He shrugged. "It is war my friend and it is what happens. You ride your luck." He nudged me, "You, my friend, are lucky. The men all want to be with you."

"Be with me? What do you mean?"

"You are the one who has the luck and you don't

get injured. They want to ride with you." He could see my confusion. "Take the other night; when I returned I thanked God that you wanted me with you and it was Jimmy who got hurt. Do you see what I mean? You are lucky!"

I had never thought of myself as lucky, rather the opposite, my parents had been murdered, my sister sold herself and I was press-ganged on to a slaver, but, as we headed for the camp I reflected that he might be right. I could have died in the fire at my home. I could have fallen from the mast. There were many other instances; the fact that I looked like the captain's brother. But if I was lucky I would not ride my luck. As we all know, luck can run out.

The invalids were generally better when we returned; apart from the captain who had drifted into a sleep and was feverish. David and Danny thought this might be a good thing. The fever might cleanse his body. I was not so sure.

We were taking nothing for granted and we kept vedettes out. This was good for two reasons, it gave us early warning and it taught all of us to be watchful and resourceful. While we ate Danny secured the latest money in a place of safety. We had decided, early on, that it was not a good idea to carry money with us. We were all single men and any money from a dead man would be divided between the rest. I was now confident that, when time allowed, I could send the money back to Ireland for Caitlin. The problem was where would I send it? All the people I knew who could have carried it for me were now dead or missing. It was a problem I wrestled with over the coming year.

On the second day, the captain had taken a turn for

the worse and, when we examined his wound, we could smell the putrefaction. Even David did not know what to do. Luckily Danny did. He sent us all off to find maggots. It was summer and there were plenty. When the men came back with them David and I looked at him curiously. He gave a half smile. "My grand da was with Wellington in the Peninsula. They found that when you had a bad wound then maggots would eat the dead flesh. When the maggots died then you were healthy."

We couldn't argue with that as it made a kind of sense and we packed the greasy little blobs of white around the ugly angry wound and bound it again. We were now in the hands of Danny's granddad and the men who marched to war fifty years earlier on the other side of the world.

Harry took a patrol out at dusk to see what he could see on the Berryville to Winchester road. While he was away we made our camp more secure by putting trip wires and alarms up. So far we had been unobserved but I could not believe that someone would not use the stand of trees for hunting. Danny and David fretted and fussed over the captain. When we caught some rabbits we made a soup which we could feed to the semi-conscious officer. I let Danny sleep while I took the midnight watch with Dago. I was not sleepy and I found myself worrying over Harry. The trap laid for us by the cavalry had nearly succeeded. Had they used guns rather than swords then the outcome might have been different.

Harry and his men arrived back a couple of hours after midnight. Since we had relieved some of the Yankees of their watches we could all now tell the time and I had a fine hunter, courtesy of a dead sergeant from Illinois. It made me feel more civilised being able to tell the time.

I had a pot of coffee going and Harry strode straight up to it. "I could use a cup of that." As he sipped the scalding liquid he said, "Actually I could do with a cup of tea but never mind."

"Find anything?"

"There is a convoy camped the other side of the town." He pointed. "It is only about two miles from here. We found it as we were heading back. The roads are empty but the convoy has a company of cavalry guarding it." He grinned. "We must have annoyed them and," he flourished a piece of paper. "I found this and a bunch of others pinned to buildings and trees all over the county."

I read it.

Notice

$500 reward for information leading to the capture of the Partisans and bandits known as Boswell's Wildcats.

Colonel William S. Fielding
Officer Commanding Berryville Military district.

It brought a smile to my face. We had irritated the Yankees after all and we now had a name of the military commander. Perhaps, when the captain was recovered we could pay him a visit. It would be interesting to see his reaction when he met the actual Wildcats.

When Danny awoke we updated him. He looked down at the captain. "It seems a shame to let the opportunity go by, just because the captain is a little poorly."

I sensed he was looking for support. "They will have to go down the Valley Pike and, once they are south of Berryville, they will think they are home free. We could hit them there, from behind."

"Or," suggested Harry, "we could have half a dozen attack from the flank and draw off the escort then the rest attack from the rear."

"Even better. " He turned to look for our medical expert. "David!"

The recruit joined us. "We are leaving you here to watch the captain and Jimmy. We are taking the rest on a raid." He saw, as we all did, the disappointment on the face of the young man. "Don't worry son. Just as soon as the captain is fit again you will be fighting with the rest of us but it is important that the captain gets well. You can see that can't you?"

"Yes, Sarge."

It did not take us long to organise and Harry took his five troopers for the diversion. He would come from the direction of Winchester and lead them in that direction. We would attack ten minutes after we heard the firing. The road they were following was not a turnpike and had twists and turns affording numerous opportunities for ambush. In addition, it did not have a continuous wall boundary. Both of these factors would work in our favour. Harry left before we did; he had to go far further than we did. The sergeant was still not fully fit and I could see that he would not be able to fight as well as he normally did. We rode along the road and we could see the blue of the cavalry as dots in the distance with the white wagons between them. Suddenly we heard the crack of the pistols and then the reply from the cavalry. We could see, even four hundred yards away, the smoke and then we heard the bugle. The cavalry began to thin out as their commander chased Harry and his raiders.

Our plan was to get as close as we could before we fired and so we only had four men using their carbines. They would be the marksmen who would target the drivers. They had left only ten riders with the six wagons and their attention was fixed on the pursuit ahead of them. The first they knew of our presence was when two of their riders were pitched from their saddles. I took a risk and shouted, "Surrender! We are Boswell's Wildcats!" Miraculously it worked and the other eight threw their arms in the air. Working quickly we trussed up the soldiers and guards, including the two wounded men and then ordered the drivers to head due east.

"Let's head for Boyce." Wounded or not Danny could still think and plan.

"Right, Sarge! Come on get those wagons moving." The men urged and whipped the draught animals as hard as they could. There was urgency about our actions which had been lacking in the Yankees who had been charged with protecting the convoy. We had intended on destroying the supplies but this seemed too good an opportunity to miss.

"Jack, you keep ten men at the rear of the wagons. When the Yanks come then form a skirmish line and slow them down. I don't think they have repeaters and Harry should be able to join us."

With the ten men left with the wagons, we were only outnumbered by four and a half to one. For us, that was good odds. Besides which our carbines would cut that down and it would become a battle of wills to see who wanted to win the most. We had the advantage that we were fighting for our country and profit; two powerful incentives.

As we struck the back road leading to Front Royal I wondered how long they would chase Harry. The distance to Winchester was almost the same as the distance to Front Royal. If the pickets of our own army were alert then this hare-brained scheme might just work. Every mile we rode brought us closer to safety. When we passed through the sleepy hamlet of Boyce we were just five miles away from safety and then Dago shouted to me. "We have company."

"Rearguard on me. Dismount!" We leaned our carbines on our horses as the cavalry galloped down the road. They were in an eight deep line and I could see that they had ridden their horses hard; they were frothing and foaming as they laboured on. Once again they had adopted the sabre although I could see a few of those behind trying to aim their own carbines. They had more chance of either the ground or a bird than they did us. I waited until they were a hundred yards away and then gave the order, "Fire!" I wanted volleys and, although it meant a slower rate of fire, it was a wall of lead heading towards the advancing cavalry.

The smoke made it hard to see the effect and suddenly an officer reared up before me, his sword poised to strike. I had no idea how many shots I had left but I raised the barrel and fired. It struck his horse and the dying beast fell backwards. I looked at my gun. I was out of ammunition. I sheathed it and took out my Colt to shoot the next rider I saw looming up. Before I could fire I heard Harry shout, "Whoa there! We are on your side." Our raiders had returned and we were now a troop once more.

The smoke began to clear and we saw the Union cavalry drawing up a hundred yards away. There were a handful of dead men and horses as well as a couple of wounded ones between them and us. "Mount!" I checked to see that we had suffered no casualties and we mounted."Let's find the Sergeant eh boys?"

They all gave a rebel yell and we rode after the wagons without the Yankees pursuing us. I suspect their commander was dead pinned beneath the dying horse and the withering fire had made them reluctant to charge us. Even so, we retreated cautiously, watching for any sudden movement from the enemy. There was none and soon we reached the pickets outside the Confederate lines south of Front Royal.

The quartermaster was even more delighted with our latest haul. Much of it was ammunition and would fit the muskets. In addition, there were Sharps rifles which were much better than those the south had to hand. Finally, there were bayonets and boots in one wagon. It was a mixed cargo but, with the horses and prisoners, a valuable one for Boswell's Wildcats. We were anxious to return to Berryville and Stuart's aide sent a company of cavalry to escort us to Boyce. The last thing anyone wanted was to be ambushed by the cavalry we had defeated. As we rode north I could see that there were wounds; none of them serious but Harry's men had suffered the most and it made me think about Dago's words; was I lucky?

Rebel Raiders

The captain looked much better when we returned and he was both awake and eating. David and Danny looked at the bandage and saw that all of the maggots were dead. It had worked. We all saw a visible improvement in him when we told him of our latest raid. "It seems I am now redundant. You do better without me than with me!"

I could see that he was joking and he looked to be proud of us. "Well sir, if this keeps up we'll have the Yankees whipped by Christmas."

Danny was wrong but that was not because of our efforts. Nor was it the fault of Generals Jackson and Stuart but we did begin to have drawbacks and they began at that moment. The Yankees began streaming north from Front Royal when General Jackson launched his attack. I don't know how much influence we had on the outcome of the battle but I like to believe that we weakened the Yankees somewhat. The result was that we could relax a little for a few days while General Jackson prepared to advance upon Winchester.

The captain was raring to go. We had done so well already that he thought we could shoot for the moon. We were all fit again, even Jimmy's broken arm did not slow him up much and the captain decided to take us back to Leesburg. We knew that there was a barracks there and any disruption we could cause would slow down the Union reinforcements. Once Winchester was recaptured then the Valley would be secure and we could march on Washington. We left before dark ready to strike when the soldiers were tucked up in their beds. The captain had briefed us well before we left and he intended to take us around Leesburg and approach from the Washington side. That strategy had worked before and we saw no reason why it should not work again.

We struck the Potomac well after dark and located the spit of land in the middle of the river known as Harrison Island. We were to split into two groups. The captain would take Harry and half of the men and scout the northern half of the town. The rest of us would cover the south. We would rendezvous back at the island.

We kept the river to our left as we made our way south. There were still lights on in the houses and we each kept a cocked Colt in our hand. We had suffered one ambush at Leesburg already we would not make the same mistake twice. Dago whistled and pointed. It was an artillery park and there were cannons. They were the Parrot Rifle, a weapon superior to most of the ancient cannons we had in the south. There were caissons and limbers but no horses so there was no way for us to capture them. Danny waved me over. "We'll have to spike them. I've done it before. I'll take a couple of lads. You and the others find any guards and deal with them."

I left Barton with the horses and we went quickly to the dark building which was close to the corral containing the six guns. The door was shut and I could hear noise from within. I signalled to my men to be ready and then I tried the door. It was open. I opened it as quietly as I could and eased it so that I could enter. I slipped through and smelled the foetid air of sweaty unwashed men. I moved into the room and the rest of my men followed me. Suddenly Jimmy tripped on something and a Union voice said, "What the!!

Someone else struck a flint and lit a candle. The thirty artillerymen found themselves looking down the barrels of the Colts held in our hands.

"Now, gentlemen we are Boswell's Wildcats, you may have heard of us. If you have then you know that we are dangerous. If you cooperate then you will live. I would like you all to stand and put your hands on your head." I noticed that Dago and Jed had placed themselves in the dark area at the back of the room. Most of the men obeyed me but two tried to turn and run. They were both felled by my men's Colts. "Pick up your comrades and do not try anything again or we will be forced to do more than wound next time."

They were suitably chastened and they filed out. I picked up a uniform; they were from New York. As one passed me I asked, "Irish?" He gave me a sullen nod. Strange, we were from the same island and yet on opposite sides; much like the Americans where brother sometimes fought brother. I could not just shoot them out of hand. I saw that they were all in their underwear and I had an idea. "Dago, march them to the river. We'll join you there." I heard the clang of a hammer on metal and knew that Danny was spiking the guns. "Jed, go back inside and bring out any papers and other items of value. Jimmy, go and help him."

It did not take Danny long to complete his task. He then placed a charge in each cannon and jammed some mud in the barrel, finally, he made a trail of powder to one of the caissons and then to the outside of the corral. "Everything go off all right Jack?"

I saw Jed who waved. "Yes, Danny. The prisoners are by the river."

"Then get the horses. This is going to go bang very soon."

We were mounted and ready to ride in a heartbeat.

Danny raced up to us. "Ride like the devil is after you!"

There was a flash and then a crump and then a series of bangs and explosions. It was still erupting when we reached Dago and the prisoners. Danny looked at me and I winked. "Right boys I want you to wade into the river up to your chest and face the other side. When I give the word you can turn around. You can leave the two unconscious soldiers here."

Faced by the revolvers and hearing the explosions they obeyed. I turned to Danny. "I figure by the time they turn around we'll be long gone and a man in wet underwear neither thinks nor moves swiftly."

He patted me on the back. "I like it. Let's go!"

As we headed back to the island we could hear the explosions in the distance. The guns would be repairable but it would take time. We hoped that the limbers and caissons would be beyond repair. It had been a stroke of luck finding the artillery park. Obviously, they had found the most convenient place for men and guns anticipating a short journey to the front. The island was deserted and I, for one, was a little nervous about waiting. Any Union troops in the area would be racing to the scene.

Danny shook his head, "We wait, Jackie boy. Sure and you aren't nervous, are you? Not Lucky Jack!"

"Not you too Danny; you know there's no such thing as luck."

"I don't know. I talked to the Captain about it and you know what a well-read man he is. The great French General Napoleon said of one of his generals '*I know he's a good general, but is he lucky?*' The lads agree with Napoleon a lucky soldier is better than one who has no luck."

Dago, who had the sharpest ears of any of us, hissed,

"Someone coming."

There was the sound of ten guns being cocked and then Harry and his horse loomed up out of the dark. There were just three men behind him. He shook his head. "What a cock up!"

Danny looked beyond the huddle of panting horses and distraught soldiers. "Where's the captain?"

He pointed behind him. "We were just off the main street and we saw a general's horse. The captain decided that we could capture him. I was sent with these lads to watch the end of the street. The rest followed the captain in the door. There were shots and we raced back. Poor Alex came out gut shot. He managed to tell us they had been ambushed and the captain captured and then he died. We came here."

CHAPTER 10

Jack

The silence around us seemed to be deafening. Yet in the distance, we could hear the crackle and crack of the fires and the small explosions from the artillery park. Harry said quietly, "We can't leave him there."

Danny looked hard at the distant town. "He would tell us to go back to Berryville; no he would order us back to Berryville." He sighed and took a deep breath, "And that is what I am ordering. Back to Berryville. We might be able to exchange a prisoner for him."

I shook my head, "We are fighting for him, Sarge. If he isn't with us then what is the point of fighting. Besides, you saw the notice. The Yanks think we are bandits. They might hang him rather than exchange him. They have been desperate to get their hands on one of us and we let them have the leader; the Boswell of Boswell's Wildcats." I sensed his dilemma. "Look, Sarge, you take the men back and Harry and I will take a few lads and see if we can spring him. If it is impossible then we will follow you. That way we are only risking half a dozen of us and not the whole troop."

I could see Danny weighing up the options and he came to a decision. "Only volunteers mind."

Every hand went up. I chose the men I knew that I

could rely on. I did not want too many; a smaller number would be easier to command. "Dago, Jed and David."

Harry and Danny both looked at me. Harry said, "David?"

"If Alex was shot then the others might be. Do you know anyone else who could fix them up? Besides, "I grinned at David, "we promised him some action didn't we?"

"Away with you and be lucky!"

As we trotted away Harry said, "Do you have a plan then or is it thinking with the seat of your pants?"

"I reckon that they will have heard the explosion and sent some of the men to investigate but they would keep a good guard on the Captain. It's a pity we don't know how many there are still we can try a trick." I reached behind and took my hide jacket made by Aaron. "If I put this on," I pointed at my white slouch hat. "Some Yanks have white slouch hats too; they might think I am one of their scouts. I can knock on the door I can pretend to be one of the Irish from one of those New York regiments. They will hear the accent and see the jacket. They won't look down to my trousers. Once I am in then…"

Harry threw me a sceptical look, "Then what?"

I shrugged, "I haven't got a clue but I can think on me feet Harry boy."

We reached the end of the alley and Harry pointed at the building. We had peered down the alley and saw that there were two guards there now. "If you hear any shots then come a-running. I am sure that those two will look inside the door and you should be able to sneak up on them." I tucked one of my saddle Colts in my boot and put the second in my waistband.

Harry shook my hand, "Take care, Jack. I would hate to have to break in a new partner."

I grinned and strolled down the alley as though I had every right to be there. "Halt who goes there?"

"Private McGinley, First New York battery." I made sure I sounded Irish. I kept strolling and gestured behind me with my thumb. "I was up there where the fire was. I have been sent with a message for the General."

As soon as their guns dropped and they smiled I knew that they had accepted my story. "We heard the explosion. What happened?"

"Some dozy bastard was having a quiet pipe near the caissons." I looked up at the skies. "I guess God is giving him a bollocking right now."

They both laughed and one said, "They are in the back room." He lowered his voice. "We caught that Mosby tonight, you know, the Grey Ghost?"

"Really? I should like to see him."

"Aye well, we killed two of the others and there are a couple of wounded so watch out for the blood."

I was relieved to see that the door they opened was not locked. I knew then that Harry and the others would be able to reach me easily enough. I took a deep breath and stepped through the door. After the dark of the alley, it seemed unnaturally light and I wondered if my disguise would work. I saw a blue slouch hat on the hall stand as I passed and I exchanged it for my white one. It might make all the difference. There was another guard on the door, to what looked to be the kitchen and I could hear voices beyond.

The guard did not seem suspicious as I had passed the first two. "Yes?"

"I am from the Irish Battery I have a message for the

Rebel Raiders

General."

"He's inside. Let me see." He knocked on the door and opened it a sliver, "General, a messenger from the Irish Battery."

A voice said, "Bring him in."

The sentry preceded me and I saw that there were two soldiers with guns but the guns were pointed at the ground. There was a General and an aide. Seated around the table were the Captain, Barton and Davy. I could see that Jem was lying on the table, wounded with a bloody leg. As I entered I slipped my gun out of its holster and as I fired into the stomach of the sentry I threw my waistband pistol to the captain. Barton jumped up to punch the aide and I fired at one of the soldiers, who was slowly bringing his gun up. My bullet took him in the face and his gun fired as he fell backwards. The captain shot the second armed soldiers and then we pointed our guns at the general and his aide. I heard two shots from outside and then Harry and the others burst in.

"David, see to Jem."

The smoke was clearing and I saw that the general had been shot. I looked at the captain who said, "It was the musket, it shot the general by mistake."

The aide knelt down and began to tear at the general's trousers. He looked pale. "Harry, get some horses." I gave Barton my boot gun." I looked at the captain who seemed confused, "Sir, I think we have ridden our luck enough for one night. Let's get the hell out of here. The aide here can look after his general."

"You are right. Dago, Jed, carry Jem out." He looked at the aide, "And for your information, sir, you can tell your general that I am not Mosby, I am Captain James

Boswell the leader of Boswell's Wildcats." He grabbed the satchel full of papers and maps and we strode out. I checked the bodies in the room as I left and took two watches and an Army Colt from the aide. I noticed that the other bodies had been cleared already. I switched my hat and closed the door behind me.

After the smoke and the noise in the house, the outside seemed unnaturally quiet. I saw that the captain sat astride the General's horse and he was now grinning. "Thanks for that boys. Let's get the hell out of here!"

Just then a small patrol appeared at the end of the alley where we had hidden. I fired my last three bullets and the others emptied their guns. When we looked back the end of the alley was empty.

Harry shouted, "Down Main Street then!"

Dago and Jed were in the lead and they wheeled into the Main Street. I heard the pop of their guns. I drew my carbine. As we turned into the street I saw that there were many soldiers milling around and making their way towards the distant fire. The captain drew the general's sword and the rest of us opened fire. The sudden appearance of horsemen and the crack of the guns sent everyone racing for cover. Soon we had cut a swathe through the terrified troops who had fled in all directions. There were only a handful of us but the horses and the rebel yells made it sound like a company. In what seemed like a heartbeat we were heading west towards the gap in the Blue Ridge while behind us we could see the glow that was the devastation of Leesburg.

We could not slow down for poor Jem and David rode with him on the front of his horse as we galloped up the Blue Ridge towards Berryville. We knew we were not out of the woods yet for we had to get around Berryville and dawn was almost upon us. I urged Copper next to Harry. "Harry, you and Jed had better take the lead in case of an ambush. I'll take Dago to the rear."

Harry's teeth flashed white. "Perhaps I should be with you, Lucky Jack!"

We found that Sergeant Murphy awaited us just the other side of the gap. He and the rest of the men were waiting in ambush position as we rode along the trail. His relief was obvious. "Well done lads." He looked apologetically at Captain Boswell. "I couldn't risk the entire troop, sir."

"I know Danny and I am pleased although what would have happened if these mad lads had been killed in the rescue attempt I don't know." With our escort, we made the camp without further incident.

Jem was badly wounded and we were not certain if he would be able to fight again. David worked hard to save the leg but the bullet had shattered the kneecap and part of the tibia. The balls that were used were enormous. Jem looked up with a brave smile on his face. "I can always get a wooden leg, sir."

"Whatever happens with your leg you will have a home for life on my plantation, Briardene. David, take a couple of men and escort Jem down to Front Royal. See what the surgeon there can do. Take these maps and the reports we took from Leesburg. Stay with Jem until you know what is going to happen about his leg."

When they had gone Captain Boswell became morose. Danny, Harry and I sat with him after supper. "It is my fault. I should have scouted first and not gone haring in." he pointed to me. "Jack's plan worked, didn't it?

I should have used that idea."

Danny shook his head, "Jack only came up with that as a last desperate act and we know what a lucky bastard he is."

He and Harry punched me playfully on the arms. The captain shook his head, "No, he planned well. He only risked himself and he had Harry and the others as backup. I just charged in and assumed they would all roll over and surrender."

"Up to now, they have."

"Yes, Harry, but things will be changing. After this battle I want a couple of volunteers to take Jem back and I want you to lead them, Danny."

"Me? But my place is here."

"No Danny, your place is where I say it is. We need another ten men and you are the best judge of men I know."

"Jack here, he could go. He is a good judge of men."

"True but the men regard him as a talisman don't they? Anyone who rides with Lucky Jack will survive. That's what they believe and I don't want them looking over their shoulder rather than blindly following this mad bugger eh?"

I took out the Army Colt I had taken from the aide. It was much bigger and heavier than my own and fired a bigger ball. "That's a cannon, Jack!"

"I know. I took it because… well, it looked useful."

"You'll need to get some ammunition for it."

I showed him the cartridge case I had taken. "I have fifty rounds in here. I will use it for one of my saddle guns and keep the other as a spare."

Matty returned before nightfall. "General Jackson was really happy to get those maps. He is going to attack tomorrow and he asked you to be a nuisance." He looked quizzically at the Captain. "I wasn't sure what he meant sir."

"He meant let's annoy the Yankees from their rear and their flanks."

We left well before dawn and headed down the Berryville Pike. There were just sixteen of us and, as a cavalry force, we could do little of major significance but we could draw off valuable forces from the attack of Jackson. We crossed the Opequon Creek at dawn and heard the rumble of cannons to the south. There looked to be a fog in that direction but the air was clearer where we were. The cannonade was obviously the softening up phase of the forthcoming battle. We could see blue uniforms in the distance moving from Winchester towards the south. Those of us who had been there remembered Kernstown; that had been a slaughter but this time we were in a better position to help and this time our help had been requested. We were no longer the beggars at the feast.

We headed across country over the hills and hollows which surrounded Winchester. We knew that if we kept the creek to our left and the city to our right we should come upon them. It was becoming foggier and Captain Boswell ordered us to carry our carbines to avoid being surprised. Harry had the flag unfurled for today we would not be mistaken for Mosby; we would fight under our own banner; Boswell's Wildcats.

I could see a vague line of dark shapes approaching in the fog and I shouted, "Captain! Up ahead!"

The Captain halted us. "Right boys, form line and move up slowly. When I give the command then begin to fire. Be ready to retreat when I say so."

We edged forwards. I would have preferred to be on foot as it gave a better platform to fire but I had learned how to use Copper as a firing stand. She would stand as still as a rock and I could lean across her neck. Suddenly the air cleared and we saw the third, rear rank of a brigade of infantry. There were a thousand men before us but they had neither seen nor heard our approach. Grinning with the joy of battle, the Captain shouted, "Fire!"

Resting my elbow on my saddle and my forearm on Copper's head I began firing at the same spot reasoning that men would fill the gap created by the man I would have hit. They were so surprised that it took some minutes for them to react but then their officers made them turn and aim. We heard the order, "Front rank…"

"Right boys, run!" The three hundred balls would have cut us to ribbons and we galloped away before they could fire. I heard the crack of the muskets which sounded like paper tearing and then it sounded as though a hive full of wasps had taken after me. I heard at least one of the men cry out but then we were out of range of their guns. Matty had been wounded and one of the horses was wheeling around in pain from a ball in the rump. David was still with Jem and we had to fix Matty up as best as we could.

Suddenly we heard a bugle and heard, "Charge!" A company of cavalry had been detached. I suspect they thought that we were a company as well. "Give them a couple of volleys." Fifty balls flew in their direction as we saw the ragged line, with sabres drawn approaching. Our bullets punched a hole in the middle of the line. I saw a mad look in the Captain's face and he yelled, "Follow me Wildcats! Charge!"

I just had time to sheath my carbine and draw my newly acquired Army Colt before we charged towards the gap. It was the one thing they had not expected and their own charge was propelling them quickly in our direction. It meant we came together at a prodigious speed. There was no chance of aiming; you pointed a gun at the nearest blue and fired before the next one was upon you. They were using sabres and I felt the blade of one slice into my saddle. I blasted the trooper and the huge ball took off the trooper's head. The sabre was left embedded in the wood of my saddle. And then we were through their lines and the battlefield seemed much quieter. I could see a few empty saddles but Harry, Danny, as well as Dago and Jed were still together.

The captain was almost out of breath but he had time for one more order. "Ride north to Winchester!"

We saw some Union soldiers trudging towards the town and when they saw us they thought that we were the cavalry who had broken through. They fled screaming north adding to the chaos. We took pot shots at any organised soldiers but our aim was to get away from the cavalry before they regrouped. I could tell what the captain was thinking. If the hundred cavalry were chasing us then they couldn't fight Jackson. If the rear rank of the brigade of infantry was looking over their shoulders then they could not support their comrades. The fourteen men we had begun with had had a disproportionate effect.

We galloped through the town which was a supporter of the south. As we did so we saw Confederate flags being unfurled from windows and those who had collaborated with the Yankees fleeing with all that they could carry. We did not stop until we were on the Berryville Pike and then we assessed the damage. There were just nine of us left. We had left five comrades on the battlefield. We had lost more men in an hour than we had lost in weeks of partisan work. There were still three men at Front Royal but we were now down to eleven effectives, the war was taking its toll.

Dago laughed, "Jack. You have a souvenir from the fight." He pointed at the sabre still embedded in my saddle.

I took it out with some difficulty. It was a fine sabre and had been engraved. ' Given to Lieutenant Wilcox by the grateful citizens of Dover PA.' The brave young officer would now be buried on the battlefield and the burghers of Dover would, no doubt mourn the loss of a fine young man. War is a waste.

We returned to the camp to pack up. It was no longer necessary as we were too few to function as a force. It felt sad to be dismantling the tents and collecting together the prized possessions of our dead comrades. The captain said that we should head for Front Royal and see Jem. Hopefully, we would find out what the Army of Northern Virginia had in store for us.

Interlude

Atlanta 1862

Atlanta suited the ex-redcoat. His fine accent matched his manners and dress. He was invited to all the best parties and, as the eligible men were all away, he had the pick of the ladies. Had he been American he would have been scorned as a coward but his impressive record in the Crimea meant that he had no cause to defend himself. Of course, that record was embellished and added to at every dinner party. He was able to dine out each evening and enjoyed the finest of foods and wines. He also cultivated the older and richer men of Atlanta and was able to profit from their acumen, knowledge and assistance. Soon he was richer than his dead father had ever been and was well on the way to making enough to return home to England and beard his detractors. Of course, as the faithful Neil pointed out, he could never do that as he had deserted and, as such, was merely a pipe dream. The money was not enough for Arthur wanted power and that meant marrying into some rich American family who would give him the springboard to become more powerful than the men in England who had shunned his father. Only then would he really be able to return and rub their faces in his success.

Washington

Jackson's campaign had stabilised the Shenandoah Valley and given Banks and the other generals sent by Lincoln, a bloody nose. The Union was on the defensive and General Robert E Lee took command of the Army of Northern Virginia. Jackson had shown that the valley was the dagger they could hold to the throat of the Union. The war was going the South's way.

In Washington, there was a hurried meeting chaired by Abraham Lincoln. "These Partisans are causing more trouble than enough. What can be done to halt them?"

A staff lieutenant brought out a map with red marks where there had been incidents. "You can see Mr President that there appear to be about four groups and they operate here and here." He pointed to two places on the map.

"But they are behind our lines."

"Yes, sir. But they are mounted and well armed."

The normally placid President slammed his hand on the table. "We will lose this war unless we can curb these bandits. I want a regiment of cavalry arming with the new Henry carbines I have been hearing so much about. I want the best men and the best leaders." He strode over to the map and pointed, angrily, as he spoke. "Put a company here, here and here. They are to scour the land and capture these bandits."

"And when they are captured, Mr President?"

"Then hang them for the thieves and robbers they are!"

Boston January 1863

Kathleen O'Donnell had died of a fever and Sean, her husband became a shell of his former self. Caitlin found herself taking on more of the duties of running the South Boston bar. She learned about buying beer and how to make the maximum profit from it. She introduced food to increase the takings and, over time, was becoming a good businesswoman. In the odd moment she had to herself she would think of Jack and wonder where he was but then there would be a new demand on her time and her little brother would drift a little further from her mind.

CHAPTER 11

Jack

While we awaited the return of Danny and the new recruits we were bivouacked in the house of a Union sympathiser who had fled north when Jackson returned to the northern valley. Stephens City was just south of Winchester and sat astride the Valley Pike. It enabled us to keep in touch with events in the army whilst allowing our wounded men and horses to recover. I knew that both Harry and I had been fortunate to avoid injuries both to us and our horses. I did not ascribe that to luck but to a deep sense of self-preservation. I knew that some men panicked; even the captain had shown that he was not immune from reckless behaviour. Harry and I tended to be cooler and more dispassionate. I did not know the word until David, who was quite well read, explained it to me. It was when he was comparing Harry and me to Danny that he brought it up. Harry and I burst out laughing when he looked over his shoulder wondering what the joke was.

It was not all sleeping and grooming our horses. Harry and I took small patrols up as far as Maryland to get a better picture of the land we would be traversing soon. We rode in pairs. I took Dago and Harry took Jed. The captain still had issues with his wound and David had not wanted him to risk further injury. The Captain did not waste his time either and he spent many hours closeted either with John Mosby or Stuart and it paid dividends when we did go to war again for they could almost read each other's minds and we operated far more efficiently.

Dago and I headed towards Charles Town. There were many Union sympathisers in the town and we would have to be careful but it was an important town as it was close to Harper's Ferry and we knew how crucial that would be if we were to invade the north. Once again we skirted Berryville. The Union had now put troops there to guard their left flank. Knowing the area, as we did, there was no danger to us but we were vigilant nonetheless.

The land between Berryville and Charles Town had few people. We did not see many farms at all and those we did were without a sign of life. The land around the town rose and we halted just below the road leading to the Main Street. I was wearing my hide jacket over my shell jacket and I was wearing my white slouch hat. I hoped that I would be taken for a drifter or a farmer. When Dago took off his hat his curly black hair made him look like one of the many itinerant Italians who still travelled in the area looking for work. The giveaway was our grey trousers with the yellow stripe but we both hoped that no one would notice them.

We found a stand of trees where we could observe the comings and goings on the main road without being seen ourselves. We tied our horses to a nearby tree and climbed up into the branches of an oak which had enough foliage to hide us. We could see plenty of traffic heading along the busy roadway and we saw despatch riders galloping along too.

"We could easily ambush one of those fellows. There'd be no danger and we could find out more than some of the risky raids we have done." Harry, like me, wondered at some of the unplanned attacks we had made. He liked caution.

Just then a voice from behind us made us start and go for our pistols. "Now what is a pair of badly dressed Southern boys doing halfway up to a tree then?"

When we turned to face the voice we saw that it was a ruddy-faced woman of at least forty. We dropped down to the ground. "Sorry, ma'am. We didn't know we were trespassing."

"You weren't boys." She pointed behind her to a small house in the distance. "That's where I live. I was on my way to the market to buy a bushel of flour." She held out her hand. "Annie Fowler's the name. So boys, who are you and what's your regiment?"

I tried to play dumb. "We are just heading west to find work on farms."

"Don't think I am as dumb as I look, son. I know cavalry when I see them," she pointed to the yellow stripe on our trousers, "and you both have fine Colts on your hips and your horses are as fine a piece of horseflesh as I have seen in many a month. Besides," she drew herself up to her full five foot of height, "my boy is in the Twenty Seventh Virginia, as was my late husband who was a sergeant so I am on your side son."

"I am sorry for your loss ma'am. Where did he fall?"

"Kernstown. He and my boy were on Sandy Ridge."

I nodded. "We were too. It was a bloody battle."

Suddenly her face lit up. "Say you aren't the boys who held the line so my son could escape. The

Wildcats!" Alarmingly she raced towards Copper who looked at her in surprise when she approached her. The woman took my carbine from my holster. "It was you. My boy said you kept firing and firing until the Yankees had to stop. Bless you, boys." She threw her arms around me and kissed me and then repeated it with Dago. "You two boys come back with me to my home and I'll put on some coffee."

"I don't know ma'am."

She lowered her voice. "Son, there is a company of Yankee cavalry billeted in the town and they are looking for you Wildcats and Mosby's Ghosts."

Dago and I looked at each other and I could see fear all over his face. I gave a slight nod and he said, "In that case ma'am, we would be delighted."

Annie had a stable at the back and we put our horses in there with a bucket of water and some hay to chew on. The coffee was bubbling away when we entered her two-room house. The kitchen also served as a sitting room and a dining room. "Make yourselves at home boys. 'Taint much but there's no mortgage and I'm beholden to no man."

I smiled, "Ma'am the house I grew up in had one room and it was half the size of this."

"You are Irish aren't you?"

"Yes, ma'am. County Wexford."

"My folks came from Tipperary. They're all dead now. Indians. I came back from the frontier with Abe Fowler. He was a good man. Ah well, I guess I am a widder woman now." She leered at Dago. "You fixin' on getting a wife young man? I could set you up real well in the back place."

Dago blushed and mumbled something unintelligible.

I grinned, "Sorry ma'am. We are all single men until the war is over."

"Pity. A waste of fine young men."

"You were saying about the cavalry..."

"That's right son, keep me straight. They come here a week ago and have been scouring the land twixt here and Berryville for you. The reward for you is up to $1000. There's many a miserable soul would like to get that. You are safe here and welcome but don't trust too many others. There's a bunch of them want to become West Virginia."

"Any infantry or artillery?"

"No just the cavalry and they have repeating carbines too so watch out."

She then told us of her son and asked us to recount the battle. She became tearful when we described the death of her husband but there was pride too that he died well. We had not known that we would meet Annie Fowler but it made helping her son even more important than it had been at the time.

By the time we returned to Stephens City we had a full picture of the company. They were obviously specially selected for the task and seemed to be more efficient than the cavalry we had met before. We had spent a whole day watching them training and they knew their business. These would not charge in with sabres rattling; these men were hunters and we were their prey.

Captain Boswell seemed flattered rather than worried by the news. "Well, I guess our reputation is building. When Danny gets back I reckon we'll take a trip up to Charles Town and see if we can't tweak the bear's tail eh boys?"

He was more confident than I was but he was our leader and we would walk over red hot coals for him. Harry also brought back similar news. It seems between Mosby and the Wildcats the Partisan Raiders were attracting a great deal of attention. He brought captured Yankee newspapers filled with stories about the Ghost and the Wildcats. I did not believe all the stories for we would have needed to be in two places at once to commit all the atrocities we were credited with. They also seemed to suggest that we had spies working in every town which, of course, was not true.

A week after we had visited with Annie, Danny arrived with more men, uniforms, horses and supplies. The captain told us that we had banked our profits and our little company was doing quite well. To a poor boy from County Wexford that sounded good but it paled into insignificance when compared with the war and the risks we were taking. When the war was over then I would think about the money and saving Caitlin; until then all I could concentrate on was staying alive.

"Do you think that this Annie Fowler would help us?" Captain Boswell had learned from John Mosby that safe houses were better than a camp.

"She is a feisty little woman sir and I am sure that she would help us but I would have thought that Charles Town was the last place we would go. There are Union cavalrymen there and they are armed as well as we are."

Captain Boswell leaned back on the hay bale. "Well boys, it seems to me that the one place they won't expect us is in their own back yard eh? It's like where is the best place to hide a valuable book? In a library!

From what you have said they have been there some time and I would assume that they have checked the local area thoroughly. They won't expect us to be so cheeky. Besides, I would like to bloody their nose a little. Think of the effect on their brass if the soldier boys they sent after us were whipped by the men they were hunting?"

I have to confess that it sounded like a reasonable idea when explained like that but I wondered if we were taking one risk too many, again.

We reached Annie's farm just before dawn having ridden through the night to avoid any enemy patrols. Her dog began barking as we rode into the yard and she came out with an antique shotgun. When she saw me and Dago she snapped to the dog, "You get inside, Scout, and stop bothering these boys." She grinned up at me and Dago. "I wondered when you boys would show up again. I didn't expect all your friends though."

"Ma'am, this is Captain James Boswell the leader of Boswell's Wildcats."

The Captain stepped off his horse and lifted Annie's hand to his lips. He kissed the back of it. "Thank you, ma'am, for looking after my boys."

She glanced over at Dago. "I am afraid, Dago that good looking as you are, this is the boy for me."

Rather than being embarrassed as I would have been, the Captain laughed. "They told me you had spirit ma'am and I can see that they are right. Could we use your barn? We will try to avoid attention."

"As I told Jack here, I am a supporter of the South, besides which, I can always say that you forced your way in."

Sergeant Murphy shook his head and said quietly, "I

can't see anyone believing that."

We spent the day resting after our night ride while the Captain explained his ideas. "I want the Yankees to think that we are further north than we are. I intend to raid into Maryland. We are but three miles from the river here and we can cross north of Harper's Ferry. We will hit Sharpsburg and then return here. By the time the Yankee cavalry hear of it and head up the road, we will be back in the safety of the farm. If the cavalrymen are any good they will split their men to patrol the Harper's Ferry road and the road to Kearneysville. Assuming that they have to keep some men in Charles Town then we will have reasonable numbers when we ambush them."

The new men just listened but the veterans like Jed, Dago and Jimmy knew that we could question the Captain to clarify issues. "What if they don't leave men in Charles Town sir? Then we would be outnumbered heavily and I hear those new Henry carbines are real good guns; better than ours."

"Good point Jed but if they don't leave men here then we raid their camp. I am sure they will have remounts and supplies that they need."

I could see the new men nodding at the thought that had gone into it. I leaned over and said to one of them, "The Captain is a real clever man."

We left in the middle of the night and headed towards Harper's Ferry. We did not use the road and after a mile, we veered towards the Potomac and followed it north until we found a shallow place to ford. We spread the new men next to the veterans to help them when they crossed the river. We had done it before and found it easy but it would be hard to cross a river at night time. Once we reached the other side I saw the relief on their faces. Dawn was breaking as we saw Sharpsburg in the distance. It was a prosperous Maryland town and, so far, had avoided any distress as a result of the war. We were about to change all of that. Harry and I were sent with two men each to scout the west and east of the town to see if there were any soldiers there. We returned at nine to report that there was nary a blue coat to be seen.

"Good, then we shall find whatever this town has to offer and steal it." He pointed to the telegraph pole and said, "Cut the wires. We want no word of this to get out."

With the wires cut the town of Sharpsburg was isolated from the rest of the Union. We boldly rode down Main Street. The inhabitants were too shocked to do anything but stare. "Sergeant Murphy, take your men and destroy the telegraph office. Jack, take your boys and find the stockyards. Harry, see if you can do some damage to the lock on the canal." He smiled at us, "I am going to rob a bank!"

I took my four men and rode to the stockyards. They were easy to find from the earthy smell of animal dung. When we reached them we saw that there were forty head of cattle there and we drove them from the yards down the road. I also found ten horses which I quickly roped together and led myself. I knew that the cattle would slow us up and I sent Dago and Jed to drive them towards the river whilst I went to see if the captain needed any help. I reached the bank just as they were emerging with bags of money both paper and coin. When the captain saw the horses he laughed and shouted, "Perfect Jack. I wondered how we would get all this loot home." His men began to pack the sacks on the horses' backs.

Danny and Harry joined us both flushed with their own success. I could see the effects of Danny's handiwork by the column of smoke rising in the distance and Harry just kept chuckling. "It will take them a few weeks to repair those lock gates." He looked for my men. "Did you have any trouble, Jack?"

"No, I sent the lads south with the cattle. They will need a head start."

With the captured horses mounted the captain led us away. As we left he shouted, "Thank you Sharpsburg; Boswell's Wildcats appreciate your donations to the Southern cause."

We caught up with the cattle at the river and, with the extra men had no difficulty in fording it. We only lost one cow during the crossing. When we reached the other side the captain said. "Harry and Jack, you two take your men and drive these cattle to General Lee. Rejoin us at Annie's."

As we headed south Dago shook his head. "How come we always get the shitty jobs?"

I couldn't help laughing as one cow had just deposited the biggest pile right in front of Dago. "I guess we are his go to guys. You know you wouldn't have it any other way."

"True but with the cavalry looking for us this is going to be a tough thirty miles."

I had to agree with Dago. We should really camp with the cattle but that would be too risky. I sent Jed out ahead and we rode down the road once we were clear of Charles Town. I wanted to make Berryville and hope that our forces had secured the town. It was a long and smelly day following the fifty or so lumbering beasts. I was delighted when Jed galloped up to us. "I found some soldier boys. Up ahead. It's Stuart and his cavalry."

"Thank the lord. It is getting dark and I couldn't have driven them much further."

The General himself rode out to greet us with a company of his cavalry. "Well done boys! I'll have these delivered to the Quartermaster myself." As I told him of our raid he wrote out a receipt for the cattle. "Tell the Captain he and Major Mosby are doing fine work. Will you bivouac with us tonight? We would be honoured."

I leaned in to speak quietly, "As would we sir but the captain is trying to trap a hundred Yankee cavalry armed with Henry carbines so he needs all the help he can get."

"He surely does. Well God speed young man." He paused, "Are you the one they call Lucky Jack?"

"I am sir."

"Well stay lucky, we need all the luck we can get."

Even though we were tired we just rubbed down our horses, watered and fed them with grain and then remounted to head back north. We chewed on venison jerky to ease the hunger pangs. We had found that, so long as you chewed something, your stomach thought you had been fed.

We reached Annie's well after dark but Danny was watching for us and Scout did not bark. "You boys will be plumb tuckered out I expect."

"Too right Danny." I handed him the receipt from Stuart. "General Jeb seemed pleased."

"As he should be." He gestured with his head. "Annie left some stew for you boys. It's in the Dutch oven."

Even though we were desperate for our beds we devoured the stew and homemade sourdough bread. We all fell asleep over our dirty plates. We were awoken by the noise of the rest of the boys moving around. David, ever polite, said, "Sorry boys. The captain said not to wake you but..."

"I know. And we did get a couple of hours sleep. Come on boys rise and shine. The Wildcats go to war again!"

Harry threw his metal plate at my head, "You Irish are just too damned cheerful."

By the time we had dressed and thrown water on our faces the rest of the men were assembled and mounted. Danny galloped in, "You were right, Captain, They sent forty men towards Sharpsburg and another forty to Harper's Ferry. There are about fifteen left in their camp."

"Then let us ride to Harper's Ferry."

One of the recruits, Paul, asked me, "How will we know where to attack them, Corporal?"

"The thing is they can go anywhere once they have crossed over the river and they will spend all day looking for us because that is where we hid last year but when they come back, they have to come down this road and we can just wait."

We halted just half a mile from the river. The road crossed a wooded ridge. The Union boys would have to approach a blind summit and then the road jinked left. It was a perfect place for an ambush. The Yanks would think they were safe as they were close both to Harper's Ferry and their own base and they would be relaxed and off guard.

Captain Boswell and Sergeant Murphy took their men to hide behind the trees on the road below the summit. Harry and I had our men on the Charles Town side. It would be our task to open fire when the lead pair reached us. In that way, we could surround them with enfilading fire. The others would attack the men on their side of the summit. Once we had built small barricades with fallen logs to afford us some protection I allowed our men to have a sleep for a couple of hours. Harry and I knew we needed our men as alert as possible. We had surprise on our side but we would be outnumbered two to one and this time the cavalry would not be using sabres.

I had just dozed off, or so it felt when Dago roused me. "Jack, it's the Yankee cavalry. They are coming."

We all cocked our carbines and rested them on the logs. A steady platform for our guns could be the difference between success and failure. Our advantage lay in our first three shots before they could react, draw their weapons and fire back. We were deadly silent and we could hear the jangle of their horse furniture and the buzz of tired conversation. I was on the extreme end of the line on the left and it would be Harry and me who initiated the ambush. I saw the two officers at the front and could hear their conversation.

"I don't care what the Major said, John. These raiders will be near Kearneysville. There were no cattle tracks leading to the Ferry."

"Yes sir but there were no tracks leading to Kearneysville either. How many raiders do you reckon there were?"

"Well the reports said forty but I would estimate they would need at least fifty to have done the damage they did. It is a good thing we have these Henrys or I wouldn't fancy meeting fifty reb raiders."

The Yankee captain was close enough to me for me to touch when I fired. A heartbeat later, and the lieutenant was also flung from his horse. My second shot hit the space where the standard bearer had been before Dago shot him. I saw the puff of smoke from the Yankees as I fired my third shot and then I heard Danny yell, "Cease fire!"

When the smoke cleared, I saw three dead horses and ten dead and dying men. We had little time to waste as the noise would have been heard in Harper's Ferry and Charles Town. "Quick boys, strip the bodies of anything valuable."

I went to the dead Captain and took his Army Colt and saw, to my disgust that he did not have a Henry carbine; and they said I was lucky! He did have an expensive sabre, a fine watch and two twenty dollar gold pieces. It more than made up for the lack of a carbine.

Danny led the rest of the men over the rise and I saw that we had three horses in tow. He grinned at me. We got three more on the other side and there are half a dozen who will be wounded. Get your men moving, Jack. We have a ways to go."

We left the road three hundred yards from the rise. There was a long lick of water about forty yards wide and four hundred yards long. We rode through the water, it only came up to our boots but it would cause them a problem trying to find our where we emerged. We kept going south with the river to our left and a low ridge to our right. We wanted them to think we had returned to Berryville. When we hit the Charles Town road we used it for fifty yards and then headed back to

Annie's. We did not ride in column but in single file. Once we reached the woods leading to her land we all split up and went in every direction through the trees each of us trying to find a route which did not leave tracks. It would take a better tracker than the Yankees possessed to follow us.

When we reached Annie's we were proud of our actions and the result. The Union had sent their best after us and we had beaten them. We still had supplies taken from Sharpsburg and we ate well. Annie's larder was as well stocked as any rich industrialist in the north and we enjoyed a hearty meal. The captain addressed us all after we had eaten.

"I do not want to put this good lady into any more jeopardy. Tomorrow we make our last raid in this area and then we will hightail it back to Winchester. I am anxious to report to the general and discover what he has planned for us."

I, for one, was disappointed. I saw no reason why we couldn't stay in the area. The enemy had yet to do anything to harm us and I saw no reason for that to change. Harry was less convinced. "We all know that you ride your luck Jack but one of these days these Yankees will get the drop on us and then…"

Jed and Dago were sent out early the next day to view the cavalry from the hill overlooking their billets. When they returned it was with good news. "Looks like they just left ten men in camp, the wounded and a couple of others. The rest headed south towards Berryville."

"Right boys saddle up." The captain went to see Annie. "Thank you, dear lady. We will not inconvenience you any more. Remember if things get tough here, just ask for me and I will find somewhere safe for you until this unpleasantness is over."

"You are a kind man Captain and I will miss you and my boys." She kissed him on the check and then did the same to Dago and me. To me, she said, "May you be in heaven half an hour before the devil knows you're dead." And she grabbed me and cuddled me until I thought I would burst. "You do remind me of my boy and I hope that someone looks after him too."

I was sad to be leaving Annie. She had been like another mother to me. She was carved out of kindness and love. Leaving that rock of a woman we rode through the woods and reached the hillside overlooking the billet. There was nought to be gained by caution and we galloped in with pistols cocked. As soon as they saw us the sentries dropped their guns and raised their hands above their heads.

"Sergeant, search the tents for papers. Harry, leave the tents for the wounded but burn the rest." He grinned at me. "Jack, take the boots and the weapons off these lads. Then search the camp for ammunition." The captain turned to his four men. "Gather the spare horses."

One of the wounded raised himself on one arm as I was collecting the boots. "You the boys who cold cocked us yesterday?"

I looked over at him. He was little more than a boy."We were that son, Boswell's Wildcats."

"Where are the rest of your boys? There were twice as many of you yesterday."

I winked at Dago who was shaking his head. "They are off chasing your Major and the rest of you Yankees." The boy shook his head in awe.

By the time we left, there was just the infirmary standing and the rest was an inferno. I was delighted to find that there was a huge quantity of ammunition for my two Army Colts. I had found that they were more powerful than the lighter Navy Colt. We headed south on the pike, riding through Charles Town and the shocked citizens.

As we left we congratulated ourselves on our success. We had beaten the vaunted Yankee cavalry twice and not lost a man. We rode all morning and were approaching the Berryville Pike when the day went from joy to despair. We suddenly found ourselves facing the rest of the cavalry who were hunting us.

CHAPTER 12

Jack

The road had taken a turn and come towards a slight rise so that neither the Union cavalry nor we could see each other. The first we knew was when Copper neighed. That was always a sign of danger and I whipped out my Army Colt in anticipation of danger. The rest of the troop had learned to watch me and every hand reached for a gun so that, when we crested the rise and saw the sixty horsemen we were, at least armed. The captain reacted quicker than the Union officers. "Charge!" If we were riding faster than the enemy then we had a chance of breaking through.

We spurred our horses and all of us took a different target. My Army Colt boomed and bucked but I saw the bugler fall to his death despite the hurried nature of the shot. I cocked and fired a second time, hitting the trooper who was trying to draw his Henry from beneath his leg; his Colt would have been quicker and that error of judgement cost him his life. I almost shook my head in despair. In this kind of action, you wanted your pistols and we had them ready. As soon as it was empty I drew my second Army Colt and kept firing. Suddenly a trooper appeared out of nowhere, almost next to me and I saw, less than two yards away the gaping barrel of an Army Colt. It looked as big as a nine-pound cannon!

I saw the flash and felt it strike me and then I was in the middle of the smoke. I put my hand to my cheek, expecting to come away with blood but, instead, it came away black- a misfire.

I was now charging blindly because of the smoke and confusion, I shouted, "Wildcats! Yeehaw!" The cry was taken up and I knew that I was not alone and then suddenly there was no one left before me. I reined Copper in and looked over my shoulder. I could see horses and men lying in pools of blood and gore on the pike. Some of the bodies had fallen over and onto the wall which lined the roadway. Although they were mainly blue I saw a couple of grey coats among the dead.

"Keep firing!"

I heard the captain's command and I fired for all I was worth. When I had fired all of my Colts I heard the command. "Form up and follow me!"

The captain led us at a trot south on the pike. I dropped to the rear, which was my usual position; partly to watch and listen for pursuit and partly to see who had fallen. My heart sank when I counted the survivors: the captain, Danny, Harry, Dago, Jed, David, Jimmy, Davy and Johnny. With me that made just ten. The rest were now empty saddles trotting dutifully behind their fellows.

I turned to look at the road behind and the dead comrades we had left. I heard the voice from behind me. "Unless you want to join them Jackie boy, let's get the hell out of there." Danny's voice brought me back to reality and, grabbing the reins of the horses I kicked Copper round to follow Harry and the others. We rode in silence to Winchester. Each man tended to his own wounds as we rode. We could not slow down for we didn't know if the Yank cavalry would follow us.

We reined in next to the old courthouse. Normally we would have found somewhere to camp but not after the disaster of the Berryville Pike. We tied our horses up and went into the tavern which was on Main Street. No-one spoke until we were inside and then Danny said, "Beers and a whisky chaser for all of us." He slapped down a handful of coins and we stood, each man lost in his own thoughts. When the drinks came we all took off our hats and at a nod from Danny picked up the whisky. "Here's to the dead! God bless you, boys!" We threw the whisky down and inverted the glasses and then took a swallow from the beer.

The toast released the tension. It was Dago who spoke first. "I think we killed more of them than they did of us Captain Boswell."

Jed wiped his moustache with the back of his hand and said, "Damn straight we did. I was at the back and I counted at least fifteen we hit. They'll remember the Wildcats."

The captain finally spoke, "The trouble is each one we lost is worth ten of the damned Yankees. I just keep getting good boys killed."

Danny put his huge arm around the captain's shoulder. "All of us fight for you Captain Boswell knowing that we might die but we are doing good work. Jesus, we took on three times our number and bested them. We have a regiment tied up watching for us and they think there are over fifty of us. That is some achievement captain and no mistake. If they had more men like us and Mosby the war would be over! And it is just feckin annoying that it took so long for them to realise that!"

We finished our beer in silence and then the captain waved his arm around and more beers were pulled. Then Danny laughed, "And what about Lucky Jack here? Bejesus he's the only man I know to look down the barrel of a Colt before it is fired and survive!"

Everyone laughed and I self consciously wiped my face with a bar towel. "I thought I was dead too! It was a weird experience!"

Danny pointed up to the sky and, crossing himself, said, "Sure and someone is looking out for you and that's no error!"

We reported to General Stuart who was delighted with the results of our raids and the supplies we had acquired. The captain had taken Danny and Harry and me with him. He was even more impressed by the losses we had caused. I could see that he was curious about Captain Boswell's reaction.

"But James you have completed an outstanding patrol. You should be proud of yourself." He was shaking his head in disbelief that Captain Boswell could be so upset by a handful of dead men.

"But General, I have lost almost twenty of my boys since the war started."

General Stuart shook his head, "My dear fellow, twenty dead men against your successes? It is negligible."

The captain's face was infused with a look of pain. "But their faces haunt me at night."

I could see that General Stuart did not understand how this could be so and it was one of the differences between the two men. The captain cared about each of his men while to the General the men he lost were a means to an end. I knew who I would rather follow. The general seemed to dismiss the captain's concerns with a wave of his hand. "We cannot afford for you to go back to Charleston to recruit men. There are many men in the Valley who would love to serve with Boswell's Wildcats. Mosby has had great success recruiting men for his raiders. We will have some posters made and you can select while you are here. Now that you have the captured Henry carbines and the other weapons then you can equip your men just as well here as back in Carolina. You need to promote your sergeant here to lieutenant. We want at least forty raiders this time, not just twenty!" With that, we were dismissed and we began to recruit soldiers to replace the dead.

    Danny became a lieutenant and Harry and I were promoted to sergeant. Dago and Jed became corporals. It felt like we were losing something. The men's opinions of each of us would not change but the bigger we became the less effective we appeared to be. Perhaps that was just me, I don't know but the skirmish at Berryville marked the low point for me in my time with Boswell's Wildcats. Looking back on it now I can see that it was all tied up with leaving Annie and losing the men. It seemed I couldn't hang on to anything I really cared about and that set me thinking about Caitlin. Where was she and was she surviving?

    The posters were put all over the town and we soon had a line of young men wishing to join what they thought was an exciting force. The captain insisted that the four of us, officers and sergeants alike, interview the prospective troopers. We relied heavily on Danny, or as we now ribbed him, Lieutenant Murphy, for he had chosen all of the previous men and he had not chosen poorly yet.

Some were easy to weed out. They had the shifty look of someone who was out for a fast buck; they were the criminals who believed the lies about us being murderers and bank robbers. Some were patently unfit while others couldn't ride. We asked the thirty ones who made it beyond the initial inspection to wait while we went through all of the applicants. Dago, Jed and the other boys spent some time chatting to these thirty and, when we began to ask more probing questions we had their opinion to guide us. Gradually we weaned out the weaker ones and selected the better ones until there was just one young man left. He was shorter than the rest and had the most flamboyant moustache I have ever seen that was not worn by a general. His name was Cecil Mulrooney although he did not pronounce it as we did, rather he made the first syllable sound like 'cease'. When the captain called him Cecil he snapped, "My name is Cecil!" I thought that Danny was going to punch him. The young man went on. "It's a family name and I will lay out any man who mocks me for it!" He balled his fists ready to fight.

I heard an Irish lilt to his voice although it was not as pronounced as my own accent. I could see Danny readying himself to get rid of the boy but there was something about him I liked. I held up my hand. "Mind if I ask a question or two of the young man lieutenant?"

I saw Harry smother a smile and Danny nod as he held his hands together to prevent him using his own mighty fists!

I asked, calmly, "So Cecil," I ensured that I pronounced it properly, "what if one of the boys in Boswell's Wildcats says your name wrong. Not to mock you but because he knows no better? Will you punch his lights out?"

"They'll soon get to know my name!" I wondered why I was trying so hard for him; he was doing himself no favours.

I changed tack. "Do you have family?"

His eyes filled up. "Not any more. Ma and Pa died of the fever when we first come over and my wee brother died a month ago." He looked at me carefully. "Why?"

I smiled and spread my hands, "It seems to me that you are upset and I wondered why you would pick a fight with the toughest man in the Wildcats, Lieutenant Murphy. Now that I know that I can begin to assess you properly. You see, Irish," I saw the Captain nod his approval and Harry smile, "we don't operate like other cavalry. We have to rely on each other and watch our comrade's backs. We can't afford to have someone who will fly off the handle every time someone gets their name wrong." I saw his shoulders sag as he prepared for rejection. "I take it you have tried to enlist before?"

He nodded, "Four times."

"And have you ever donned a uniform?"

"Twice."

"And?"

"And I was sent away in disgrace because I punched out someone who got my name wrong."

I let his own words sink in. "And what does that tell you?"

In answer, he said, "It was my da's name and his da and... well, it's like disrespecting my family."

"I can see that so how about we call you Irish. Do you object to that?"

His hands knotted into fists. "Just so long as they

don't mean anything by it."

I shook my head. "What do you mean by that?"

"Well, sometimes they use Irish as an insult."

"Oh I see; because the Irish are mad buggers and not very reliable, like me and the lieutenant here?"

For the first time, I saw the ghost of a smile on his lips. "I suppose."

"Well let me tell you, Irish, we are mad buggers and that is why the enemy fear us. Now the decision to take you or reject you is not mine but for myself, I would give you a chance." I leaned over and shook his hand. He grinned at me, "Because if you cock up it will be the lieutenant here who will punch your lights out and I think he would quite enjoy that!"

Of course, we took him. As Danny said, later on, I had done so much work that they couldn't reject him. He was one of the best recruits we ever had and he never let us down. He was loyal, fearless and brave but the only one who ever used his Christian name was me. The rest all called him Irish and he seemed to like the name and the ideas associated with it.

Once we had our new twenty-five men we had to equip and arm them. Luckily we had not yet taken the new horses to the Quartermaster and we were able to mount them all with our better spares and the ones we had recently recaptured. We also had enough Navy Colts to give each man one Colt and we gave one man in two a good carbine. The rest had to make do with the single shot Burnside carbine. The uniforms were made for the captain by a woman in Winchester, called Barbara Sandy who appreciated the extra money. Within two weeks we had equipped the men and taught them the basics. We did not need to go in for complicated marching and parades; they just had to learn to fire their weapons and follow orders. We divided the men between the four of us. Dago and Jed were with the captain and the sergeant. I know both of them were unhappy for they had become used to me and both of them felt that Jack's luck rubbed off on them a little. I still had Jimmy and Davy from the old crew and, of course, Cecil. None of the others wanted him but I was happy for him to be with me. This was despite the fact that he had a habit of following me around like a little dog.

August was unbearably hot and our woollen uniforms itched like you wouldn't believe. We were, therefore, grateful when Generals Stuart and Jackson asked us to head towards Harper's Ferry and, as General J.E.B.Stuart said, "Do your normal trick of annoying the Yankees and we'll start to win this war."

We did not bother to use tents this time as we wanted to travel light and any rain, especially at night would be a blessing. We decided to head, first, back to Charles Town. It was only a couple of miles from Harper's Ferry and we knew the area well. One lesson we had learned from the Berryville disaster was to have a couple of men as scouts. This naturally fell to Dago and Jed both of whom took it in turns to scout, each time with one of the new boys. This improved the skills of all of our troopers.

It felt strange to be riding with so many more men. We had almost double the number we had had previously. Man for man we were lighter armed but, as Danny said, we would soon have better equipment, courtesy of the enemy.

We decided to swing by Annie's place and approach

Charles Town from that direction; it was hidden and safer. It was Dago and one of the new boys who were scouting. When we were half a mile from the farm they suddenly returned, their horses whipped to a lather. Dago threw himself to the ground and began beating his hat against the floor.

This was so unlike the normally calm Dago that we were all taken aback. "Dago, what's the matter?"

"I'm sorry Captain." Dago began to cry and just waved his arm towards the farm.

We rode on wondering what horror awaited us. When we reached the farm it was burnt out and there, swinging on a rope were the emaciated remains of Annie Fowler. Around her neck was a board upon which had been burned the following inscription. "*This is a spy and a traitor. This whore helped the Confederates and we hung her. Charles Town Militia.*"

The captain was white with anger. "Danny, cut her down. Jack, get your boys to dig a grave."

Dago joined us when he was composed and he sidled up to me. "Sorry about that, Jack, but she was a kind lady and did not deserve this. Those bastards are going to pay."

I put my hand on his arm. "She wouldn't want us to do anything to sully her name anymore and she wouldn't want us getting hurt. You know that."

"I know Jack, but…"

"We will make sure that the people who did this pay but the innocent should not be harmed."

When we had laid her in the ground and covered her with earth the captain spoke a few words. "Take this fine lady lord, Annie Fowler. She was a good lady with a kind heart and she deserves to be with you. She was a good wife and a good mother. Hopefully, she and her husband will be reunited in heaven which is surely where this good lady will be. We commend her soul to you."

We looked at each other. The new recruits could sense the latent anger we all felt. They had only seen the captain, Dago, Jed and the rest of the old timers smiling and happy. Now they saw angry faces and I could see that they wondered at the change.

We decided to stay on the farm. We knew all the routes in and out and we were close enough to Charles Town to get there quickly. "Jack, take Jed and a couple of your new boys and scout the town. I want to know if the Yank cavalry is still there. If you can see where the militia is then so much the better."

I took Irish and Georgie with me. I looked at the new boys. "This is your first time as a scout so watch Jed and me. Keep your holster open and draw when you see me and Jed draw. If we fire then you fire and you keep on firing until we say stop."

"Yes Sarge," they chorused. It was a harsh world in which to learn but there was no other way.

We headed through the trees and emerged at the hillside above the Yankee camp. The blackened earth showed where their tents had been and the small mounds of earth showed where they had buried their dead but of the cavalry, there was no sign. I led the four of us down through the trees towards the edge of town. There was an old deserted timber mill and we dismounted just behind it. I left Georgie with the horses and we took our carbines. I pointed to Irish and then to Jed. Irish nodded and he placed himself between us. We walked cautiously down an alley leading to the main street. I took off my hat and peered around the corner. I could see at the northern end of the street, a barricade and half dozen men who were on guard; they were militia. I ducked back and we retraced our steps to our horses. We mounted and we rode down to the southern end of the street. Jed checked and he nodded when he returned. The militia had the town bottled up. They were obviously doing the job the cavalry had done.

We managed to return to Annie's without detection. "No Yank cavalry captain but the militia," I saw Dago's face tighten and frown, "have barricades at the end of the street. Of course, the dumb asses don't know you can get in, like we did, in the middle and there they have no barricades."

"We'll attack tonight. I'll take Harry and his men and we'll attack the southern end, Lieutenant you take Jack and attack the northern end. We leave in ten minutes."

I gathered my new men around me. "You will be using your carbines. Choose your target and aim well. Once the firing starts then you will see nothing because of the smoke and you will be firing blind. Keep your holster open and if it gets close work then draw that hog leg and keep firing until you have no more bullets. Remember boys the brave man wins and the coward ends up with a ball in his back. Stand your ground and you will prevail." I gestured to Jimmy and Davy. "Watch these two boys. They are as good as it gets."

I led the column the same route I had taken before and we hid behind the Timber Mill. Captain Boswell nodded and led his half down the back of the Main Street towards the south. It was getting a little darker but it was still as hot as Hades. We left four men with the horses and then Danny and I led the thirteen men towards Main Street. We had to give the others time to get in position but the wait allowed us to see where the militia were and how many there were. Irish proved his worth by pointing to the roof of the building opposite; there was a man with a rifle. I nodded and patted him on the shoulder. I would take him out.

Danny looked at his watch. It had been decided that we would begin the attack. I pointed to the man on the roof and then at myself. Danny nodded his approval and then he led us on to the street. We formed a half line and then Danny said, "Fire!" My carbine bucked as I squeezed the trigger and the sniper screamed as he fell to his death. The militia turned around and began to fire at us but they were outmatched. Soon they all lay dead or wounded.

"Jack, get to the barricade with your men. Jed, check the buildings and see if there are any more militia hiding there. I'll go and see where the captain is."

I could hear the intake of breath from my new men as we stepped over the bodies of the dead and the wounded. The bullets we used were big and made a mess of anything they hit. The street was slick with blood. "Davy, Jimmy, get to each end of the barricade and watch for movements. The rest of you fill in the gaps between."

I went to the militia and began to collect their weapons. They were, as I expected poor in quality and not worth taking. I collected their bullets and powder as we could reuse that. One young man, who was gut shot reached up to try to grab my hand, "For the love of God help me!" His hand was slick with his own blood.

I stood over him and said coldly, after shaking his

hand away, "Like you helped a poor widow woman? You killed a good woman and you deserve to die. You can bleed painfully to death for you are a murderer."

He coughed up some blood, "She was a whore and a spy!"

I spat in his face, "Which shows how little you know. She was a kind woman and she hurt no-one and I have wasted enough spit on you. Rot in hell you Yankee scum!" By the time I had reached the barricade I heard the sigh of death as he died.

We heard the crack of pistols as Jed found militia willing to fight. After a while silence filled the street. I turned as I heard footsteps behind me. I saw Danny and the captain following Dago who his carbine pressed into the back of three militiamen. Jed and his men emerged from a side street with another two.

The captain faced the five men. One of them wore the insignia of a captain; he was an unpleasant looking man who looked as though he would be a typical officious bank official. "Are you the leader of these men?"

He growled, 'Twas the Major until you bandits killed him."

"Who led the raid on Annie Fowler's farm?"

The man leered, "You mean that Southern whore? The Major but we was all there when she was a screaming and a yellin'. We had to give her a good slapping to quieten the bitch down."

Danny grabbed Dago's arm for he could see the pent up fury in his shaking shoulders.

"Sergeant Hogan, get me five ropes." I hurried across to the hardware store. I heard as I kicked in the door, "I sentence you all to death for the murder of Annie Fowler. Punishment will be carried out immediately."

The militia captain yelled, "You can't do that!"

"I guess I just did."

At that one of the men tried to run but Dago blasted his kneecap in two. As the man lay on the ground Dago took the man's bandana and tied a rough tourniquet. "Can't have you bleeding to death before we hang you can we? You yeller piece of shit!"

I threw four of the ropes to my men and then threw one end over the crane beam outside the livery stable. I quickly made a noose and Dago grabbed the wounded man who was screaming and crying. "For the love of God! I just followed orders."

I put the rope around his neck and Dago said, "Well so am I."

He nodded at me and we both hauled on the rope. He did not break his neck but he died none the less; he slowly choked to death his legs twisting and turned as he fought to live and his face contorted and blue as he was slowly strangled. The last to die was the militia captain. "I hope you rebs rot in hell."

"If we do we'll be sure to speak with you."

The captain's face was a mask of anger. "Lieutenant, I want every citizen of Charles Town in Main Street! Now!"

"Sergeants! You heard the order!"

"Quick boys, take the houses to the north!"

Within a few moments, our men were rousting the citizens of Charles Town and they stood fearfully shivering before these avenging rebels who looked so angry. When they were all gathered and surrounded by the carbines and Colts of our men the captain spoke. "You may not have murdered poor Annie Fowler, a fine lady who tried to live her life well, but you supported those men who did. I should slaughter you all for the murder of that fine woman…" I knew that he would not do so but they did not and I saw the terror in their faces. "We will not do as you did and murder innocent people. The Confederacy is coming north and when it does you have a decision to make. Union or Confederacy? Make your choice well, for my Wildcats do not forgive nor forget insults." The captain should have been an actor. He held them there and then fired one round from his Colt into the sky. It sounded like the crack of doom. "You have been warned!"

The people dispersed, terror written all over their faces. The bodies of the hanged men were now still, the last twitches of life now gone.

CHAPTER 13

Jack

I noticed a change in Captain Boswell as we spoke. He became far more serious. I think we all grew up that night. I know we were vindictive and had taken revenge, but we felt that we were justified. The next day we scoured the town for military supplies. There was not a great haul but the muskets, ball and powder would aid the Confederacy and add to our funds.

The next day, Jed was sent back with a report for Stuart, and Harry and I were sent out with our men to scout. The previous day had been a good lesson for the recruits and I noticed a much more serious attitude amongst them later on. Cecil rode his horse next to mine, ignoring the angry looks from Davy and Jimmy. "Sarge, sir,"

I smiled, "Just Sarge will do Cecil."

"Why did we hang those men? They were just doing their duty."

"No Cecil, they weren't. Annie was not given a trial, she was lynched. She had done nothing wrong but they didn't want to know. It is a cruel world and the Wildcats do not forget an injury."

"People say that the Wildcats are bandits."

"Is that why you joined then?"

He became indignant and the pugnacious recruit

appeared once again. "No! Why!"

I became the sergeant, "Quiet! Until you have served with the Wildcats for a decent time then do not criticise them! If you want to ride now and leave us then do it but otherwise, watch and learn."

He was silent and I sensed the outrage from Davy and Jimmy behind me but I remained silent. This was the only way the recruits would learn. In a small wee voice, he said, "Sorry Sarge. I want to be a Wildcat. Give me time and let me learn."

I smiled ruefully, "I am sorry Cecil but this job does not allow for learning, it is a case of the quick and the dead!"

We took shifts patrolling the town during the hours of darkness. The next day I was summoned along with Harry to the town hall which the captain was using as an office. "Harry, head up to Kearneysville. See how far you can get before you are seen. Jack, you have a more difficult task. I want you and your boys to scout Harper's Ferry. General Stuart and General Jackson will need to know how many troops they are facing."

Harper's Ferry was the gateway to the north and I knew that it would be well defended. I took my eight-man patrol along the river to avoid detection. I noticed an island in the river. There appeared to be some cover from some spindly trees and I marked it for future use. I had taken a pencil and some paper with me. Dago, who had accompanied, Jed Hotchkiss on his map making trip, had shown me how to make rough maps which helped when explaining things to senior officers. I led the men up the hill known as Bolivar Heights. We went cautiously for I expected to find Union soldiers entrenched there. To my delight there were none. We dismounted to make us less visible and I ordered the men to lie down and count the Union forces. I sketched a map. There were hills to the north of the river, Elk Ridge and one to the east, Loudon Heights. They all appeared to be devoid of any blue uniforms. Perhaps the Yankees had abandoned Harper's Ferry?

The men came back to me. The recruits were a little wary of committing themselves to a definite answer and I had to be quite curt with them. "All I want is a rough figure. It isn't a test!"

Jimmy and Davy grinned at the squirming recruits who shuffled their feet as they mumbled their responses. By my estimate, there were about twelve to thirteen thousand men in the area but they appeared to be in the town. Whoever was commanding there did not have the first clue about defence.

I led my patrol back and reached Charles Town at the same time as Harry. Harry could not believe what he had seen, "There's no Yankees 'twixt here and Maryland. It's as though they have all left."

"Well there are plenty at the Ferry but they are not prepared for an attack." I showed the rest of them the rough map I had drawn at Bolivar Heights.

The captain was excited and he scribbled a report for General Stuart, "Dago, take this immediately to General Stuart."

"And where will he be... sir?"

The Captain sighed his exasperation. "I am sending you Dago because you are bright enough to find the General. Jed found him south of where we are now so I would assume he is between here and Winchester but just find some cavalry eh? For all I know he could be north. Just do your best." Dago nodded and left.

When Dago returned in the middle of the next morning he was clutching a letter. The captain tore it open eagerly. "It seems we have set things in motion. The whole army is heading north. General Lee is invading Maryland! They are at Frederick already!" Harry and I grinned at each other like schoolboys; Frederick was north of the Potomac. "General Jackson and General McLaws are heading here and we are ordered to find a way across the rivers."

Danny asked, "What about Charles Town?"

The captain shrugged, "We leave it. There are no militia here and nothing of any military importance. We will take the militia horses and arms and deliver them to the quartermaster when we can."

We rode out of the town in the early afternoon. The inhabitants of the cowed town hid behind windows and peeped at us as we trotted from the small burgh. We later heard that they made up all sorts of exaggerated stories about us. They had us raping women and dragging children along the street for fun. It was all lies. We hanged five men and one was wounded but they were soldiers. In our defence, I think it was justified but I could see how it would get us the title of Boswell's Butchers. Whatever the reason the effect was that the enemy would come to regard us as savages and treat us accordingly. As we rode towards Harper's Ferry we were blissfully unaware of our tarnished reputation.

When we were out of sight of the town, the captain split us up. "Lieutenant, take Sergeant Hogan and see if you can make contact with the forces to the north of the Potomac. I will take the rest to the west to find Jackson. This way we can ford the rivers and give the information directly to the generals."

As we trotted east I said to Danny, "There's a small island in the Shenandoah. It should make fording the river easier."

I led us down the trail towards the river. We crossed the railroad tracks leading to Winchester. We had neither seen nor heard a train whilst at Charles Town; the war was too close to risk a valuable train. We found the river easier to ford than we had thought. We only had to swim for a few feet and the horses could cross quite easily. As we rested the horses on the island Danny said, "I am not sure guns would get across there."

"True but the cavalry and infantry could."

We climbed the hills to the east of the Shenandoah. It was a perfect place to defend whilst affording a clear view into Harper's Ferry. "If the general gets here quick we could take Harper's Ferry quicker than you could skin a rabbit." Danny enjoyed watching me skin a rabbit. It was a skill I had acquired when I had lived in Ireland.

"Well, it seems to me that if we have troops over at Frederick then we might be able to find the general there."

We rode east along the Potomac looking for a ford. One of the recruits reckoned that White's Ford was close by. We had our carbines in our hands for we were now in Union country. There was no front line here and we all remembered our encounter near Berryville. We were close to the ford when Copper neighed. We reined in and levelled our weapons. To our relief, we met a few scouts from the Thirty-Fifth Virginia Cavalry. The sergeant saluted Danny. I think Danny was taken aback. We didn't go in much for saluting.

"Who is your general and where is he, sergeant?"

"General Walker is back there with the Colonel."

Neither of us had heard of General Walker but they were Confederates and they would do the job. "Take us to him then. We have some information he might find useful." As we rode with the sergeant he told us what he knew of the campaign. His cavalry were there to escort a brigade sent by Lee to deny Loudoun Heights to the Union forces. We did learn that it was Jackson who was heading from the Valley to take the crossing. It was good to know that we had arrived in time to help the men secure the heights with their guns.

We never actually got to General Walker for, when we rounded the next bend, we met Colonel White and his cavalry. As soon as he saw us he seemed to take an instant dislike to us and our unit. We couldn't work out why.

Danny saluted, "Lieutenant Murphy of Boswell's Wildcats. We were sent to scout the hills around Harper's Ferry sir and the Loudoun Heights are unoccupied."

I think we expected some praise or a thank you but it was as though we had not spoken. "You are the ragamuffins who work for that scoundrel Stuart, aren't you? Well, I don't take advice from bandits and thieves. I know this country and I will advise General Walker on where to place his men and guns. Now get out of my sight before I have you arrested."

To say we were dumbfounded was an understatement but luckily for me, Danny knew when to back off. I think I would have been tempted to say something but that might have resulted in our arrest.

"Thank you, sir. We'll be on our way." Danny wheeled his horse around and led us back the way we had come.

When we were out of earshot I asked, "What the hell was that all about?"

Danny shrugged, "All I can think of is politics. A lot of people don't like the partisans and, from the way he talked about General Stuart, I get the impression that he doesn't like Stuart either. We did our job Jackie boy. The rest is up to them."

We recrossed the river and headed south along the railroad line. "We'll have to find somewhere to sleep soon."

"We are close enough to Annie's..."

We headed back to the farm where we slept in the ruins of the Fowler Farm. The next day we heard the sound of marching boots on the nearby road. We were not sure whose army they were but we mounted and rode to the tree line. To our horror, there were three thousand soldiers marching to Harper's Ferry and they were all Union!

"I reckon we need to find General Jackson. This increases the garrison in the town and if that fool White keeps wandering around the hills they might even occupy the heights."

We kept to the woods bordering the road and, when we reached the end of the column we risked crossing the road. We would not risk the road for fear of running into more enemy troops. Suddenly a shot rang out and I glanced over my shoulder to see two companies of Union cavalry trotting up the road. I drew one of my Colts and fire blindly as I shouted, "Union Cavalry, ride hell for leather boys!"

Every trooper turned and fired whilst kicking their horses hard. There was little chance of hitting anything but the smoke would add to the confusion and we had learned that Yankee cavalry did not like being fired upon. We headed up through the trees and twisted and turned to avoid the branches and roots which threatened to unhorse us. I was not worried that I might be hit by a stray bullet for the odds were in my favour that they would miss but, being the last man did put me in danger.

Copper was a sure-footed horse and I found that I was gaining on some of the recruits. I stopped and turned. I could see the nearest troopers were some hundred yards behind me. I drew my Colt and rested the barrel on my forearm across Copper's neck. I cocked and fired four times. One of the pursuing horses fell and the others slowed to draw their own weapons. I holstered my Colt and followed my men. I had bought us some time. By the time we had reached the crest, the pursuit had stopped. They obviously thought we were not worth the effort. The nervous recruits were grinning at their brush with death but they had reacted well to the danger.

We descended to the road on the other side of the hill and headed for Martinsburg. There had been Union troops there but we hoped that by now it was Jackson who held it. When we saw the grey column snaking along the road we knew that the Union had left the vicinity.

Not only did we meet General Jackson but we were reunited with the captain. He could not believe that Colonel White had behaved as he had. "I will never understand why some men put themselves before the cause. You stay with the men Jack and Danny and I will report to the General."

The grey column progressed towards the distant Harper's Ferry and we attracted many curious looks. We were obviously cavalry but we looked different from all the other units in the army. Soldiers being soldiers I knew there would be much speculation about us. The Partisan Rangers were something of a legend and few regular soldiers could claim to have seen one. I suppose for the foot cavalry of Jackson's army we helped to pass an hour as they tramped up the road.

When our officers returned we found that we had another task. The captain explained as we left the army to head north, into Maryland. "The general wants information about the land to the north of the Potomac. We know Sharpsburg and he wants us to find out how many Yanks are there."

Danny always liked his food and it was he who pointed out one of our problems, "We are running short on supplies sir."

Captain Boswell grinned, "Food you mean?"

"Well, food and ammunition sir."

"Then we had better find some closer to Sharpsburg." At least we were no longer encumbered with the animals and weapons we had taken from Charles Town. They had been handed over to the Quartermaster and our funds had risen again.

We crossed the river south of Williamsport. Those who were veterans knew the country well but I could sense the apprehension of the newer troopers who just knew that we were now in the land of the Union and far from friends.

We found a track leading into the hills and we followed it. There was a farmhouse which looked deserted. Farms normally had a fire going and this one did not. Harry sent two of his men to scout the house and they waved to show it was empty. We hid the horses in the barn and then searched the farm for food. It had been deserted for some time and whatever supplies they had had were long gone.

"Jack, take Jed and Dago. Head down the Shepherdstown Pike. Get some food for us."

I took it as a compliment that the lieutenant thought that we would manage to have some success but it put pressure on me again to deliver. It was dark as we clip-clopped along the road. The walls to the side of the pike always made me apprehensive. I liked the freedom of the hills in case I had to make a sudden escape. Ahead I saw a cluster of lights. There was a hamlet of some description. We slowed down to approach as quietly and unobtrusively as possible. I sent Dago around the hamlet to approach from the other side and Jed to cover the back. After giving them a few minutes to get into the position I boldly rode up to the front.

As I reined in Copper I heard, "Get off your horse you damned Reb or I will shoot you where you stand."

Then I heard Jed's voice, "Not if I shoot you first you peckerwood!"

And I heard the report of a Colt being fired. I just drew my two Army Colts and kicked Copper. As we turned the corner I caught sight of a couple of blue uniforms and I fired; I saw the flash of three other guns and I sprang from Copper's back. A Yankee sergeant's face suddenly appeared and I fired both guns blowing his head from his body as though it had been a watermelon and then there was just the groans and moans of men dying.

"Dago!"

"I'm alright, boss. I just got clipped!"
"Jed?"
"Never even got close!"

As the smoke cleared I saw the six dead Maryland Cavalrymen lying in ungainly heaps. Dago was clutching his left forearm. I rushed to him. "Sorry about that sarge, I had just cleared the woods and they had the drop on me. Luckily Jed arrived and..."

I shook my head. "If you hadn't spooked them then we would have all been dead or prisoners. Jed, check the back of the main buildings and I will cover the front." I glanced at Dago who was busy trying a bandage around his arm. He waved me away with his good arm. I kicked in the front door and saw a woman and her children standing behind a man with a shotgun. As the back door splintered under Jed's boot I lowered my gun. "Sir, there have been enough killings and I would sure hate to kill you in front of your children. Lower your gun, you have my word you will not be harmed."

His wife's terrified face nodded and the shotgun's barrel was lowered. Jed's gun clicked ominously as he holstered his weapon. "How many more were there?" They just stared at me. "There were six out there. Were there any more?" The woman shook her head." "Good, now you folks sit down whilst we clear up a little for you." I gestured to Jed. "Clean up outside and then check the kitchen." I nodded meaningfully so that Jed would know to check for supplies. I could see, now that my eyes had adjusted to the dim light that it was a tavern. I smiled, "I sure could use a beer." No-one moved and so I put some coins on the bar. "And one for each of my two friends would not go amiss."

Again the woman reacted first and she nodded

without taking her arms from around her children. The man went behind the bar and began to pull three glasses of ale. I holstered my gun without covering the flap. I was taking no chances. I had sunk the first sweet beer by the time Dago and Jed returned. Dago's left arm was in a sling. They looked at my empty glass. "Yours are on the bar and," I threw down some more coins. "We'll have three more."

The woman had become more confident and she moved the children to sit on the wooden settle by the fire. "Who are you bushwhackers?"

"We are Boswell's Wildcats ma'am."

I saw her eyes widen and the man made the sign of the cross. He murmured, "Sorry if I upset you, boys."

"No, sir. You were just defending your property. We understand that." I finished my second beer. "Now we will be leaving and you will understand if I ask you to wait at least ten minutes before you venture out. I would sure hate to end this pleasant evening on an unpleasant note." The two adults nodded for all they were worth. "Now the bodies are covered," I saw the imperceptible nod from Jed, "but I think you had better keep the children in and save them the unpleasantness." I tipped my hat. "Then thank you for the beer. I sure appreciated it."

When I stepped outside I saw that the six horses were loaded with assorted packages and sacks. Jed grinned, "They are going to be real unhappy when they see that we have taken all of their food."

As were riding back Jed reached into his shell jacket and pulled some documents out. "I guess those Maryland boys were acting as couriers. Here's a letter to McDowell."

"The captain will be real interested in that." I resisted the urge to open the letter.

CHAPTER 14

Jack

When we returned to the farmhouse, they were pleased to see us and the extra cavalry mounts and guns. While Harry organised the food and David dressed Dago's wound the captain read the letter. His face darkened. "Damn! It seems the Yankees have got wind of Lee's plans and they are setting to ambush him." He looked at Danny. "Get a rider to take these to General Lee. He should be up around Boonsboro way."

Danny sought out Barton who had proved himself to be a sound rider and a steady man, not prone to panicking. He leapt on his horse and, with a piece of bread in his hand, galloped away toward the north-west.

The next day we headed north, deeper into Union-held land. To the south, we heard the rumble of cannon fire and the crack of muskets. "Sounds like General Jackson is beginning his attack."

I wondered if Colonel White had finally reached the top of Loudoun Heights. It would be a disgrace if Jackson lost men due to one man's pig-headed attitude. We had more urgent matters to deal with for Matty and Jimmy, who had been riding ahead as scouts came galloping in. "Captain. There's a bunch of Yankees up the road! It looks like a regiment of infantry and a company of cavalry."

In the distance, we heard the battle at the Ferry. "These will be reinforcements." The captain looked around and pointed to a spot where the turnpike turned. "Follow me." He galloped and led us to the wall. There was a stand of trees about forty yards from the wall. "Danny, get four men to take the horses there. The rest of you get behind the wall. We are going to ambush them. We need to at least delay them and give General Jackson time to attack."

I glanced at Harry as we took our places. I could see what he intended but it was risky. If it had been just infantry then we could have escaped easily but cavalry meant that they could move as quickly as us and they wouldn't have to run forty yards to get to their horses either.

"Cecil, you stay close to me."

Dago joked, "It's the safest place to be Irish. That is Lucky Jack!"

We spread out along the wall with our carbines at the ready. We would be firing at point blank range and, hopefully, would achieve complete surprise. "Take off your hats boys and get as low to the ground as you can."

It was nerve-wracking to hide, waiting; we could hear the jangle of the horses and the singing of the marching soldiers as they approached our place of concealment. Their singing was a good sign indicating that they were not suspicious. Danny was at the extreme left and it would be his job to fire first. We had no idea if the cavalry were just at the front or the front and rear. I hoped that when we fired at least some of the horses would bolt. I checked, yet again that my carbine was cocked and my Colt ready to be pulled. I saw Irish chewing his bottom lip nervously and I gave him a smile and a wink. He attempted a smile back. By now the recruits would be wondering how come the soldiers didn't see us and the simple fact was most marching soldiers look ahead or at the ground. The turnpikes all had walls and they all looked pretty much the same.

I heard one of the sergeants say. "Callaghan, can you not march in step? You are making me feel sick the way you wobble out of rhythm."

I heard his comrades laugh and then I heard Danny shout, "Now!"

We all stood and began firing. The cavalry were further up the road and we poured shot after shot into the hapless infantry. They were taken completely by surprise. When my carbine was empty, I pulled my Colt and fired a couple of rounds.

The sergeant I had heard before was ordering his men into line and I heard the captain yell, "Back! To the trees!"

"Right lads, run like the devil himself is after you." As my boys ran I fired one last round at the sergeant who was busy organising his men. He spun around as though pulled by an invisible rope. Then I ran. I heard the ragged crack of an attempt at a volley. The balls buzzed around me like angry hornets. I saw one of Harry's boys fall and Harry and Matty picked him up. Then Cecil tried to turn and fire. It was brave but it was stupid and a ball struck him. He too fell. I picked him up; luckily he was not a big man and I was able to throw him over my shoulder. I ran but I ran slower than before. By the time I reached the horses the rest were mounted. I threw Cecil's body over his horse and flung myself into the saddle.

Dago pointed and yelled, "The cavalry." I could see

beyond his pointed hand the company of cavalry who had been at the rear and they were charging across the fields towards us. I fired my last three bullets in their direction and then joined the rest of the Wildcats as we galloped away. I saw, to the right, that some of the cavalry hit by Danny and his men, had also joined the chase but they were further away. Dago had Irish's horse and was struggling to control it. I saw Cecil raise his head. He looked around and realised what had happened. He managed to slip his leg over the saddle and grab his reins. I could see the blood dripping from his arm. He was tough all right. The captain and Danny were at the back and they were both firing behind them. I slowed down to join them.

"Captain! How about a charge? It'll slow them down and give the lads a chance to escape."

He grinned, "It's just mad enough to work." He took out a second Colt. I had two as yet to be fired and at a nod, the three of us wheeled around and, with a rebel yell, charged the hundred men of the Maryland Cavalry. We emptied our guns and then wheeled again before we reached them. They had stopped to fire at us and by the time they were ready, we were gone, hidden by our own smoke. As we raced after our own men I saw that the charge had slowed down those men but the remnants of the fight at the wall were closer and there were six of them trying to cut us off. I had no loaded weapons and I drew my expensive sabre. It was some time since I had used it but it felt lighter and more graceful than the cutlass I had last used on board the Rose.

They were coming at us from our right which suited us for it meant we could use our swords before they could. War is not a sport and the only aim is to win. I veered towards the first trooper who eagerly raised his sword. I slashed upwards with my blade and ripped through his horse's neck. As the beast collapsed in a fountain of blood he was thrown from his horse and the rider next to him had to veer away to avoid the dying beast. I straightened up and increased my lead.

Harry had led the rest of our men a safe distance away and it was time to end the pursuit of these horsemen. I edged Copper to my right and the corporal who came at me tried to strike me with his blade; the problem was his horse's head and it made his movement awkward. I chopped down with my sabre and severed his left hand. He screamed in agony and fell writhing to the ground. Behind me, I could hear the captain and Danny fighting their opponents. There was still one trooper trying to get close to me. He tried to stab with the tip of his sword but I smacked his blade with mine and then swung the edge of my own sword across his body. I didn't mind where I hit him, any blow would make him falter and so it was. The sword ripped across the top of his arm and I saw the blood begin to flow. When I swung the sword backhand he decided he had had enough and he wheeled his horse around, returning to the rest of the cavalry who had, themselves, halted.

I saw Harry and the others waiting for us, their carbines reloaded and ready but it was unnecessary, the pursuit was over. Copper was flecked with sweat and her breath was laboured. I reined in and slowed to a walk. I turned to look at my two officers. The captain had lost his hat and they had both received cuts to their faces and hands. None looked serious but they showed how close we had come to disaster.

Dago burst out laughing, "There you are Irish. I told

you Lucky Jack could fall in a shit hole and he would come up smelling of roses. The captain and the lieutenant have more cuts than someone who visited a blind barber and Jack here looks like he has just come from a parade!"

We walked our horses to a ridge from where we could observe the Union brigade. They had halted close by the road and we could see that they were tending to their wounded. David too was kept busy dealing with our injuries. Three men had died and apart from Cecil, there were three others who had wounds. It had been a costly encounter but those reinforcements would not be heading for Harper's Ferry any time soon. It had been a price worth paying.

The captain looked at our small band and shook his head. "I guess we'll head back to Harper's Ferry. We need to lick our wounds and regroup." He looked north towards Sharpsburg. "We know there are Union soldiers here and that was what we were sent to discover."

We limped along the pike, heading, all the time, towards the sound of firing. Having scouted Elk Ridge and Loudon Heights we hoped that we would find our own forces in position. As we rode along the road we saw grey uniforms on the crest of Elk Ridge and the captain led us in that direction. To our surprise, there was just one regiment there. The colonel was pleased to see us as he had no scouts of his own.

"General Jackson sent the rest of the division over to South Mountain; it seems Robert E Lee is under attack there." We exchanged looks. Perhaps Jed had not reached the general in time. "You boys are welcome to bivouac with us. I could use some scouts." He pointed to the town below. "They have, as near as makes no difference, almost fourteen thousand men there. If they decided to attack us tomorrow, well it will not be pretty."

Have you any idea where Stuart is?"

"Last I heard he was with Jackson." He pointed to the heights on the other side of the town. "Yonder."

"Any way across the river?"

"There's a pontoon bridge a half mile along the Potomac."

Captain Boswell turned to us, "Danny, I'll go and report to General Jackson. You are in charge here until I return."

As he galloped off I went to check on Cecil and the other wounded. The ball had struck him in the shoulder blades. It must have been spent as it had not penetrated. It had bled a little but I suspect the fall from to the ground and the rock he had hit had done more damage. He tried to raise himself on one arm. I waved him back down.

"They say you picked me up and saved my life." His face showed the pain of the effort

"More likely just saved you from a Yankee prison. How are you feeling Cecil?"

"Sore and stupid."

"The sore I can see but the stupid?"

"I got hit didn't I sarge?"

"Lots of fellows get hit but you survived and, hopefully, you will; learn to weave and duck a little more next time. Get some rest. We may need to ride again soon and I would hate to have to leave you here."

His faced filled with fear, "No sir. You ain't leaving me here. I'll crawl after you if I have to."

I smiled at him. "Just get healed first eh?"

When I rejoined Harry and Danny I heard the thunder of hooves and Jed wheeled in to a stop. He leapt from his horse. "Message from the Captain. He wants Jack and Dago at the General's headquarters." He pointed just beyond the guns which were still firing spasmodically. "He wants you now!"

I looked at Danny who just shrugged, "Better do what he wants. Dago, get your ass over here and get your gear."

Jed pointed us in the direction of the pontoon bridge and we rode down the trail to the river. I noticed that Dago no longer had his sling on. "How's the arm?"

"Just stiff. If I use it too much it aches but I can still hold the reins. Any idea why he wants the two of us?"

"Not a clue." I ran through all the reasons why we might have been summoned but could think of none. The pontoon bridge moved alarmingly as we rode across and I think I would have preferred to swim but we reached the other bank and we were dry at least. We kept the town to our left and rode beyond the sporadic firing. I saw the flags and standards indicating the staff tents and asked a Virginian Cavalry trooper, "Which one is General Stuart's tent?"

"The one yonder with the light inside."

We tied our horses next to the captain's. How do you knock on a tent? I coughed and said, "Sergeant Hogan reporting as ordered sir."

Stuart's voice sounded, "Come in both of you."

They were both seated and hatless, the general gestured to two seats. "Please take a seat and you may remove your hats." Both he and the captain looked serious and I began to wonder if I had committed some offence or other.

Stuart nodded at the captain who began, "We are going to ask you to do something for us but before it is explained you should know that you are not being ordered. If you do not wish to undertake this mission we will understand and it will not be held against you. Do you understand? What you do is voluntary."

I looked at Dago who shrugged and I replied, "Of course sir."

"And me." Dago just grinned.

The general half closed his eyes and leaned back, "I have a nephew. One of my nephews, Archie Stuart, a lieutenant in the Second Virginia was captured this morning." There was a pause and Stuart opened his eyes. "I want you two to rescue him."

The captain smiled and nodded. I had many questions and they spurted out in no particular order. "Where is he? How will we know him? Why us two?"

Stuart laughed, "The why you two is easy. You are Lucky Jack Hogan and the two of you have proved more than resourceful many times before. Your captain said you two were the men for the job as soon as I mentioned it. As for where he is well the Yankees have a holding prison for officers at Gettysburg. He will be kept there for a while and either exchanged or sent to a prison camp at some future date. So you can see that we need this expediting sooner rather than later. Every minute increases the chances of his being taken out of reach. They will know he is my nephew and this would be a coup for the Union brass."

I asked the obvious question, "Why not exchange him then?"

"He is only a lieutenant and it would not look good to have a general use his influence for family."

This didn't explain why we were thought to be expendable but I let that one slip by. "Why Dago, why not Jed? Dago was recently wounded."

The Captain spoke. "That is precisely why. You two will be travelling on Union horses in Union uniforms. The story will be that you are escorting your wounded friend back north."

I was not sure that the story would wash."We could be shot as deserters by the Union, that is if our boys don't kill us first."

"This is why you are being given the choice. You would, of course, travel in your own uniforms until you were clear of our lines. As for how you would know him." Stuart smiled, "Like his uncle, he affects a red neckerchief and his hair is long and over his shoulders. He does bear a striking resemblance to me."

I looked over to Dago who nodded. "We will try then sir but suppose he has given his parole and refuses, as a point of honour to return with us?"

Stuart's face became grim, "Then you will bring him back forcibly. You have my permission, in writing if you like. For the purposes of the rescue, you outrank him."

"And any other officers?"

"If you can then bring them back too but the priority is Archie."

"We had better start now then sir and travel through the lines while it is dark."

"We have three Union horses outside; I believe they were the ones you captured recently."

The captain handed us two uniforms, mine was the uniform of an officer and Dago's that of a sergeant. "These are from the Twenty Fourth Maryland. They are based in Harper's Ferry. Here is an order from the colonel of the regiment authorising the two of you to travel to Dover." I looked at him quizzically, "Dago's new home town. It is north of Gettysburg and gives you a reason to stay overnight in Gettysburg."

I was all out of questions save the big one which lurked like a storm cloud in the back of my mind. How the hell would we manage to pull this off? We packed our new uniforms in the saddlebags of the horses and I put my own Colts in the saddle holsters. I also replaced the carbine. I wanted familiar weapons with me. I clipped the sabre to my belt; I was an officer now and would need to look the part.

As we left the Captain said, quietly, "God speed boys. I know you can do this if anyone can."

CHAPTER 15

Jack

We did not even notice the swaying pontoon bridge as we crossed over the Potomac for a second time. Both of us were too busy working out how we would pull this bizarre mission off. We headed for the road to Frederick. I decided that we had to take it one step at a time. First, we had to get through Frederick that would be our first hurdle. It was a large and busy town. I had a map given to me by the captain. It was a copy of a Union map we had captured and if found would not arouse suspicion. I could see that once we were beyond Frederick then we might avoid detection but there were sure to be troops in such an important and strategic town. When we were a few miles from our own lines I reined in my horse.

"Time to become Yankee cavalry, Dago."

We quickly changed and stuffed our old uniforms into the saddlebags. If we were searched then that would be a giveaway but I wanted to have the option of changing uniform if it became necessary. We both had a sabre as this seemed to be the weapon of choice.

"I think we will try to hit Frederick at about nine in the morning. It will be busy and two more blue uniforms won't be considered strange."

"But two blue uniforms heading north might be."

"Then you had better put your sling on." The wound on his arm was still angry looking and any cursory inspection would confirm that he had, indeed, been wounded. The sling would merely draw attention to the wound.

We rode slowly along the road and I was acutely aware that it would look strange to be travelling at night but we had no option. It was just less than twenty miles to Frederick and we made the outskirts before dawn. We tied our horses to a tree and lay down to await the dawn. I fell asleep almost immediately. I have no idea how long I was asleep but something woke me and I sprang to my feet my hand on my Colt. The first silver glimmer of light was in the east and I peered around looking for the source of the disturbance. Suddenly the deer which had wandered close to us heard me and sprang away. As it did so Dago awoke.

He rubbed his eyes, "I guess that was dumb sir, falling asleep."

"Then we are both dumb Dago for I fell asleep too. We had better get a fire going and we'll make some coffee. If anyone comes by it will look natural and I need something to keep me awake."

By the time we had made and drunk the coffee, it was daylight and we saddled up and headed up the road to Frederick. We were now in Pennsylvania and far from any aid and support. "We better look relaxed Dago. We are supposed to be in our heartland. If we meet anyone then let's tell a joke or a story. We have to appear casual."

There were many side roads which joined the main pike and we found ourselves overtaking wagons, carts and mules heading into the town as well as meeting others leaving. Our blue uniforms attracted many supportive comments.

"Show those Rebs your steel lieutenant!"
"Hurrah for the Union!"
"God bless you, boys."

It struck me that if this was the greeting we would receive all the way north then our task would be simple. At the edge of town, where the buildings became closer together, there were two soldiers lounging at a rough barrier. The barrier was up. I nodded to Dago who began to talk, "So Irish, being the dumb Mick he is tried to put a second ball in the barrel. Well, I said to him," I gave a casual salute as we passed the two privates but appeared to be too interested in Dago's story, "that is the quickest way to blow your hand off." I laughed and then we were beyond the two sentries.

I breathed a sigh of relief and said, "Well done Dago. Now comes the difficult part."

We had to appear to be keeping up with the traffic in the town. To go faster, which we both wanted to do, would have been to invite attention. Soldiers saluted as we rode through and we returned them. This was hard for two soldiers who rarely saluted anyone. Suddenly a captain of the judge advocate's department stepped out in front of us. He smiled and said, "Where are you boys going?"

I saluted. "Going back for a little leave, captain. My sergeant here got wounded down at Harper's Ferry."

"I heard that you boys were down there. How about I treat you to breakfast at Dave's over there? He cooks mighty fine ham and eggs."

I knew that to refuse would be seen as suspicious and I grinned, "That is a fine offer, captain."

As we tied up our horses he asked, "Why the third horse?"

I grinned conspiratorially, "It's my spare and if I had left it with the regiment then who knows who might have taken it. I like my horses; they have got me out of trouble more times than I care to think about."

Once inside Dago said, "Sir, there are some sergeants over there..."

"Go ahead sergeant," I took out some Yankee dollars. "Here have a treat on me!"

"Thank you, sir."

The captain ordered breakfast and when it came, it was enough to feed my whole section. "Dig in lieutenant. This is the best food in Frederick, it's famous."

I nodded my mouth full. He was right and I didn't realise just how hungry I was. When we had finished he lit up a cigar. "Care for one?"

"No thank you, sir, I never acquired the habit."

He leaned back in his chair, "So how is the war going?"

"General Miles is still holding out at the Ferry and General McClellan is whipping Lee at South Mountain." I was glad that I could give information which, if checked, would

He slapped the table, "Damn good. I don't like to see the damn Rebs this close to Pennsylvania. I prefer to fight in their precious valley."

"Did you fight there sir?"

He coughed and looked embarrassed, "No lieutenant. I keep asking for a transfer but they insist on keeping me here. I have to interrogate Confederate prisoners when they come through." He leaned forwards, "Believe me it wins battles."

"Really sir?" I gave him my most innocent of smiles.

"Oh yes indeed. We pick up little bits here and there and it all paints a bigger picture. You see I knew about Lee at South Mountain. Yesterday I questioned Jeb Stuart's nephew and he kept blabbing about how his uncle would be going to Lee's aid and when he did then we would be beaten." He shook his head, "Little firebrand, full of piss and vinegar." He took out some bills and threw them on the table.

"No sir," I began to take out my own bills.

"I insist lieutenant. It's the least I can do for two heroes."

I nodded to Dago who smiled at his companions and left. We mounted and waved our goodbyes. "Well the food was good Sarge but it tasted like sawdust I was so nervous."

"Remember Dago, I am supposed to be a lieutenant and I know what you mean." I jerked my thumb at the back of the departing officer. "He confirmed that Archie Stuart was here yesterday so he should still be at Gettysburg."

"The sergeants told me that the captain you were speaking to isn't worth spit. He has a cosy little job here and he loves ordering them around. He is about as popular as a rocking chair in a room full of cats."

I laughed and we both began to relax as we headed north out of Frederick. Once we had left the outskirts we kicked on. We had about thirty miles to go and we needed to make up lost time. At least we would not need food again until we reached the small Pennsylvania town.

It was late afternoon when we saw the town ahead. There appeared to be ten roads entering and leaving the town. This was now the tricky part for we had to find where they held the officers and avoid detection. There appeared to be a number of blue uniforms visible and we halted at the inn which bore the name, Gettys, it appeared to be both popular and busy. We tied our horses outside and entered. The noise in the dining room stopped momentarily when we walked in. I could see that the officers and sergeants were seated separately. Dago and I would stand out if we sat together but there was no way around it. The buzz of conversation soon began again and a rosy-faced women strode up to us. "Table for two or two tables?" She looked at Dago's stripes.

"As this brave sergeant recently saved my life I think we will share a tablê as we shared danger on the battlefield."

She nodded her approval. I had said it loudly enough for the other soldiers to hear. I suspected that this far from the front these were not combat soldiers but those who supplied services for the men who fought. I noticed that their gaze was now averted as they accepted my decision to eat with a sergeant.

We ordered food and then watched the soldiers who entered and left. I noticed that two of the officers had the white shoulder board fields which identified them as being part of the judge advocate department. I suspected they would be the ones who would be involved with prisoners. When they left we paid and left after them. The knot of officers stood on the boardwalk talking and Dago and I fiddled with our horses and saddles. We slowly mounted and I heard the major say, "I'll just walk by and make sure that those lazy bastards aren't lollygagging!"

He walked away to the northern end of the street while his fellow officers headed south. A lieutenant shouted, "We'll be at the billet, sir. We'll set up the card table."

That told me that once the major had visited the prison then they would be ensconced in their billet playing cards. It now depended upon how many men there were at the prison. We rode down the street slowly and overtook our officer. We exchanged salutes and he then carried on walking. I saw the prison. It was the only building which had a Union flag flying. There were four guards outside, wire along the top of the walls and there was a central watchtower peeping up from inside. I could have climbed the wall, if needed, from the back of my horse but I suspected that once inside there were locks and bolts. Just beyond the prison was a livery stable and we headed there.

An old negro came to the door. "Yassuh?"

"How much for the night?"

"With feed and water that'll be two bits each."

I threw him double what he had asked. "The rest is for looking after them real well."

"Yassuh!" He beamed a toothy grin at us.

We took our two Colts from our saddle holsters and, once we had emerged we tucked them into the waistband of our trousers. We strolled back beyond the guardhouse where the major was berating the men. "How many times have I told you that I want two men patrolling the perimeter and two on the gate? You are not here to gossip like a bunch of washerwomen. If I come back and find this state of affairs again you will be on a charge!"

As we passed them I said, "Evening."

The major gave a half smile and said, "Nice night for a stroll."

"It is."

We walked along a little further and heard the officer say. "I know we only have two officers in there at present but that makes no difference. Vigilance at all times!"

He then turned to follow us. I nudged Dago and winked, "Damn it, sergeant. I have left my sabre on my horse."

"Sorry, sir. I'll go back and get it. Sorry, sir!"

The officer gave me a sympathetic look and said, "These non-coms have it too easy, you know?"

"Don't they just." I strolled slowly back towards Dago who had disappeared into the livery stable. There were just two guards on the gate; both were looking unhappy about the tongue lashing they had received.

I nodded at them in an absent-minded way. "Evening sir." Having spoken to their officer I was considered safe.

"Evening boys." I saw Dago emerge with my sword. "Come on Sergeant there is a card game waiting for me."

He ran towards me and I saw the smirk exchanged by the two guards. They enjoyed seeing a sergeant belittled. As Dago reached me I pulled my Colt just as Dago drew his and we pressed them into the stomachs of the surprised guards. "Now then boys. How long for your two friends to walk the perimeter?"

They hesitated and Dago punched one hard with his pistol. "The officer asked a question boy."

The other said, "Ten minutes give or take one or to."

I nodded to Dago who cold-cocked the man he had

punched. He took the piece of rope he had in his pockets and tied the man's hands and feet and pushed him into the guard room. Finally, he gagged him with his own bandana. That done he opened the door into the exercise yard and shook his head.

I put my gun to the head of the sentry. "Is there anyone in the tower?"

"Not tonight. We only have the two prisoners."

"Who is with the prisoners?"

"The sergeant." He looked fearfully at the huge Army Colt. "Don't kill me, sir. I am just married and would like to see my pretty little wife again."

"Then do exactly as I say. Stand outside the guard house and when the first guard comes around tell him the other guy has gone for coffee; don't do anything to spook him. I have an Army Colt here and I will use it." He wasn't to know that I had never killed a man in cold blood before now and it was unlikely that I would start soon.

I heard the first of the sentries as he crunched on the gravel which ran around the outside wall. "Bill, where's Joe?"

"Went for coffee."

"He had better be quick then otherwise Major Pain-in-the-ass will chew him out." As he reached me I jerked him forwards and Dago cold-cocked him too.

"Well done and now the last one."

Dago had trussed the second captive up and was ready with his gun for the third. This one appeared to be less curious than the other and just wandered up to Bill. Before he could say anything I jerked him onto Dago's gun. While Dago tied him Bill began to plead, "Don't cold cock me, sir. Please." Dago shook his head

256

and tied Bill's bandana around his mouth. He tied him up while I got rid of the guns. We now had to work quickly or someone would notice the lack of sentries.

Knowing that there was no one in the tower we ran to the main building where we could see the light from an oil lamp. I decided that a bold strategy might work. The sergeant would assume that anyone entering had been sanctioned by the men at the gate and I rapped smartly on the door. "Lieutenant Hogan with another prisoner. Open up, sergeant."

I heard a chair scrape. Dago stood off to one side. "Where's the Major? He ought to sign him in."

"He left for a card game with the lieutenant. Come on man I want to get to my bed. I have been riding all day from South Mountain."

"Typical officer," I heard him mumble. The key turned in the lock and a grizzled unshaven face peered out at me. He looked at me and said, "Where is he then?"

I pointed at Dago, "Here!" The sergeant looked at Dago for a second and then Dago's Colt cracked against his skull. He fell like a sack of potatoes. We dragged his body inside and grabbed his keys. Behind the desk, I saw two Henry carbines and I grabbed them both.

"Lieutenant Stuart!"

I heard a voice from the back say, "Here. Who is it?"

We unlocked the first door and saw two cells. One of them had a young lieutenant and the other had a captain. Both looked as surprised as any. I think the uniforms confused them for the captain said, "Who the hell are you?"

"Sergeant Hogan of Boswell's Wildcats; the general sent us to rescue you." I didn't want the captain to feel slighted that we had been sent for a mere lieutenant.

The captain sat back down. "I am sorry sergeant but I gave my word that I would not attempt to escape."

"I respect that sir. Dago, open both doors."

"But I said I cannot go with you."

"I know sir and this works in your favour because it shows that you kept your word. Lieutenant, are you ready?" He hesitated. "We haven't got long and the guards will be coming round."

Dago made the decision for him. He pushed him out of the cell and I thrust the Henry into his hands. "I sure hope you know how to use this." I grabbed the sergeant's frock coat. "Here put this on, it will cover your grey uniform."

We quickly ran to the gatehouse. No-one was in sight. We walked along the street as calmly as we could. We almost fell into the livery stable. The old negro just smiled. "We won't need the stables after all." I found a silver dollar and thrust it into his hands. "For your time and trouble."

He chuckled, "I knew you boys were real soldiers not like the ones we have here. You take care now sir."

We mounted swiftly and galloped out towards the south. The stable boy just waved and then closed the gate. It was as though we had never been there. There were no guards at the end of the road, as there had been at Frederick. We rode hard until we were clear of Gettysburg. We had too many miles to go to reach safety before morning and I decided to try to get beyond Frederick and then rest up for a few hours. Our horses had been fed and watered and had some rest. If we did not push them then they would see us through. That was the trouble with strange horses you did not know their strengths and weaknesses but the horses had aided our disguise.

"Was the general who sent you my uncle by any chance?"

"You got it in one. I didn't want to upset the captain back there by telling him we came just for you."

"How did you manage to overcome the guards? There were at least five."

"It's one of our specialities, its called lying through your teeth. We do that a lot."

"You'll have to excuse my friend Dago. He tends to call a spade a shovel!"

"Are you with the cavalry?"

"Sort of. In an unofficial way, you might say."

"Are you two with the Partisan Rangers then? Mosby?"

"No, we are the other ones, the Wildcats."

"I heard them talking about you. They said something about hanging a bunch of soldiers in Charles Town."

"They weren't soldiers, they were militia and they had murdered a woman. Don't believe all the bullshit you read and hear."

"There's a price on your heads you know."

"There has been for some time. What is it up to now?"

"$1500!"

Dago whistled, "For that kind of money I think I would turn myself in!" The joke eased the tension and we rode steadily on. I wondered how long it would be before they found that the bird had flown his coop. We still had over twenty miles to go and I had an itch at the back of my neck. I saw a slope to the right and I kicked hard, "You two, follow me." I turned towards the hill. There was a shallow stream running from it and I led the two of them up the stream bed until we came to a rocky patch. We walked along there and then we turned to enter a shallow valley which led up into the ridgeline. We were out of sight of the roads and I dismounted.

"But I thought you wanted to push on?" Our cocky little lieutenant had become more confident since we had escaped the prison.

"We did but I have a funny feeling and this is a good place to hide." I was not about to explain to the shave tail what my plans were.

We waited in silence and Lieutenant Stuart said impatiently. "There's no one there. We are wasting time."

Dago clicked his teeth. "The sergeant is called Lucky Jack by the boys in our outfit and for good reason. If he gets a twitch then we listen."

"But I am an officer and you two ..."

"And we have permission from your uncle to do whatever we have to get you back safely. And we will. So do me a favour, son and shut up!"

The silence seemed to go on forever and then we heard the unmistakable thunder of hooves. I took off my hat and slowly raised myself to peer over the rocks. I knew that I could not be seen but I wanted no sudden movements to give me away. I could see ten horsemen riding hard. It looked to me as though they were led by the major and the lieutenant we had seen earlier. That boded well for if they were the leaders then we could easily best them in a fight. I waited until they were well out of sight before I rejoined my companions. Stuart's nephew looked shamefaced. "How did you know?"

"I didn't but I had a feeling and in this line of work

that is almost as good as an extra gun. The trouble is they will reach Frederick before we do which means we need a different route home from the one we had planned."

I mounted again and we rode back to the bottom of the hill. "If we head due west we should drop down on the other side of this rise. I think this is called the Blue Ridge Summit. We can do the hard work at night time when we won't be seen and then I think there is a road on the other side. We can skirt Hagerstown and cut across the Potomac to Kearneysville."

Dago nodded but Lieutenant Stuart looked appalled. "That will take us two days!"

"Maybe three!"

"But what about food? What about shelter and a bed?"

I shook my head, "Son, no one said it was going to be comfortable but this way is safe. The Yankees will have barricades and checkpoints all through the big towns. Your uncle is a famous man and they would have made much of your capture. Anyway, that's what we are going to do. Dago, lead off."

I took the rear. We found a road of sorts which made the going easier than I expected. It meant that we cut across the ridge lower than the summit. I would have hated to try the road in a wagon or a cart but our horses made little of it. When we reached the crest we could see a flicker of lights about ten miles away. By my reckoning that was Waynesboro; a small town but one worth avoiding. We began our descent and the rough road led us inexorably toward the south-west which was our direction of choice. It was coming on to dawn and we were tired. Dago held up his hand. "Jack, there's a spring up ahead and a stand of trees. Good shelter."

"Then let's camp there." We took the saddles off the horses and rubbed them down. We gave them water first and some of the grain we carried. I noticed that Archie just watched us. He was obviously a soldier with servants and, like his uncle, in it for the glory. We took off the bedrolls and laid them out.

"You two get some sleep and I will try to get us some food."

Dago nodded and rolled over to begin snoring almost immediately. Archie looked despondently at the bare roll and sighed. I had no time for those who played at soldiers. I had seen rabbit holes nearby and I took some leather thongs, the type we used to repair saddles and made a couple of traps. I placed them at the entrance to three of the burrows and then returned to the camp. Dago was snoring away and Archie was still struggling to get to sleep. I took the opportunity to gather some dry wood and kindling. If we caught any rabbits they would need to be cooked. I couldn't see Archie eating raw rabbit.

I heard the squeal that told me I had at least one bunny. I slowly made my way back to the traps and saw that I had snared two. I took them back and began skinning the rabbits. When the guts were disposed of and the attendant disgusting smell had dissipated, I threaded a branch through them. My work was completed. As dawn broke I woke Dago. "Two rabbits there and kindling; it should be dry but make sure it is before you light the fire." I couldn't risk firelight in the night but dry wood would not give off smoke.

Dago snorted, "You trying to teach your grandmother to suck eggs now?"

"Sorry, its being with the shave tail I guess. Give me a couple of hours eh?"

CHAPTER 16

Jack

I awoke, surprisingly refreshed and the smell from the rabbits brought me fully to my senses. Dago was grinning at me from across the fire while Archie Stuart looked bleary-eyed and mournful. "I don't know how you can sleep on the hard ground like that."

"Practice." I looked expectantly at the food. "Well, Dago, are the rabbits ready?"

"Just waiting for you, boss."

I poured my canteen over my face and then refilled it from the icy spring. It tasted as good as any beer, icy and clean. After we had devoured the rabbits we all felt much better, even the grumpy lieutenant. We rested for the morning and then set off in a southern direction. We kept the Catoctin Mountains to our left knowing that the Union would be looking for us in that direction. Dago rode point, keeping a sharp eye for blue uniforms. I wanted to avoid a fight at all costs. The valley we were in looked to be deserted although there was the occasional farm to be seen. We gradually descended until Dago spotted a road and we risked riding along it. I intended to keep going as long as we could for Frederick was just some ten miles to the east.

It was late afternoon when we struck Middletown. This was a sleepy one road town and we rode through it as casually as you like. We waved to the old men standing, chewing the fat and struck the Burkittsville road to the south. Once again we kept a range of mountains between us and any Union cavalry seeking us. We still had plenty of daylight and I rode next to Dago for a while. "I think, looking at the map that we can follow this road to Brunswick."

"There are or there were Union troops there, boss."

"I know but we can turn off before we hit the town. Brunswick is almost on the Potomac and I would like to get over tonight if possible." We both glanced at our charge who looked exhausted already. "Have you ever swum a river on a horse?" The look of horror on his face gave me the answer.

Dago spat in disgust, "Then we'll have to follow the river to Harper's Ferry. Are you still planning on getting there tonight?"

"They will have spread the word by now. It will be more than the ten-man patrol I saw last night. As soon as we reach Brunswick we'll ditch the blue and revert to grey."

It took us ten miles to strike the main pike leading to Harper's Ferry. We could see the lights of Brunswick in the distance. "Right time to become rebs again!"

Archie had been quiet for most of the afternoon and, when we had changed he asked, "Do you fellows do this sort of thing often?"

"What sort of thing?"

"Well, this... "He spread his arm around at us and the horses, "riding behind enemy lines living off the land, living on your wits."

I looked at Dago and we both laughed, "Pretty much!"

"I will be glad to get back to the cavalry."

"Don't count any chickens just yet." I pointed at the carbine I had given him. "Can you use that?"

"I have used it but I prefer a sword."

"If we meet anyone and we start firing then you fire that thing until it is empty and if we meet anyone we will not be running from them, we will be charging through them because whoever they are they will be between us and your uncle!"

He looked at Dago and said quietly, "He is joking!"

"He most certainly isn't! You'll enjoy it lieutenant and you can dine out on the story afterwards."

Dago and I both had our Colts in our hands as we gingerly trotted along the road. We hoped that Jackson had won but, for all that we knew, the battle could still be raging or the Yankees could have won. It was getting close to midnight and I hoped that, on this cold September night, the Union vedettes were wrapped in their greatcoats and not listening for the movement of horses on the road.

I was beginning to think that, perhaps, they were tucked up asleep when out of the dark three Union troopers appeared. "Halt who goes...?"

That was as far as they got. Our guns were cocked and ready and theirs were not. Dago and I got three shots off each and the road was clear. "You two ride. I will cover you."

Dago slapped Stuart's horse and I swapped my half-empty gun for a loaded one. Harper's Ferry was but two miles away and I had no intention of losing my charge now. The rest of the cavalry were bivouacked nearby and they came at me piecemeal. I fired calmly and slowly until my gun was empty. I was stationary and they were not. Their bullets clipped the trees around me but never came close to me. I took out my last loaded gun and fired three shots and then kicked my horse hard to wheel away into the darkness. I heard their bullets but they had fired too quickly and the shots zinged around me and my horse; we both appeared to bear a charmed life.

I heard Dago give a rebel yell and knew that, up ahead, were friendly forces. I glanced under my arm and saw twenty cavalrymen whipping their mounts for all they were worth. My brave beast was tiring but she kept going. I pointed my pistol under my arm and steadied it on the rump of the horse. I squeezed off a shot and one of those pursuing me fell from his horse. I heard my horse whinny and saw the red mark where a stray bullet had nicked her hindquarter. "Keep going, bonnie girl! You'll get there."

Up ahead the road rose to a crest and my two companions had disappeared. My pursuers were now less than thirty yards away. Lucky Jack's luck was about to run out. I crested the rise and saw, to my delight, Boswell's Wildcats, a solid line of carbines. There was a gap left for me and I scuttled through it just as thirty carbines bucked and hit the cavalry like grapeshot. We had made it!

I reined in my wounded horse and patted her neck. "Well done, lass, well done!"

Dago was standing next to his horse and I leapt off to shake his hand warmly. He grinned lopsidedly at me, "Lucky Jack again!"

Lieutenant Archie Stuart stepped from his horse and I could see that he was shaking. His eyes were wide with terror. "How did we get through that alive?" He looked at my uniform, searching for bullet holes or wounds. "And how did you escape injury?"

"More men die or get wounded because they worry that they will die or get wounded." I shrugged, "If it happens, it happens."

Just then there was a clattering of hooves and General Stuart galloped up with his personal escort. Even at this late hour, he was immaculately turned out. He leapt agilely from his horse and threw his arms around his nephew who appeared to be totally embarrassed. "You made it! Thank God!"

Archie to do him credit stepped back and said, "I owe it all to these two men uncle. They did things that I did not believe were possible."

The General grinned, "They have been doing that for me for some time but, seriously, gentlemen, I am in your debt. If you ever need anything then you just ask. I would promote you or give you a medal but," he glanced over my shoulder at Captain Boswell and Lieutenant Murphy who were approaching, "I know that the Wildcats do not go in for such things." He shook me and then Dago by the hand. "Come Archie you will have much to tell me and I know the Wildcats will have things they wish to say."

After they had ridden off it seemed very quiet. Captain Boswell nodded very slowly, "I was not sure you would manage to bring this off but you have both done well." He looked at the back of the departing general. "If you wish to be promoted..."

I shook my head, "We only need one lieutenant and besides I like being a sergeant."

Harry and the rest of the men returned with the horses and weapons from the dead Yankees. "Quite a tidy haul here sir. I think we are in profit again." He looked at me. "And did you bring anything back with you?"

"Will two Henry Carbines do and a couple of Army Colts?"

He laughed, "That'll do nicely. Come on lads lets get back to camp. I found a jug in one of the saddlebags."

The next day we caught up on the news of the army. Jackson had captured the garrison and the guns of the defenders of Harper's Ferry. The set back of South Mountain had been reversed and the Army of Northern Virginia was marching into Maryland.

"The generals were so pleased with us they said that we can recuperate and re-supply here before we begin operations around Berryville again."

"Berryville?"

"The generals want to put pressure on Washington and the Blue Ridge is the perfect place for us to operate. We are going back there next week." He pointed at the wounded who were still bandaged. "They are recovering and when we heard the shooting the other night they all wanted to help out."

"How did you know where we would be?"

"The cavalry scouts of General Stuart reported lots of activity around Frederick and the only reason we could think of was your escape. We knew you would avoid Frederick and that meant coming along through Brunswick. Harry and Danny have been leading patrols in every direction looking for signs." He shook his head. "Every man knew you would make it back. Even when we heard they had a regiment chasing you. Tell me, how the hell did you break him out of prison?"

I told the others the tale and they nodded at various points. "It's a good lesson, sir. The troops who aren't at the front have little or no battle experience and some of them are hiding out there in the rear areas. They seem to be afraid of battle. Even Archie, Lieutenant Stuart seemed a little gun shy. Instead of targeting combat troops we should be harassing the quartermasters and supply corps. We will be much more effective."

We left for Berryville before General Lee sent the Union army packing at Antietam. I know they say the battle was a draw but Lee had fewer men and he did not lose as many. I know that he had to come back to Virginia but it showed the Union what he could do and it meant that the Army of Northern Virginia could winter in the Valley.

Although Berryville was still close to the Union lines, they no longer occupied the town. The Blue Ridge was the extent of their influence although they had, apparently, increased their patrols. That would be one of our tasks, to tie up cavalry which would otherwise be engaged with Stuart and our own horse warriors.

Harry and Jed led a small patrol ahead of us to find a suitable site for our base. Captain Boswell wanted to be within easy reach of Leesburg and Charles Town and the area eight miles or so from Berryville seemed perfect. Harry found what we all thought to be the ideal base. There was a large pond or small lake nestled in a natural dell. There were forests on three sides with an aspect to the west. It was as though we had ordered it. We hid the tents amongst the trees. You would not know it was a camp until you were in the middle. We cleared some trees further back to make a corral for the horses and we were set. Harry and I went shooting the first day there and bagged a couple of deer and smaller game. We would eat well.

The captain allowed us a couple of days to establish our routines and then called us together. "We have all learned much in the past few months and we will now put that to good use. Tomorrow we will take four patrols over the Blue Ridge. We will not engage the enemy. We will be invisible but we will choose good targets." He grinned at us. "We have been very successful so far and, when you are ready there are funds for all of you but this gives us the chance to really hurt the Yankees and line our pockets at the same time. The people we will be attacking will be northerners; the more we hurt them the less our people at home will be harmed."

I was given the task of scouting the Potomac and I led my section northwards. Davy and Jimmy scouted ahead and Cecil, who had become somewhat attached to me tagged just behind Copper. After crossing the Blue Ridge I skirted Leesburg; the lieutenant would investigate the forces there, and I headed due north to the river. We knew the river well to the west but it was largely unknown to the east. Here it was much deeper and fords were less frequent. The southern bank was a mixture of forests and more open woodland. Had there not been a war it would have been a pleasant excursion. We crossed a couple of small rivers and, as dusk approached I found a wall of stone rising about two hundred feet from the river. There was a sparsely woody and shrub covered island and we made camp there. I could see no signs of life on the bluffs and we felt safe.

We had good rations, having only left that morning and I split the watch so that we all did two hours. I lay, resting my head on a dead tree trunk listening to the Potomac bubbling away. Davy, Jimmy and Irish were seated nearby and they must have thought I was asleep for they began to talk about me.

"Is it true that the Sergeant was a pirate once?"

I heard Davy laugh, "Where did you hear that Irish?"

"When we signed up I heard that there was an Irishman who had been a pirate and he jumped ship to join the captain. Apparently, he killed a pirate over an argument about a woman!"

"I can see how that story came about but he worked on a ship which carried slaves and the captain offered him the chance to leave the ship and join him."

"Ah, that makes sense. I couldn't see him as a pirate."

"He can be dangerous Irish; I know they call him Lucky Jack but he is a tough bugger and he can be ruthless. Just remember that."

As they turned in to sleep I wondered at their perception of me. I did not see myself as ruthless but perhaps they had a better view of me than I had of myself.

We headed over the bluff the following day. I sent Georgie, one of the new boys to scout ahead and he trotted back after an hour away. "Sergeant there's a farm up ahead."

He paused and I said, "And…?"

"Well, I know the owner. He was a friend of my pa." Georgie's dad had been killed nearby at the Battle of Ball's Bluff in the early days of the war. "His name is Thomas and he is a good man."

We all knew that a good man meant he was a Confederate sympathiser. "Let's stop there for a while then. We may get some useful information. Well done Georgie."

Thomas and Lydia Miskel were honest farm folk. They had to hide their Confederate sympathies as most of their neighbours favoured the Union. He allowed us to put our horses in the barn and he gave us some feed. His wife gave us ham and eggs with fried chicken for breakfast; washed down by a pot of coffee.

"See much Union activity around here Mr Miskel?"

"We didn't but," he pointed east, "yonder is the town Dranesville and they have recently put some Yankee cavalry there." He chuckled, "I reckon it's because of Mosby." I know that the captain and the lieutenant would have rankled that John Mosby seemed to be seen as a hero while the Wildcats were largely unknown. I did not mind the anonymity. North of the Potomac there was a price on our heads!

"How many men?"

"More than you have."

It was always difficult asking civilians to estimate numbers of cavalry. We would have to scout them out. "Thank you for your hospitality sir. We will leave by the back fields; we wouldn't want you identified as southern sympathisers." At the back of my mind was the fate of poor Annie Fowler who had helped us and paid for it with her life.

As we left I called Georgie over, "Do you know where this Dranesville is?"

He pointed to the east. "A few miles over there."

I turned to the others. "We are going to see how many Yankees are at Dranesville. We need to know where their camp is and how man men. Keep your eyes open for ways in and ways out. No talking from now on." Even though it was daylight it paid to keep silent for the human voice carried long distances and we needed to be as unobtrusive as possible.

The town lay to the south of the Leesburg Pike and looked to be a small settlement with some woods and farms surrounding it. We saw an old tavern just on the edge of the woods; it looked like it was the oldest building in the area. We dismounted in the trees and left our horses behind the tavern. Drawing our Colts we left the safety of the woods to inspect the tavern. Without entering we saw that there were a man and a woman preparing for the day. They were oblivious to our presence and were wiping down the bar top and the wooden tables. I left two men to watch them and the horses and then we remounted and rode down the road towards the centre. So far we had not seen a sign of the barracks or the camp but Cecil suddenly raised his hand and pointed to an area to the north of the road. I glanced and saw the blue uniforms. We quickly headed for the shelter of some shrubs. The advantage of grey was that it blended in well with green whereas blue stood out.

I could see that there were enough tents for about a hundred and fifty men. There was an open fence running around it. As an obstacle, it would not stop a determined attacker and I suspect it was more to demarcate the boundaries and to enable sentries to patrol. When I looked at the standard, just outside the command tent I saw that it was a Pennsylvania regiment. I stored that information for future use. Having seen all that we needed to see we returned to our men and the horses. We did not speak another word until we were on the pike.

"Well done Cecil. I made it about a hundred and fifty cavalry from Pennsylvania. Anyone see anything else?"

Davy spat at the ground and said, "I think I saw a cannon, looked to be a four or six pounder."

Although I hadn't seen that I trusted his eyes. "Well done. Let's get back to the captain then."

It was late afternoon when we returned to our camp in the Blue Ridge. Our return journey had been without incident but then we had been as discreet as we could and used every scrap of cover. The captain liked the idea of raiding Dranesville. "It will send a message to the Union that we are getting closer to Washington and warn them that they are not good enough to find us."

"Captain? How about if we raid somewhere further south first. This Dranesville sounds like a long way off. Jack, could we get there and back in one day?"

"No Harry, but we could get there in a day and raid at night."

"Either way if we can have them looking for us somewhere else then it would help."

"That's a good idea sergeant. Any ideas?"

Danny scratched his stubble, "We found a stud farm at Upperville. It's only a few miles away and there are no Union troops there. We could get remounts and make a tidy profit."

The captain was not so certain and I could tell that from his expression and his next questions. "The owner could be a Southern supporter. We don't want to hurt our own people, do we?"

"He has a Stars and Stripes hanging from his porch."

"Perhaps that may be to make the Yankees think he is one of them. Still, we can ask him who he supports. We ride first thing."

Later, when I spoke with Danny I asked him what he thought of the captain's comments. We had fought long enough together for him to know I was not being disloyal; I just wanted to know my leader's mind.

"This is close to the captain's home and it is Virginia. The captain believes that every Virginian supports the south. I am not so sure. I think the flag tells us all that we need to know. Besides, whoever the owner is, he will get more money from the north than the south."

That was true. The Union bought remounts for the cavalry; the southern cavalryman had to provide his own mount. If he was unhorsed, he had to get his own remount. I agreed with Danny but at least I now understood the captain's reasoning.

The area we were visiting had been the centre for horse breeding for the past ten years at least. It was, horse country, and our journey there was easy. The farm we were seeking was enormous and we could see many corrals filled with horses as we rode out of the forested slopes of the Blue Ridge. The Stars and Stripes flew prominently above the white imposing house. The collonaded portico and the huge mansion told us that this was a rich man. It struck me that the owner was making a bold and brave statement that he was a supporter of Abe Lincoln. This was despite the fact that he was close to the Confederacy and the fluid border and frontier between the North and the South.

"Harry, you and Jack keep your sections here and watch for trouble. We'll ride up to the house and see what his politics are."

As they left and trotted up the fence lined drive Harry agreed with me, "Waste of time talking. We should just take the damned horses. This way he could cause us trouble."

We watched as the two officers dismounted and climbed the steps to the colonnaded porch. They knocked and I saw a negro butler let them in. "Well, they are in, at least. I half expected him to come out waving a shotgun or a sabre."

We waited and watched the house. Suddenly, out of the corner of my eye, I saw a horse and rider almost explode from the side of the house. "Davy, Jimmy, come with me."

I did not need to explain to Harry he had seen the rider too and knew that it meant one thing; someone in the house was sending a rider for help. The rider was heading for the turnpike. "Davy, go straight along the road in case we miss him. Jimmy, you stop him going into the hills."

I leaned over Copper's head and spoke to her. "Come on old girl; let's see just how fast you can move."

The rider made the classic mistake. He did not make his mind up and stick to it. He tried to change his mind and direction halfway towards the road. He saw Davy and halted. I could almost see his decision making and he chose wrongly he headed up towards the Blue Ridge. That would take him away from any help and towards Jimmy who was now eating up the ground on his chestnut mare. I turned Copper's head slightly to intercept further along. I saw that Davy was also now heading in our direction. The rider's horse was a fine beast and it was built for speed. It was not built for twisting and turning in woodland. Nor was the rider good enough to cope with the undulating ground and the natural traps which lay along the ground. We were well used to this and the three of us had done it many times. From his frequent glances over his shoulder, I could see that he had no military experience for if he had he would have ignored us and concentrated on escaping. From his build, I could see that he was little more than a boy. Something must have spooked his horse for he suddenly found his mount rearing. He was a good rider and kept his seat but, by the time he had it under control again, there were two Colts aimed at his chest.

He was about fifteen years old and was well dressed. He was also brave as he tried to face us down. "Who are you, bandits? This is my father's land now be off with you."

We didn't bother answering. I nodded at the reins and Jimmy led the horse back down the slope. Davy rode behind the boy and I rode next to him.

"Who is your father, son?"

"Colonel Richard Dulay and he is a magistrate. You will go to jail for this. My father has friends in Washington."

"That's the trouble, son, you see we have none but we do have someone in Richmond who thinks well of us."

He suddenly seemed to see our uniforms for the first time. "You're Rebs!"

Davy added, dryly, "The boy is quick, I'll give him that."

The boy flashed an angry look over his shoulder. I shook my head at the impetuous youth. "So where were you off too in such an all-fired hurry?"

"I was going to bring the cavalry and the Marshal from Middleburg. They know what to do with thieves and robbers; they hang them!"

That was useful. Middleburg was less than ten miles away and we did not know there were cavalry there. "Well now you needn't bother, the cavalry are already here." Soon enough we had reached Harry and the rest of our men. His face paled as he saw the weapons. "You two stay here and I will return this young man to his father."

I rode up the drive and found the house even more spectacular close up. Dago and Jed were in charge of the rest of the men and Dago grinned, "Throwing one of the little fishes back in the pond Sarge?" The men laughed and the boy coloured. I felt sorry for him. He had not been afraid to ride for help despite the danger to himself.

I helped him down although he shrugged off my hand. We reached the door and I grabbed his arm. He tried, again to free himself but this time I was not offering aid I was restraining him. Pulling on wet canvas in a gale builds your muscles and gives you a grip of iron. I used it to good effect."Son I do not wish to hurt you but, unless you do exactly as I say, you will be hurt." I opened the door with my other hand and led the boy to the open door I could see. The black butler stood with open mouth and I held a finger to my lips and said, "Ssh!"

I could hear a voice, I presumed was the boy's father, speaking, "Well if you gentlemen would care to have a bite to eat then we can look at the horses later on this afternoon when it is a little cooler. How does that sound?"

I thrust the boy into the room. "Fine by us sir, but the cavalry from Middleburg won't be here to give us a warm welcome now and it would be a waste to let the food spoil."

He grasped his son to his chest and his face changed from the smiling benevolent one he had shown to a mask of reddened anger. "If you have hurt this boy..."

"He has not been touched and you can be proud of him he is a good boy." I turned to the captain and a grinning Danny. "He was riding for help. Apparently, there is a cavalry regiment just down the road."

"And they will catch and hang you horse thieves!"

Danny looked at the captain and spread his hands, "There you are sir. Does that answer your question?"

The captain nodded and turned to me, "You and Harry know what to do. Send Dago and the boys in here."

I saw that the butler was still there. "I think they all need a stiff drink in there." He gave a slight bow and hurried off; I think he was just glad to have some orders to obey. At the door, I said, "Dago, take all the boys in there. I think the captain agrees with Danny now. Oh and make sure no one else tries to run off. We are going for the horses."

There were over eighty head of horses. I left the breeding stallion and a couple of mares in their corral. I was not being deliberately kind or soft in any way. Had we tried to take the stallion it might have caused us more trouble than enough and no-one would want a stallion as a mount. We tied them together in strings of four. This would make it easier to move them. I hitched two of them to the open wagon we found. I suspected that the captain would be liberating other items from the house.

Harry led the men back towards our camp with

sixty of the horses. I tied the other horses to the back of the wagon and Cecil drove it. He swelled with pride when I selected him. The main reason was that the others were all better riders than he was and I did not want to risk losing him and four horses.

As I had expected there were boxes and piles of goods taken from the house waiting for us on the porch. There were some fine guns, coffee, flour and tinned goods. They were all the things we could not easily get and which we needed. I picked out some men to lead the horses and sent them after Harry while Cecil and I helped to load the wagon. The captain and the lieutenant kept their Colts on the Colonel, his son and the staff. I had no doubt that the boy would soon go to Middleburg but by then we would be hidden from view.

CHAPTER 17

Jack

We took the wagon towards Berryville. The horses could go directly to the camp but we wanted our pursuers to think we were based on the other side of the ridge. Once we reached the bridge over the Shenandoah, we emptied the wagon and packed the two spare horses and ours with everything we had taken from the horse farm. Then we pushed the wagon into the river and watched it float downstream. By the time the cavalry reached the bridge, it would be gone from view and they would search in vain for our crossing point. We rode along the rocks of the river bank and then made our way through the woods back to our camp.

It was almost dark by the time we arrived. We had travelled carefully to avoid leaving a trail which could be followed. While some of the men prepared our supper the officers and non-coms held a meeting. The captain was reasonably democratic and allowed us to discuss our plans. Harry was the bluntest of us all, "I think that we delay the Dranesville raid, sir until we have dealt with Middleburg."

Captain Boswell nodded and said, "Any other opinions?"

I coughed and said, "I agree with Harry. We can still

raid Dranesville but the Middleburg cavalry are closer. If we attack them and then retreat west, that will confirm that we are at Berryville. The other thing is I don't like the idea of inquisitive cavalry being so close to us. There is still the reward being offered for us and they may just search the Blue Ridge. We aren't far from Upperville and the herd is a big one."

"How about this sir?" It was Dago who had the brainwave. "We whip these Yankee's asses. That normally makes them less inclined to look for us." We all laughed, mainly because it was true. "Then we take the horses to the Quartermaster and then we go to Dranesville and raid them there too."

We all sipped our coffee as we ran the plan through our minds. "I can't see a fault in it, sir."

"Nor can I, Danny. We'll leave four men to guard the horses and then take the rest to Middleburg. We'll get there for dawn. They should be tired after searching for us all night."

Choosing four men was hard as they all wanted to be on the raid but, by picking one man from each section, it was deemed to be fair. It was Georgie from my section who I left behind. I knew that we would need his local knowledge for Dranesville and this minimised the likelihood of his being hurt in the raid. We had not scouted the town before but we knew that it was very small with just the main road running through it and two minor roads heading north and south. We were aided with identifying its location by the sound of the bugle at reveille. As soon as we saw lights appearing in the field to the west of the hamlet we knew where they were.

The captain halted us. We were thirty experienced

troopers and all of us were fully armed. He addressed us all calmly. "We have them cold. We charge through the camp. Empty your guns at the men you see or the tents. I will lead my section first; the second section will be the lieutenant then Harry and finally Lucky Jack." The men all laughed. "Then we turn and come back through their camp. If we have been successful then we will strip the camp but if they are returning fire then follow me and we will take the Berryville Road. No noise until I open fire and then yell as though you are Stuart's Brigade!"

As we lined up I said to my section, "Just use one gun and aim. I don't want any of you falling off your horses!"

We rode silently towards the camp. We were hidden in the darkened west while the first hints of dawn and the lights of the fires in the camp gave us a vague picture of the place. Being at the rear gave me more chance to estimate numbers. From the tents, I guessed that there would be about a hundred men. We would be outnumbered by over three to one but they would be the ones being surprised and that counted for much in a battle.

Suddenly the captain and his section leapt forwards and began firing. As soon as they did so Danny and his men yelled and followed. Then it was Harry's turn. He still had the standard and he held it proudly. I heard his section yell, "Yee haw! The Wildcats!"

I turned, "Remember boys they will be expecting us, keep low in the saddle. Now ride! Yee Haw!"

The camp was indeed up and I saw numerous bodies already lying in the walkways between the tents. A trooper emerged from his tent and I blasted him at point blank range and then I was firing almost blind as I entered a world of gun smoke and chaos. As quickly as we had started we were through the camp and the dead and the dying.

"Reform on me! Change your weapon. Despite what I had told my men I now drew two Colts and tied the reins to my pommel. Copper would follow Harry's horse and I could protect my men better. I knew that they would be waiting for us. "Charge!" I let my men get a step ahead and then released Copper. Four Union troopers were kneeling down and aiming at my men. I fired both barrels, cocked them and then fired again. I kept up a double fire all the way through the camp. I suddenly caught a glimpse of the flag; this was another company of the Second Pennsylvania; they were the regiment sent to find us.

When we reached the other side I saw that there were a couple of empty saddles. There were still Union soldiers firing and we had done enough. The captain said, loudly enough for the whole camp to hear, "Well done Wildcats, back to Berryville."

I grabbed the reins of one of the spare horses and we galloped off into the dawn. Once we had cleared the hamlet, we headed north-west towards our Blue Ridge camp. I saw that one of the empty horses belonged to Richard, a new trooper but a hard worker. He had been in my section and I had had high hopes for him. The other had been the mount of one of Harry's men. It was as I had thought; they had been prepared for the last riders to come through. We had paid the price with dead and wounded.

We knew that the raid had been a success but losing two men took the gloss off it. We all knew that it was possible to die, indeed, it was quite likely but we all hoped that it would be someone we didn't like and we all liked each other. We were doomed to mourn for our dead comrades.

The camp guards had not been idle and we had a good meal waiting for us. The captain came over to speak with Harry and me, "I know the risks you boys took and your troopers. It won't be forgotten and next time it will be Harry or me who has the shitty detail."

We both nodded and Harry said, "It always hurts when one of the lads gets it. We would feel as bad if it was someone from your section sir. Every one of them is as important to all of us."

"I know I just wanted you to know my feelings too." He shook himself as though to clear his head. "Dago, take Jed and a couple of my boys and make sure we aren't being tracked."

I saw Dago looking fondly at the food as it was being heaped on the waiting plates. He enjoyed his food but I knew that the cooks would not let him go short. Dago was worth three ordinary men in any fight.

We took down our tents the next day and hid them. We would be going directly to Dranesville from Berryville, or wherever we found the quartermaster. We had chosen the best mounts for those of us who needed them. For myself, I would not exchange Copper for Bucephalus himself. The trail we took was not a well-worn route. We had discovered it ourselves. It emerged at a huge oxbow on the Shenandoah and we had found that we could ford it there easily. We roped the horses for the crossing as we did not wish to lose any of those valuable creatures. We were paid $110 for each horse we captured. As we had over eighty it meant that each man was richer by almost $300. We were all rich men if we could survive the war.

We found that we had to take the horses to Winchester. Stuart was in town and he was delighted to see us again and to see our horses. The captain and the lieutenant told him of our exploits and although we were stood some distance from them we could see the animation on his face. I am sure it was his wish to emulate us that led to his Chambersburg Raid the following week. He was so delighted that he promoted the captain to a major on the spot and told him to recruit another fifty men such as us. After saying our farewells we collected some supplies from the quartermaster and left Winchester. We liked to be alone and hidden; even from our own army.

As we headed east to find some farm in which to shelter we congratulated the major on his promotion. He seemed embarrassed by the whole thing, "I was happy being a captain and commanding you fellows. That is all the honour and glory I wish for."

Danny shook his head, "If you don't mind me saying so sir but that is plain daft. This means that no dumb major, begging your pardon sir, can order you and us around. I would like it to be General Boswell and then we would only have to listen to Robert E Lee himself."

We applauded this sentiment and laughed. Major Boswell wagged an admonishing finger at Danny. "Of course this makes you a captain and you two smart arses lieutenants and, God help us, Dago and Jed are now sergeants!"

That silenced us all. I had not thought of that. Of course, we could do nothing really until we had more recruits and we would need to find a tailor to make our uniforms but I wondered how Caitlin would react to her wee brother being an officer. I did not make the leap to gentleman as, Major Boswell apart, I would not like to be a gentleman such as the ones I had met such as Beauregard and Colonel White.

We found an empty barn between Purcellville and Leesburg. It was like many in this part of the world. The young men had gone off to war and the elderly parents had either died or given up. There was no sign of a struggle in the house and we were careful to leave it as tidy as we found it. We always remembered Annie Fowler. We treated every home we entered as though it was hers.

When we had been in Winchester we had taken the opportunity of stocking up with ammunition. We still used a variety of guns from the two Henry Carbines to the Burnside single shot carbines. Some men had Navy Colts whilst others, like me, had Army Colts. The sabres varied from cheap pieces of metal as likely as not to shatter when first used to my wonderful sword captured from a Yankee officer. We all had a knife or two of some description although we had rarely had to use them, but we were as prepared as any regiment to face the Union and to leave the field with honour.

We took our usual loop around Leesburg to Harrison Island and the Potomac. We travelled in the early hours of the morning and lay up on the island until dusk. We needed to be at Dranesville in the early hours of the next day to enable us to scout it out. We were in no hurry; the Second Pennsylvania at Upperville would still be searching for us to the west and we were to the north. Their fellow cavalrymen would assume that they were safe from any attack. We had fled, apparently, back over the Shenandoah with our horses. We stayed at Miskel's farm again and it was just as pleasant and comfortable as the first time. They had heard of our raid and showed us a newspaper. To my horror I saw the headline, 'Wildcat Bandit Hanged!'

Richard, I was saddened and horrified to read, had not been dead but merely wounded and they had hanged him. My face set into a grimace. We all expected to die but not to be hanged as criminals. Had we not worn a uniform there could have been some justification for it but Richard had been a young patriot wearing a uniform and he had been murdered. Dago put his arm around my shoulder. "Dead is dead my friend. You thought he was dead before…"

"I know, Dago, but it is the manner of his death."

"Don't let this make you bitter Jack."

I did not answer but went to the barn to sharpen my knives and my sword; the Second Pennsylvania would pay for their act of murder. We left before dawn and headed for the garrison. I was chosen to lead the troop as I had scouted it before. I left Davy and Jimmy watching it as I made my way back to the others. "It is exactly like the camp at Middleburg but this one has a wooden fence around it and a barrier."

"Right, we will go in the same way then. We ride in four waves and turn at the end."

"Sir, if I might make a suggestion?"

"Go ahead Jack you have the right."

"If we split our force and attack from two directions at once we will achieve greater surprise."

"We might collide with each other." Lieutenant Murphy was always sensible.

"Danny, these riders are the best aren't they? That

won't happen. And I would like to take Dago and dispose of the guards. There are two at each end. We can lower the barriers and then we will have a free rein to attack without jumping fences."

I saw Harry and Danny nod. "Who would lead your men?"

"Jed can do it, sir." I saw Jed give an approving nod.

"Very well then. Each of you wave when the barrier is down and then make sure you take cover." He looked at two of his men. "You two find the herd and drive it down the road. It will stop them following us."

I had no intention of taking cover but I would not let him know that. Dago said, "I like the way you include me in your madcap ideas."

"You know you would have been annoyed if I hadn't." He shrugged and nodded. "I will take the far side, you take this side. " I was confident about Dago's ability with a knife; it was my own I worried about. I had shot men at close quarters but so far I not had to slide a knife into a man when he was close to me. I thought of Richard and steeled myself.

I skirted along the edge of the fence they had erected. It was dark and I hoped that they would not be able to see me with my grey uniform. Once I reached the corner I hunkered down and saw that the two guards were not facing each other. I slipped my knife out of its sheath. It was eight inches long and razor sharp. I had another six-inch knife tucked into the top of my boot. The two men were both looking out into the woods, both in different directions. One of them, the one on the far side, looked to be asleep or at least dozing but I could not be sure. I half stood and began to creep along the fence towards the nearest sentry. I knew that slow movements were hard to detect and I checked the ground carefully before planting my foot. When I was five yards from the man I was certain that he would hear me breathing and I forced myself to keep moving slowly. He half turned to his left, I suspect he had heard a noise from the other sentry and I leapt at him. My arms were still incredibly strong from my time on the ship and I wrapped my left arm around his mouth clamping it shut and I lifted him up. As he kicked and struggled I ripped the blade across his throat. The hot blood gushed across my arm as he died. I had no time to waste and I dropped him to the ground and hurled myself at the second guard. He may have been dozing but he came awake almost instantly and I saw his mouth start to open. I thrust out my right arm and rammed the knife through the roof of his open mouth and into his brain. There was little blood this time just a gelatinous mess which covered my hand. I moved the bodies to the side and opened the barrier. I waved my arms and then dropped into a crouch with my first Army Colt in my hand.

Even I was startled by the sudden appearance of the Wildcats who began blazing away at the tents. I waited until they had passed and then I slipped along. The first Pennsylvanian trooper who emerged from the tent had his back to me and I blew the back of his head off. I ducked inside the tent and saw that three of the four inside were dead. I put my gun to the forehead of the wounded fourth and pulled the trigger.

When I stepped out again, the camp was a maelstrom of horses, screaming men on both sides and the incessant crack of guns. I saw a trooper emerge from the next tent and I shot him in the back. I had no choice-it was kill or be killed! I opened the flap to dispose of any wounded and, to my horror, there were three unwounded men. I just reacted and shot the first in the head. The second was a huge barrel of a man and I fired my gun. It hit him but failed to stop the behemoth. He screamed in pain and anger and came on at me, apparently unharmed. I fired my last bullet at point blank range and the back of his head disappeared. My gun clicked on an empty chamber as the last trooper threw himself at me.

"Damned Yankee bandit!! I attempted to club him around the head with my gun but it lacked power and he threw his huge arms around me and gripped me in a bear hug. I fell beneath him and the wind was knocked from me. His foetid breath was in my face and his weight was crushing me. I brought my knee up with all the force I could muster and felt it connect with his testicles. He roared in rage and his grip slackened slightly. I used the opportunity to grab my six-inch knife from my boot and drive it up under his arm. I felt it strike bone and then the warm rush of arterial blood. I rolled his carcass from me and, while I was getting my breath back I recovered my gun. I was still winded as I loaded my gun again.

I stepped out and was amazed that the battle still raged. I seemed to have been in the tent for hours. I saw half a dozen troopers race towards me with guns levelled; this was it, I could not kill them all. Suddenly I heard a rebel yell and a voice shouting, "Here Sarge!"

I looked up and saw, coming in the opposite direction from the troopers, Cecil; one hand was gripping his own reins for grim death whilst the other held Copper. It was a brave act as he had no weapon to fire. I did.

I fired five bullets in quick succession, holstered my weapon and then, as Copper came next to me, grabbed the pommel and threw my legs over the saddle. I felt the air from two balls fired at me and then we were through the camp. I had survived. I could see that Cecil was shaking. "Are you hurt?"

"No Sarge." Cecil still couldn't remember my promotion but then I still had just the three stripes on my arm. "Thanks for that. It was brave of you and I won't forget it."

He attempted a weak grin. "Well, at least I didn't have to carry you!"

Dago staggered towards us, his arm bleeding. "Damned Yankee wouldn't stay dead!"

"Cecil get him a horse." I took off my bandana and tied it in a rough tourniquet above the wound. David would have to deal with him later.

"Lucky Jack still. Not a scratch on you."

I shook my head, "You will never know how close I came to being dead! Permanently!"

Cecil brought a horse and held it while I helped Dago on his horse. "Cecil, take him up the road a ways and wait there. Take him to the rendezvous point." As they left I realised that this was where we could use a bugle. I mounted Copper and yelled, "Wildcats on me! Wildcats on me!" In ones and twos, they rode up to me. Harry was there and Danny. Finally, Major Boswell appeared, pursued by at least twenty angry soldiers who were aiming their weapons.

Danny roared, "Fire!" We gave a ragged crack of fire which pre-empted the Yankee's own volley and then he added. "Let's get the feck out of here!"

We galloped away amidst a fusillade of shots. I expected to be struck down at any moment. We all halted when we reached Dago.

"Jed, watch the road." The major scanned our faces. "Two dead?"

Danny nodded, "Jeremiah and John. And I saw them both, they were dead this time." He glanced at me.

"In that case, we had better go. I am not sure how many we killed and how many are left alive but I don't want to push our luck."

We later found out that in our two raids on the Second Pennsylvania we killed forty-five troopers and wounded another fifty; a good return for just two men dead. The two men sent by the major had managed to collect forty horses which, if we got them back home, would be worth $4400. All in all, a good night's work, but we were not out of the woods yet - literally. We had to get directly back for we could not hide this deep in Union territory. We thought of Miskel's farm but it was unfair to put those good people at risk; we would not repeat an Annie Fowler. Instead, we trusted to the road and our luck. We would get as far as we could in the dark and then head for whatever cover was available. We had to hope that we had negated all the cavalry and vedettes in the area.

I rode at the front with Jed as scouts. My pistols were all loaded and ready and my carbine was in my hand. I had thought that the night's violence would have satiated me but I was still ready for more killing.

The dawn broke slowly on that October morning. When we neared Leesburg I led us from the road. In the distance, I could see the dark shadow of the Blue Ridge. Perhaps I was relaxing but, a mile along the road four Union vedettes saw us before we saw them. If I had not been carrying my carbine we might have both died there and then but Jed and I had our guns at the ready and we fired. The two remaining troopers tried to get their guns out but we shot them where they stood. We quickly grabbed their horses and the rest galloped up. Suddenly we heard, on the other side of the plantation of trees, a cavalry bugle.

"Harry, Danny take the rearguard! Get those horses moving! Take them to the camp. My section, follow the horses. You lead them, Jack. We'll try to discourage them!" The Union cavalry we had met so far had proved to be somewhat reluctant to follow us too far into our homeland- I hoped it continued like that.

We needed no urging to drive the herd hard and we whipped the captured horses for all we were worth. The Blue Ridge and the safety of its trees were less than five miles away but it would be a long five miles. I turned to the troopers of my section who were driving the herd. "Spread out in a long line. Dago, take the right, Davy, take the left." We could travel faster in a long line. When we hit the trees then there would be a problem. Behind me, I heard the pop and crack of guns. I resisted the urge to turn around. They knew what they were doing and I had to do my job too.

Even as we were racing along, I was trying to work out a plan. We could not run forever and I realised that the camp was the best place to halt them. The corral we had built was just below the ridge line and there was a wooden rail fence around it. We could put the horses in the lake with a couple of guards. We would have ten men to fire and protect the rest of the troop as they came to us. It was not many but it was all that we had. As we laboured up the slope I began to work out how we could funnel the pursuers into a killing zone; rope! I could string two ropes on either side of the defended section at head height and any riders heading there would be unhorsed while the rest would have to ride into our guns. I had to rely on the fact that the major would bring the troop towards the camp. We needed to drive the cavalry into the mouths of our guns where we could slaughter them. It was not the best plan in the world but the only one I had.

I saw the crest of the ridge approach and I shouted, "Drive them towards the lake and hold them there." I saw waves of acknowledgement.

When we reached the lake, I said to two of the major's men, "You two stand guard on the herd. They are tired and will probably just want to drink. Jed, find some rope. The rest of you back to the fence line and I'll explain what we are going to do."

I had a coiled rope in my tent and I grabbed it. Jed and the others awaited me. "We are going to put two ropes, one here and one thirty yards that way." I pointed out where I wanted them. "I want them at head height. Dago and Jed do that one. Cecil, come with me. The rest of you clear away the shrubs from in front of the fence I want our lads to see us clearly." I paused, "We are going to see how good they are at jumping fences. And us!"

They all looked at me aghast and Dago grinned and walked with Jed muttering, "Mad as a fish!"

I was grateful for Fatty's rope tying lessons and the rope on my side was soon secure enough to hold a mast in a force ten gale. Any rider hitting it would be thrown from his horse or decapitated! "Right boys, that's enough. Back here."

They all positioned themselves behind the fence. Those of you with a Burnside you will have to use your Colts. We need precision here. When our lads have cleared the fence…"

"If," muttered Dago.

"When they have cleared the fence the Union cavalry may be only twenty yards behind. Aim for the horses and the men will fall. Hopefully the major will have lost them but don't bank on it. And remember you are Wildcats!"

They gave a ragged cheer and Dago said, "That means you don't let any kind of sense interfere with your judgement!"

I shook my head and made sure I was fully loaded. I had the Colt in my holster and one in my waistband and the carbine fully loaded. I rested it on the fence. "When they come, lie down to let them jump over us and then up as fast as you can."

I heard shots and the thunder of hooves. "Here they are. Lie down now." In contradiction to my own orders, I stood and shouted, "Yee Haw! Wildcats! Wildcats ho! Ride to the corral! Ride to the corral!" I hoped they would have heard me; I think that shouting in a gale developed my lungs for my voice could carry huge distances. I had no way of knowing the direction they would take and I stayed on my feet. I saw Danny and I waved my carbine and then gestured him on. I waved my arm to tell them to jump the fence and then I dropped to the ground.

We had made an open fence for the corral and we could see, through the gaps, the wall of horses hurtling towards us. They looked to be in an arrow formation with Danny at the fore. It was hypnotic watching the hooves get slower and closer and then suddenly rise. I heard the thunder as the first horse landed and then the others all followed in quick succession. When I saw a gap I stood. The Union cavalry were thirty yards away. I yelled, "Up!" and began firing disobeying my own orders by standing in full view. I heard the ragged volley and then the charge was obscured by smoke.

I heard a Yankee voice yell. "Round the sides! Flank them!"

I grinned when, a few moments later, I heard the screams of pain as the riders who had tried to flank us were dumped from their horses. Suddenly there were another ten guns firing and we kept firing until our guns were empty. "Cease fire and reload!"

It was the major's voice; he too had survived.

CHAPTER 18

Jack

We had, indeed, broken them and when the smoke cleared all that we could see were a few horses disconsolately wandering over the battlefield and the dead and the dying. We moved, in skirmish order, to the crest of the hill and saw the remnants of the Union Cavalry heading back towards the east. We spent the next hour despatching badly injured horses, collecting weapons and live horses and burying the dead. They had been brave troopers and they deserved a burial. Harry and I searched their pockets for any identification and we carved the names on rough crosses. By evening we had buried them all and we were exhausted.

While the men cooked a rough supper we held a meeting with the officers and non-coms to get the full story of the events of the last twenty-four hours.

The major began, "There were four companies of cavalry nearby. They must have brought them forward after our Middleburg raid. We kept halting and firing our Colts when they got too close. Some of them decided they had had enough but the company that followed us had a mad bugger leading them. They just kept chasing us. He was the one with the red beard that we buried last."

I looked at my list of names, "Captain Cole from York."

"Well, he seemed determined for glory. He never took his pistol out once. He kept waving his sabre at us as though that would frighten us to death. Until you shouted, Jack, we were going to head down into the valley and try to hold them at the Shenandoah." He nodded appreciatively, "the ropes were a good idea."

Danny shook his head, "Mind I thought for sure one of us would go arse over tit when jumping the fence!"

"Don't worry captain, Dago felt the same," I asked the question I had been dreading. "How many others died on the way back?"

The major grinned, "None! They didn't even get close to us. I am not sure that we actually killed any during the chase but the wall of bullets we put up seemed to have an effect nonetheless."

"And now what sir?"

The major looked up at the night sky. There were clouds scudding around and there was a chill wind in the air. "By the time we have delivered these horses, it will be, near as damn it, November. I, for one, do not relish camping up here in the Blue Ridge with snow on the ground." We all nodded. "The general wants us to be a bigger force than we are at present which means recruiting so I guess we will head back to Winchester and winter there. I'll take a couple of you back to the plantation to get some recruits from Carolina and to get our new uniforms made. We can't have Boswell's Wildcats looking like a bunch of hicks from the west. We have a certain standard to maintain. We can also pay the men. They have earned it."

Danny asked the next question on our minds, "Who

stays here and who travels back to Charleston?"

"I'd like you and Harry to stay here with Jed and most of the men. I'll take Dago, Jack and David and four others back to Charleston. Your judgement has never let us down, Danny, and I think that Lucky Jack might find some good recruits back at home."

No-one seemed at all put out by the suggestion and we left the next day with a hundred horses and many guns, boots and other military booty. Stuart was not in Winchester but the quartermaster was delighted with our success. "You boys, along with Mosby sure save me a lot of shopping and you bring it right here. That saves me wagons!" When we looked at the receipt we could see just how well off we were. It was not bad for a pauper from Wexford.

He was so pleased that he even found us accommodation for those who were staying. There was a large house just off the main square in Winchester and the owner had made the mistake of siding with the Union when they occupied the town. His position was untenable once Stonewall Jackson had returned and we reaped the rewards. We stayed there for a week while the major paid all the men and told them how much he would invest once he got to Charleston. He even had a receipt written up so that the men could claim their money either when the war was over or when they decided to leave.

When he told us that, it was Cecil who asked the question, "Leave sir? I thought we were soldiers? I thought that we were here for the whole war."

"We are soldiers Irish, but we are irregulars. Any man who has had enough can leave and no hard feelings. All I ask is that you leave your weapons." He shrugged apologetically, "I still want Boswell's Wildcats to be the best-armed troops in the Confederacy." He paused and took a breath. "Anyone want to leave?"

We all looked at each other and roared, "Sir, no sir!"

Cecil and three others, one from each company, as we were now called left for Charleston. We were to travel by train from Richmond. I was excited as I had never travelled by the fastest transport in the world. When we were on the huge iron beast, David asked, "Why me sir? You named me. I can see why the others, the lieutenant, the sergeant, one from each company but why name me?"

"You have proved invaluable to us as someone who can heal. I have a few friends in Charleston who are doctors. You are going to spend a month finding out how to do things even better and you will be our sergeant doctor. I want no man to die of wounds on the field of battle."

All that he could manage was an, "Oh." But I think he was delighted at the prospect. David was a good soldier and could kill with the best but he seemed to get greater pleasure with healing those who were wounded.

As the two officers, the major and I sat together. "Well Jack, what about this sister of yours? Any plans to find her?"

"I think I will write to either Stumpy or his woman, Megan, and give them your address. If Jarvis gets the letter then he can forward it to me. I would send money but I would hate to think it was going to the wrong place. If the Rose had still been afloat then I would have asked Fatty or one of the other lads but..."

"I know. You have lost a lot of people close to you."

"But apart from Richard, I have not lost anyone close to me in the Wildcats yet. Do you think that is strange sir?"

He shrugged, "There are some people who believe in fate. Perhaps your fate was to lose everyone before you reached America. This is the land of promise and hope you know. All things are possible. Look at our first President; in England, he was just a small landowner and yet, after coming to America he became a General and then President. That is America, Jack, anything and everything is possible. You just don't know what your future holds!"

I held that thought close to me. Perhaps there was some higher force watching over me; perhaps it was ma and da or maybe I couldn't die until I had had my revenge and Andrew Neil and Arthur St. John Beauregard both lay dead at my hands.

EPILOGUE

Atlanta Christmas 1862

Major Arthur St. John Beauregard had, at last, secured his future. He had been courting, for some time, Clarissa Winfield, the daughter of the richest man in Atlanta. Her father, Ebenezer, owned many plantations, with their attendant slaves, as well as a fleet of ships. He had shares in a tobacco plantation and Arthur knew that his prosperity would be secured as soon as he married her. He had kept as clean a profile as it was possible. He behaved towards Clarissa and her father like a perfect gentleman at all times. He did not frequent the whore houses and gambling dens. To the outside world, he was a paragon of virtue.

Behind the scenes, however, Andrew Neil and his henchmen procured whores and slaves for orgies at the home of Major Beauregard. When one of the whores was found to have a loose tongue her ravaged body was found dumped close to the prostitute quarter. Similarly, the resourceful Mr Neil organised gambling parties behind the closed doors of two other properties they had acquired. The silence of the gamblers was assured by the ex-soldiers and pugilists employed to keep the reputation of Major Beauregard safe. They had also filled a gap in the market by smuggling in those expensive luxuries denied by the blockade. Through a series of expendable cut outs, they provided Atlanta and its upper classes with all the brandy, fine wines, expensive clothes and exotic food that they wished. Indeed, anything they wanted could be acquired by the resourceful Neil, at a price of course. Had Arthur been less greedy then he would not have needed to marry Miss Winfield but he was greedy and, on Christmas Eve, he rode in his carriage with Andrew and his other bodyguards to dinner at the Winfield's. He would ask for the hand of the lovely Clarissa, although for all that he cared she could have been as ugly as a pig but her beauty was a bonus.

When he stepped from the carriage he could not resist looking at himself in the glass of the door. He still looked lean and handsome. He frowned a little when he saw his off centre nose and the slight droop of his jaw. That peasant Hogan had done that. Of course, he had passed it off as a battle injury but it still rankled with him. Still, many others his age had allowed themselves to indulge themselves too much while Arthur watched his weight and his looks. He knew they were as big an asset as were his name and title.

As he entered the superbly appointed mansion he began to imagine himself living here. It ranked among some of the homes in London like those of the Duke of Devonshire and the Duke of Westminster. He could be quite comfortable and, once the old man had died, hopefully, sometime soon, then he would live the way he wanted to. He had worn his Guard's uniform; he knew that it impressed and he noticed the approving nods of the other dinner guests. He smiled modestly as befitted a Crimean hero.

He was seated close to Ebenezer and next to the

adoring Clarissa who seemed mesmerized by the handsome beau she had captured. During the meal Arthur was especially witty and humorous telling many anecdotes, most of them fictitious. Until he had the father's permission to marry Clarissa he would do everything he needed to; he would be the perfect suitor. He was like an actor playing a role.

When the meal was over and the ladies retired to allow the men their cigars and brandy, Arthur sought out Ebenezer. He did not like the old man. He rarely smiled and appeared to have no sense of humour but he himself had to be humoured.

"An excellent meal as ever Mr Winfield."

"A waste of money while there is a war on." The old man was a true southern patriot and had very strong views on the war and the way it was being run.

"Yes, quite, anyway I have an important question to ask you." The old man did not make life easy; he just stared at the major who began to redden. "The thing of it is I wish to marry your daughter Clarissa. I know that she is in favour of the union but I would not dream of moving forward without your permission and blessing of course." He hated playing the humble suitor but if he had to then he would.

The ghost of a smile appeared at the corners of the old man's face. "I am pleased that you have asked me. I would have disinherited her otherwise." Arthur breathed a mental sigh of relief. He had done it correctly after all. "And you can marry my daughter," Arthur was so happy he could have embraced the old man. Perhaps his face showed that desire for Ebenezer held up his hand, "just as soon as you join the Confederate Army."

Had the old man slapped Arthur or poured a bucket of cold water over his head he could not have had a greater effect. "Join the army?" He was not sure he had heard the old man aright.

"The war is going well. Lee, damned fool that he is, managed to whip the Union at Antietam and he has invaded the north. I think we need some younger blood and with your experience from the Crimea then I think we can win. So? Would you like me to get you a command or would you prefer to get your own?"

Arthur found it hard to breathe let alone think. The last thing he wanted was to join the army. He had tried it once and didn't like it. He filled the silence to give himself time to think. "Well, of course, I would be honoured to serve the south."

"Of course you would. You have spoken of nothing else for the past year. I just wondered when you would get around to it." He gave a rare smile, "Call this a push in the right direction eh, son?"

He wondered if this was a test. The old man seemed to know him a little too well. He could not have him choose his regiment; he might pick one that actually did some fighting. "Well, of course, I shall go down the day after Christmas and offer my services." He was glad that tomorrow was Christmas Day. It gave him an extra day for Neil to find out the safest option for him.

"No need to wait. I have managed to get us an invitation from the Secretary of War, James Seddon; he is a good friend of mine. We will dine with him tomorrow." He patted Arthur on the shoulder, "Consider it a favour. I know you will be able to choose any regiment you like."

Through gritted teeth and with the false smile of a

Nile crocodile Arthur said, "You are too kind sir. You cannot imagine my delight!"

Boston Christmas Day 1862

Caitlin looked at the packed bar and was already counting the takings. Since Patrick, the owner had died childless and left it to her in his will she could not believe the change in her fortunes. She felt neither guilt nor remorse at her actions. She had genuinely liked the old man and hadn't she bedded enough older more unpleasant men in her time? Her past life had led her to this point and she could not afford to regret her past actions. Following his wife's death, the life had gone out of him. The only happy time he seemed to have was when he was in Caitlin's arms. She had replaced his dead wife as best as she could. She had worked very hard to make the tavern a success. He had carefully written his will so that no-one could take it from her.

She was even happier now than she had been three months ago when she had inherited the bar. Since then, Mick had come into her life. Mick O'Callaghan was a Sergeant in the Sixty-Ninth New York Infantry, the Irish Brigade. He was older than most of the recruits but he was, to Caitlin, a reminder of home. Besides that, he was good looking and built like an oak tree. She had been swept off her feet the first time she had seen him. He had bedded her that first night.

Had she had friends they might have warned her that Mick was a gold digger who wanted part of the lucrative profits from the South Boston bar. She had no close friends and, besides, she would not have believed them. Mick showed no interest in the bar or the profits. Sure he liked to have a couple of free drinks when he came home on leave but what red-blooded man wouldn't? In addition, his mighty fists had cleared the bar of trouble on more than a couple of occasions. He had even got fellow soldiers to keep an eye on Caitlin and her bar when he returned to the front so that she now had fewer breakages and almost no trouble from troublesome customers. Her profits were up. No, she knew Mick wanted her for herself and not for her money. She was still a good-looking woman and Mick's attentions were proof of that.

The only sadness in her life was wondering what had become of Jack. She had put advertisements in all the New York papers asking him to get in touch but so far she had heard nothing. Of course, she knew that he had landed at Charleston but she couldn't advertise in the southern papers and, besides, she knew that Jack would make his way north. That was where the Irish all lived, New York, Boston, and Chicago. He would want to be with his own, as she did. He was probably in some Irish regiment. She had asked Mick to ask after Jack Hogan but it was a long time since she had seen him. Apart from his red hair how could she describe him? She just had a belief that one day, he would turn up in her life again and the last ten years could be forgotten.

CHARLESTON CHRISTMAS DAY 1862

This was the first Christmas that Jack could remember celebrating. Those back in Wexford had hardly differed from the previous days of hunger and cold. Jack and Dago enjoyed the finest foods and wines, as they stayed at Briardene, Major Boswell's Charleston plantation. Like Caitlin, the only thought which stopped it being perfection was the thought that Caitlin was in Ireland somewhere and suffering. The letter he had sent with a smuggler would now be halfway across the Atlantic and he hoped that, by the spring, he and his sister would be reunited. That would be a Christmas present worth having. Until then he would enjoy building up and training the new companies who would carry on the work of Boswell's Wildcats.

THE END

GLOSSARY

Name	Explanation
Andrew Neil	Estate manage and servant
Archie Stuart	JEB Stuart's nephew
Arthur St. John Beauregard	A former redcoat
Barton	Boswell's Horse
blackbirders	Slave ships
Blackie Jones	Sailor- Rose of Tralee
Caitlin Hogan	Jack's sister
Captain Black Bill Bailey	Smuggler and sailor
Carlton	Boswell's Horse
Cecil (Irish) Mulrooney	Boswell's Horse
Clarissa Winfield	Ebenezer's daughter
Dago	Boswell's Horse
Danny Murphy	Boswell's lieutenant
David	Boswell's Horse
Davy	Boswell's Horse
Davy Thomas	Sailor- Rose of Tralee
Ebenezer Winfield	Plantation owner Atlanta
Eddie McNeil	Top man-Rose of Tralee
Fatty Hutton	Cook- Rose of Tralee
gee jaws	Cheap barter goods
Georgie	Boswell's Horse
Jack Hogan	Farmer's son
James Booth Boswell	Slave owner and aristocrat
Jedediah Hotchkiss	Jackson's map maker

Jedediah (Jed)	Boswell's Horse
Jem	Boswell's Horse/the plantation
Jimmy	Boswell's Horse
Johnny Smith	Sailor- Rose of Tralee
Matty	Boswell's Horse
Paddy Henry	First mate- Rose of Tralee
Paul	Boswell's Horse
poteen	Home-made spirit
Sandie Pendleton	Jackson's aide
Small beer	Watered down beer- healthier than water in the nineteenth century
Toby Harris	Sailor- Rose of Tralee
vedettes	Mounted cavalry sentries
Woody Tree	Second Mate- Rose of Tralee

HISTORICAL NOTE

My heartfelt thanks to the re-enactors at Gettysburg in July 2013 for all their help and advice. Any historical errors in the book are mine and not theirs. I realise that there were few Springfield carbines in the war but the nature of the business of James Booth Boswell meant that he would be rich and, like the chaps in Silicon Valley, would have ensured that he used the most up to date technology. The irregulars I described are loosely based on Mosby's Rangers and I used William S. Connery's excellent *"Mosby's Raids in Civil War Northern Virginia"*, extensively. Mosby was called the Grey Ghost and I used that appellation as the inspiration for my title. Boswell is not Mosby and this is a work of fiction; however, the incidents such as the charges using pistols, the wrecking of the trains, being mistaken for Union horsemen are all true. I also used *"The American Civil War Source Book"* by Philip Katcher and that proved a godsend for finding who fought where, when and with what. The material for the battle of Kernstown is taken from Gary Ecelbarger's book, *"We are in for it!"*

There are many real characters I have used in the book. Colonel White did indeed have a falling out with Stuart and seemed to have led General Walker on a long roundabout route to get to Loudoun Heights. The result was that the assault on the town was delayed by two days. Although it did not adversely affect the course of the battle it could have and was one of the many examples in the war of the effects of politics within the two armies. Sandie Pendleton was an aide to Jackson in the Valley and it was he who alerted Stonewall to the dangers from their left flank.

Thanks to Wikipedia for these public domain maps made by Hal Jespersen. I used "*Civil War: The Maps of Jedediah Hotchkiss*" by Chester G. Hearn and Mike Marino for the detailed maps of the valley. (Thanks to Rich for loaning me his copy!")

The Valley campaign was a complex one and the frontier was very fluid. This was exacerbated by the movements of the Rangers and the forces who tried to capture them. The raid on Dranesville did not happen but Mosby did try to raid it in 1863 but he found that they had fled. He and his 70 men rested at Miskel's farm. They were betrayed by a local Leesburg woman and the Second Pennsylvania surrounded the building. Despite being outnumbered two to one, with only one exit to the building, thanks to Captain Flint of the Vermont Cavalry making a sabre charge, the Rangers were victorious. Mosby lost one dead and three wounded. The Union forces lost 9 dead, 125 wounded, 82 captured as well as 95 horses. As you can see, I have not exaggerated the effect of the Rangers.

The events such as the capture of a colonel, the routing of larger numbers were all well documented and Mosby's Rangers had an effect which was disproportionate to their unit size. They did profit from their raids and others, further west such as Quantrell could be considered as bandits. The Rangers did wear uniform but they were adept at deception. Having seen the Blues and the Greys on a battlefield and at dusk, I can tell you that there is sometimes little to be seen to differentiate them. The main indicator was that the Union had identical uniforms whereas the Confederacy tended to be a little more idiosyncratic. I do not know if there was a prison for officers in Gettysburg but, as officers were frequently exchanged then I assume that there must have been somewhere for that purpose. Bearing in mind its later significance I chose Gettysburg. I apologise to the purists especially as this is a Brit trying to write about American history!

I used the terms darkie, negro and nigra rather than the more offensive words which would have been used at the time. The words I have used would have been the words used to describe the Afro-Americans in the period and I hope that none of my readers are offended. I used darkie rather the others more often because, if you listen to the songs such as Suwannee River you will see that they were used by the songwriters at the time. We may question their use but this is a novel of the time and I have tried to make it as accurate as I can. Any mistakes I have made are honest ones.

I plan on another two books in this series and the third one should reference Gettysburg.

Griff Hosker August 2013

OTHER BOOKS
by
Griff Hosker

If you enjoyed reading this book, then why not read another one by the author?
Ancient History

The Sword of Cartimandua Series (Germania and Britannia 50 A.D. – 128 A.D.)
Ulpius Felix- Roman Warrior (prequel)
The Sword of Cartimandua
The Horse Warriors
Invasion Caledonia
Roman Retreat
Revolt of the Red Witch
Druid's Gold
Trajan's Hunters
The Last Frontier
Hero of Rome
Roman Hawk
Roman Treachery
Roman Wall
Roman Courage

The Wolf Warrior series
(Britain in the late 6th Century)
Saxon Dawn

Saxon Revenge
Saxon England
Saxon Blood
Saxon Slayer
Saxon Slaughter
Saxon Bane
Saxon Fall: Rise of the Warlord
Book 9 Saxon Throne
Book 10 Saxon Sword

The Dragon Heart Series
Viking Slave
Viking Warrior
Viking Jarl
Viking Kingdom
Viking Wolf
Viking War
Viking Sword
Viking Wrath
Viking Raid
Viking Legend
Viking Vengeance
Viking Dragon
Viking Treasure
Viking Enemy
Viking Witch
Viking Blood
Viking Weregeld
Viking Storm
Viking Warband
Viking Shadow
Viking Legacy
Viking Clan
Viking Bravery

The Norman Genesis Series
Hrolf the Viking
Horseman
The Battle for a Home
Revenge of the Franks
The Land of the Northmen
Ragnvald Hrolfsson
Brothers in Blood
Lord of Rouen
Drekar in the Seine
Duke of Normandy
The Duke and the King

New World Series
Blood on the Blade
Across the Seas
The Savage Wilderness

The Reconquista Chronicles
Castilian Knight

The Aelfraed Series
(Britain and Byzantium 1050 A.D. - 1085 A.D.)
Housecarl
Outlaw
Varangian

The Anarchy Series England 1120-1180
English Knight
Knight of the Empress
Northern Knight
Baron of the North
Earl

King Henry's Champion
The King is Dead
Warlord of the North
Enemy at the Gate
The Fallen Crown
Warlord's War
Kingmaker
Henry II
Crusader
The Welsh Marches
Irish War
Poisonous Plots
The Princes' Revolt
Earl Marshal

Border Knight
1182-1300
Sword for Hire
Return of the Knight
Baron's War
Magna Carta
Welsh Wars
Henry III
The Bloody Border
Baron's Crusade

Lord Edward's Archer
Lord Edward's Archer
King in Waiting (December 2019)

Struggle for a Crown
1360- 1485
Blood on the Crown
To Murder A King
The Throne

King Henry IV

Modern History

The Napoleonic Horseman Series
Chasseur a Cheval
Napoleon's Guard
British Light Dragoon
Soldier Spy
1808: The Road to Coruña
Talavera
Waterloo

The Lucky Jack American Civil War series
Rebel Raiders
Confederate Rangers
The Road to Gettysburg

The British Ace Series
1914
1915 Fokker Scourge
1916 Angels over the Somme
1917 Eagles Fall
1918 We will remember them
From Arctic Snow to Desert Sand
Wings over Persia

**Combined Operations series
1940-1945**
Commando
Raider
Behind Enemy Lines
Dieppe
Toehold in Europe
Sword Beach

Breakout
The Battle for Antwerp
King Tiger
Beyond the Rhine
Korea
Korean Winter

Other Books
Great Granny's Ghost (Aimed at 9-14-year-old young people)

For more information on all of the books then please visit the author's web site at www.griffhosker.com where there is a link to contact him.

Printed in Great Britain
by Amazon